Jealousy

LoLo Paige

Published by Avoca Press Publishing, 2022.

Jealousy

A Sisters of Sin Novel

First published by Avoca Press Publishing 2022

ISBN 978-1-7360951-1-9

Front Cover Design by T. Wells Brown Edited by Mariah Thayer and Heather Osborne Proofread by S. R. Cyres and Judy Winslow

Dedicated to all the innocents
who have been and continue to be wronged by the injustices of the world
And
To my Sisters of Sin
Together we shine.

PART ONE
SHAYLA
The Girl

For where your treasure is, there your heart will be as well. —Luke 12:34

Chapter 1
Shayla

County Wicklow, Ireland

C His name is Collin Stedman.

I've been watching him. Not as a mark. Would be regrettable to remove this magnificent specimen from the planet. He runs my favorite bookshop in Arklow, County Wicklow, in Ireland.

When the owner died two months ago, her nephew, Collin, took over. I haven't been in since she died. I wanted to vet this guy first. Only trouble is, he's nowhere online. Same as me.

This intrigues me.

Everyone's on social media. I'm not, for obvious reasons. Which makes me curious why others aren't. Surely, they're not all hired killers. Most succumb to ego and create profiles to announce their lives to the world, like a public diary.

That would be death in my line of work. Pun intended.

Every morning I get up at sunrise to be at the cemetery overlooking the bookshop. I take a muffin and my binoculars, settle in behind the imposing O'Toole gravestone, then peek around it to watch him.

He shows up exactly at seven, like clockwork. I've timed him with my phone. He's never late.

I like that.

And I like that he's shaped like an upside-down triangle and has thick hair the color of cinnamon mixed with mahogany, depending on how the early morning sun glimmers in it.

When I spot Collin's red bicycle at the end of the street, my heart beats faster, the closer he gets. His bike is like mine, with an electric motor he engages when he bikes uphill to the store.

He slows down, and like the terns whirling overhead, he gracefully swings a long leg over his bike and leans it against the corner of the

1

store. He pulls out his keys, and I watch through my binoculars as his slender fingers ease a key into the lock and turn it.

I close my eyes and envision what those fingers would feel like when he touches me. I get stirrings down low, watching every move he makes, until he pushes the door open and disappears inside with his bike.

His movements stay the same. Every single day.

I like that too.

At the back of the cemetery, I climb down the hill and weave around twisted grave markers. I get on my electric motor bike and ride home.

I've gone online and can't find anything about him, other than a news article saying Collin Stedman is the new owner of Celtic Sea Bookshop. No photo. Nothing. I'm bothered by this.

I want to know what color eyes he has.

He doesn't know I watch. I'm good at staying hidden. Unseen. Unnoticed.

The invisible loser of Arklow Town.

Chapter 2

I made my first kill at age sixteen.

Not by choice. By inheritance. I'd always been expected to work in the family business. The Uncles decided for me. They said it was time I learned the trade.

Turns out I have a knack for it. Apparently, my brain has titanium wiring in a copper wiring world, my family tells me.

I don't get emotional about things. Like killing people. Only I'm not supposed to say it like that.

We respectfully refer to ourselves as cessation specialists.

The Uncles provide room and board, along with compensation for one cessation per quarter. If there's a need for me to do more, I do it, as long as they pay me for the overtime.

Not a problem; I take pride in my work.

In my downtime, I devour books, video games, and order supplies for crafting my Celtic jewelry. The Uncles see to it I spend my off-duty time on normal pursuits.

In their words, "So our lass grows up to be a productive member of society."

I love my Uncles, and they love me. They're my only family. We survive and thrive because civilians know nothing about us other than our commercial fishing business and our cleaning and technology companies.

We're known as 'that Byrne family who keep to themselves'. To keep up appearances, our family attends an occasional *céilí* and shows up religiously on Sundays at St. Michael's for Mass.

Everyone except me. Instead, I love the quiet time; I read my books and watch my movies.

The Uncles have me tethered to our isolated cottage in Arklow, County Wicklow, on the southeast coast of Ireland. Sometimes we go to the crumbling castle our family had inherited, Bramble Hill Castle, aptly named for the overgrown brambles that surround it. A stone wall that would stop William the Conqueror—should he reincarnate and happen by—encompasses the whole thing.

No one bothers us there because we make sure it resembles a scary witch castle.

The castle is our refuge, where we have family meetings. We practice with our weapons and no one for miles around disturbs us.

I'm not allowed to travel out of town alone, even on the train up to Dublin. If I go anywhere outside of our coastal town of Arklow, either my cousin Declan or one of the Uncles escorts me.

I do the accounting for the family business, tracking everything down to the exact penny. All the figures must balance exactly. Every. Time.

That makes me happy.

Occasionally, I travel to other parts of Ireland for work. The Uncles take care of transportation, and our subcontractor, the *Shamrock Cleaners,* takes care of the rest. My cousins run that aspect of our operation.

And, as per usual, the Uncles manage the disposal end of things.

Secrecy and anonymity have made me invisible for most of my life. No one notices me by design. The Uncles make sure of it. I'm mostly a spectator, a casual observer of the lives around me. And a casual observer of my own life.

I stand outside of myself, looking in.

Lately, I'm liking how men stare at me, now that I've filled out and my hair is long. Tired of my mousy drab hair, I dyed it the color of burgundy wine. Took me some doing to get the exact color. I bought different hair dye kits and measured and mixed chemicals for the precise shade I wanted.

Nothing else was acceptable.

The Uncles only scowled. Heaven forbid that someone might notice me.

But I like how I get the double takes after a lifetime of no one giving me a first glance, let alone a second. While I'd tromped around in knee-high man-boots and colorless fashions, other girls had emulated movie stars.

Let *others* be jealous of *me* for once.

Most my age consider me a loser, and they make sure I know. What they don't know is that I could drop them like a bag of dirt, shovel them under, then go make a crispy cheese and onion sandwich.

And not think twice.

Lately, I've been edgy. I've read many books and watched all the travel shows. I want to see the world. This coastal town has closed in on me. I'm going nowhere fast—I've become an unfeeling phantom where everything presses in, burning my soul.

I wake up drenched in sweat and can't breathe.

Is this all there is? As good as things will ever be? What about becoming a wife? Or a mother? I've tried talking to the Uncles about it, but they invariably say the same thing: "We can't run this business without you—please don't leave until we get things better situated."

Whatever that means.

I've withdrawn even more and resent anyone and everyone. I seethe with desire to transform happy, loving couples into corpses. Their love, their happiness...the way they look at each other makes me nauseous.

Despite my emptiness, I'm jealous of what they all have.

And friends? I'm not allowed to have them either. I envy girls when I overhear them sharing laughter and secrets—bragging about who they have sex with and how often.

Sex. Not allowed to do that, either.

I'm twenty-two, and an unseen virgin with a skill set that would send any normal person sprinting out the door, to run screaming into the night. Not to mention a brain that prefers to follow its own unique path. A brain that ping-pongs between flawed and gifted at the same time.

Things must be in a particular order, or I go ballistic and must breathe into a paper sack. Yet I can memorize a string of number sequences most people have to write down.

When I was little, the Uncles found this wee tidbit out when they moved my stuff.

I couldn't stop screaming.

They remodeled the upstairs so I could arrange things the exact way I had to have them.

We had a terrible breaking-in period as I got older. The Uncles had egregious habits, like spitting chewing tobacco into teacups and leaving them on the kitchen table. Smoking in the house. Not showering.

I did a lot of screaming.

"No spitting! No smoking! And for the mother of all things holy, take a fecking shower!"

I trained the Uncles to accept my idiosyncrasies. We trained each other, really; they need the work done, and I'm willing to do it—as long as the house remains spotless, and I maintain order in my meticulously managed universe.

I can't stand chaos.

I've grown up believing something is wrong with my brain. When my cousins come to the house, I don't always get what they say. Their humor confuses me.

I don't laugh at their jokes, because I don't know what they mean.

They tell the Uncles I creep them out. I'm too serious. I don't smile. I don't laugh.

The entire love and fuck thing confuses me.

I've watched movies with loads of sex, so I'm not sheltered, by any means. But I'm not naïve to assume love and sex in real life is identical to the movies.

The golden perk for me in this business is that I conveniently avoid relationships.

JEALOUSY

While I haven't had sex (I'm a freak in that regard) I want to find out what all the uproar is about. But since I avoid society-at-large, I wouldn't know the first thing about how to fuck someone.

Which brings me to Plan B.

Plan A is to continue my status quo. But Plan B? *The Uncles are not to know.*

While they've never lifted a hand to me, I don't want to disappoint them.

Back to Plan B.

Let's just say, I'm mother effing good at what I do.

Chapter 3

"We have a job. This one's close to home, though," says Uncle Casen, chewing on his matchstick, eyeing Uncle Brodie across the table.

"She pissed off a thoroughbred breeder in Dubai."

I offer Uncle Casen a fresh matchstick to replace his mangled one.

"She? How close to home?" I ask, sipping tea from my mother's bone china teacup.

"Down on the coast. Almost didn't accept this one, but it pays four times the normal amount."

"The *Stormbird's* engines need replacing," Uncle Brodie cuts in. "And she needs fine detailing."

The family commercial fishing boat passed to the Uncles when Dad died in the car crash.

"Is she Irish?" I ask.

"You know we don't eliminate our own," Uncle Brodie says gruffly. "She's from across the stream."

He jerks his head toward the Irish Sea.

"My mark is English, then." I hold out my hand for the datasheet. "Location?"

Uncle Casen passes it back to me. I'm familiar with this address. "Equestrian Estates. It's gated. Video surveillance, lasers, and security for the horses."

I flick my eyes at one uncle, then the other, waiting.

"The cousins will take care of that ahead of time, as always," says Uncle Brodie.

Our family had procreated rapidly and exponentially before fucking was even invented. As a result, I have cousins everywhere. Luckily, some with tentacles stretching into Ireland's underground. Let's just say if St. Patrick would've left a snake in Ireland, my cousins could track it down.

"You mean Declan will see to it?"

Cousin Dec is the mastermind of all things high-tech. He's a genius at creating and breaking computer source code. Firewalls are mere child's play to Dec. I've seen him in action navigating the Dark Web to monitor what's *really* going on with crime in Ireland.

To find out who truly deserves cessation.

I sip my tea and set the cup down precisely on the inner saucer ring. "I'll scope it tonight. After the spring equinox, it's staying lighter later. I'll go around midnight."

"Good, Shaylee." Uncle Casen slid a box across the table. "These came today."

I open the box and lift out my new digital night vision binoculars. Not cheap, but the highest rated, according to online reviews. I fiddle with them.

"Thanks. Can't wait to check them out tonight." The Uncles make sure I'm well equipped.

They rise and ready themselves for a day on the water.

"Taking the *Stormbird* over to Geraghty's. Chart plotter is messed up again." Another trusted cousin. This one specializes in fixing all things of a marine nature.

Brodie pauses. "Take extra care, since this next job is on home turf. Extra measures will be required."

I nod. "Please don't concern yourself. I'm not someone who takes risks."

He winks. "Grand. Fill us in later. We'll be up to Avoca at a *céilí*. You should come for a wee bit. They make a mean colcannon."

I shake my head emphatically. "Not a fan of buttery mashed potatoes that give me the toots."

"No worries, wee Shaylee-Girl. Be careful."

They put on their berets and head out the door.

I luxuriate having the place to myself. I bake muffins, start a rabbit stew, then prepare for tonight's reconnaissance.

Chapter 4

Several days later, after studying my mark, I make myself comfortable, cross-legged on the grassy ground. I munch the last of my cheese and onion crisps and lick the salt from my fingers.

The lingering winter air bites my face, frosting my breath. I tug my black ski mask over my head, covering everything except eyes and mouth.

For the third day in a row, I position myself on a rise, three hundred sixty-five meters from the horse compound and mansion perched next to the paddocks. I scope every movement of my target.

The Uncles had surprised me when they said this mark was a female. I remind myself women and men have equal capacities for wrongdoing. This woman must have swindled the wrong horse breeder.

Breeding winning thoroughbreds is a high-stakes, ruthless business on the world stage.

I prefer not to know the gory details of my marks. The Uncles manage the legal and financial aspects, and frankly, I don't care to know much beyond their initial infraction.

All I know is they are bad people who deserve it.

My job is to scrutinize movements, who comes and goes, and decide the best time for my operation. I've assembled and readied my long range .223 tube gun, with scope attached.

The Uncles set me up with a single-shot weapon that's light and effective. I attach the stock, then screw on the suppressor to reduce the gun flash.

I position it on my short tripod.

To calculate my mark, I pull my range finder from my vest pocket and peer through it to get a read on the wind movement. A slight breeze moves leaves to the west, and I calibrate accordingly. Nothing like a wind gust to ruin a clean shot.

JEALOUSY

I have a perfect view of everything. The mark's bedroom tops three stories and provides me a superior angle. I watch the high-end luxury cars come and go with my night vision binoculars, their headlight beams piercing the blackness.

Tires crunch the light tan gravel, making the driveway easier to see. Horses whinny and nicker in a nearby pasture.

Activity ceases by two a.m. I note the last light going out in the mark's bedroom. She lives alone, save for two household help that sleep in a separate building off to the right, along with the security guard for the horses.

Their lights go out early.

As I lift my night vision specs to scrutinize before dropping a shell into the chamber, a movement catches my eye. An abnormally swift movement.

On the roof.

What the feck?

I twist my lens to zero in on the action.

A figure dressed in black moves along the roof ridge. Not a woman's build. The man has a similar black ski mask to mine. A well-built man, judging by the skintight spandex covering his chest and arms.

He steps gracefully, like a gazelle on a tightrope, then jumps down to a lower roof. Climbing down a trellis, he then leaps to the grass below, ducking out of sight around the corner of the mansion.

I rise from my position and scurry across the hill to get a look at the other side.

Chapter 5

I squint through my binoculars.

There he is!

Who is that? And what the bollocks is he doing at two in the morning at my mark's home?

I zoom in on the guy, a daypack slung over his shoulder. He has hold of a black bicycle, climbs on and pedals down the gravel road leading from the estate. I hear the distinct hum of an e-bike motor as it starts.

The mysterious biker becomes a dot in the distance.

In a fit of momentary panic, I can't decide whether to follow. Was he doing a hit? Was another contract let for this mark? My heart pounds so hard it wants out of my body.

I wonder what the man has in the daypack.

This is a different turn of events. I've never had an operation mess up like this. No way can I catch the guy as he races away. My e-bike is fast, but he has a head start. I waffle, wasting time—debating what to do.

Dammit! He messed up my operation!

I must finish this job tonight. An incomplete operation is not an option. I pace in a frenzy, wondering if I should continue or abort. I decide to follow through with the job when a light snaps on in the mark's bedroom.

Two white Garda cruisers with blue and yellow stripes speed toward the mansion, lights flashing. *I must abort!*

I run back to my position and frantically disassemble my weapon and shove it into my daypack, as four Gardaí jump out and head for the house, carrying batons.

A woman opens the door and lets them in. She walks outside, looks around, then shuts the door.

I clamber down the back side of the hill to my bicycle, hidden in a copse of trees.

I try not to scream. My world order is out of whack, and I fight for calm. I have no paper sacks to breathe into. The panic attack lasts forever. My veins pulsate, my head throbs, and my lungs can't get air.

I hit the ground, pull my knees to my chest, and rock. I start my sequence: *Inhale, one-two-three-four-five. Hold and exhale, one-two-three-four-five.*

Please God, make it stop.

When the attack passes, I grab my bike and run with it downhill, still fighting for calm. At the bottom, I swing a leg over and hit my electric motor starter. My bike bumps cross-country for a short distance.

When I hit the paved road, I start my motor and throttle up to maximum speed until I'm downtown. I cut the motor and pedal streets and alleys until I'm certain no one follows.

Thankfully, when our isolated cottage comes into view, I frantically pedal toward it. I bike down our long lane and hurry inside.

I tell the Uncles I had to abort and that I'll find out why the Garda showed up. And who it was that thwarted my cessation operation.

I'll make sure the guy on the roof never interrupts my operation again. Ever.

Chapter 6

I watch Collin Stedman open the bookshop as usual. But today is different.

Today is the day I'm going inside. I have a business errand, only this one is legit. In the two months since Maeve passed away, I've created an excessive inventory of Celtic jewelry designs.

It was the only way I could figure out how to grieve her loss. She was like the mother I never had, treated me with kindness and respect; she never judged.

This time I ride my bike to the Celtic Sea Bookshop, undo my front tire, and haul it inside with me. The bell tinkles on the well-worn, creaky door as I enter.

I expect Maeve to call out, "A good mornin' to ya, dearie!"

Instead, I glance up at the best-looking man I've ever laid eyes on, smiling at me. Since I haven't laid eyes on too many, this isn't saying much; but Collin Stedman is striking up close, with a quiet strength I'd sensed from afar.

"Haven't seen you in here before," he calls out in a cheerful voice.

His all-inclusive testosterone package throws me. I'm rendered helpless, and gape at his thick, wavy copper hair, eyebrows thick and proportioned to his pools of blue.

I know a thing or two about eye color, from my biology books and Uncle Casen's tutelage.

Keeping a respectable distance, I force out words.

"Did you know only seventeen percent of the world population has blue eyes? Combined with only two percent having red hair, the odds of possessing both are zero-point-one percent."

His startled expression makes me want to laugh. Instead, I freeze. Social graces are not my thing.

He squints. "Are you going to stand there all day and stare at me?"

14

His brown suede jacket unzips to just below the notch in his throat. He has freckles there. And they're beautiful.

I hesitate.

"I don't bite." When he smiles, unlimited possibilities present themselves.

Oh, no—here comes the panic—my chest constricts, and my breath comes up short.

"Are you okay?" The coppery stubble on his cheeks, chin, and above his perfectly shaped lips accentuates his look of concern.

Inhaling deeply to calm myself, I start toward him, bike tire in my hand.

"I'm grand."

His arms spread wide, his hands resting on the pay counter. I'm pulled to him like a magnet.

"You have emerald eyes. Rarer still," he says, white teeth lined up in such orderly fashion, they turn me on in ways I never thought possible.

"Two percent of the world population has green eyes."

My breath catches at his spot-on statement of fact. "Yes. They do."

I don't reveal that I'm impressed he knows this.

He shrugs with a smile that would stop stampeding sheep. "I read a lot."

I inhale deeply to hide my insecurities, that want to escape as a panic attack. But I don't let them.

After all, I'm a cessation specialist. I have skills.

Then why do I stand before him, staring like an eejit?

"How can I help you?" His Irish accent differs from mine. I place him near Donegal in northwest Ireland, with a wee bit of an American twang.

I slide my daypack off my shoulder. "Maeve used to carry my Celtic designs."

I lay out the pieces I've carefully wrapped in tissue and arrange them meticulously on the counter.

"This one is exquisite." He lifts the necklace with a silver Celtic cross and fake emerald nestled in the center and holds it next to my face.

"This peridot gemstone matches your eyes."

"Very good. You know your stones." I offer him an appreciative look.

"I dabble."

He reaches inside the display case and brings out another necklace with a dark green gemstone.

"This one's a better match. An heirloom piece from the Romantic Period."

He positions it next to my eyes, and squints to assess.

"You're good," I smirk. "Flattery is an effective sales strategy. I'll bet you sell a lot of these emeralds. Let me see."

He holds it out to me, and I tilt the design, studying it.

"This one is later than the Romantic. More like the Aesthetic Period, around 1900," I say.

He fastens his cerulean gaze to mine.

"And you also know your gems."

I lift my brows. "I do a little more than dabble."

What I don't say is how I used to imitate the elaborate designs of Victorian era necklaces.

I scan the jewelry in his collection.

"I'm not sure my designs will fit with these fancy ones."

"Sure, they will. I'll arrange yours in a separate display."

His self-assured essence disarms me as he extends a hand across the counter.

"My name is Collin."

"Shayla," I say, gently shaking it. He feels warm on this chilly day.

"Aunt Maeve mentioned a shy but pretty jeweler who makes elegant designs." His eyes probe me. "You're the one."

I shrug, wondering what else Maeve had said about me.

"Tell you what. Leave me whichever pieces you like, and what you want for them. We'll work out a consignment deal. Sound good?"

A thoughtful smile curves my mouth.

From here on out, I'll do anything Collin Stedman says.

Chapter 7

One week later, we have a family business meeting. The Uncles, my cousins from Shamrock Cleaners, and myself. Our circle is small, but effective.

I start things off. "I overheard people talking with a Garda down at Jitterbeans Coffee. A jewelry thief botched my mark."

"Doesn't matter, anyway. The contractor canceled for some unknown reason," said Uncle Casen, shrugging his round, chubby shoulders. He's the shorter of the two.

I scowl. "Bollocks. I wasted all that planning and prep time."

"It's never a waste, Shaylee," Uncle Brodie pipes up, his lankier build taller than Uncle Casen and my petite form stacked together.

I think of a sudden opportunity, and it energizes me.

"I'll work on my jewelry, then. The new bookshop owner wants more designs. They're selling steadily now that the tourists are back."

What I don't say is that I visit the bookshop each day when it opens, just to lay eyes on Collin Stedman. I need to explain further.

"Since my designs are selling, I go a few times a week to drop off more inventory and collect my cash payments."

Uncle Casen perks up. "That's grand. Never hurts to have more income."

I don't say how impressed I am with Collin's knowledge about jewelry. And art. And everything else. He's well-read like me, and for the first time, I have someone to chat with about subjects I'm interested in.

But I must be careful. I can't let down my guard; I'm risking enough as it is.

We end the family meeting, and everyone scatters.

• • • •

JEALOUSY

Collin had invited me to drive with him to Avoca this morning, to help him select scarves, blankets, and coats to carry in the touristy side of his store.

I said yes, elated that the Uncles planned to spend the day in Dublin.

After the Uncles leave, I primp before biking to the bookshop. The day before, I'd shopped for a skirt and top, a wee bit cheerier than gray, brown and black. I tug on a soft teal sweater and matching skirt, gaping at my reflection in disbelief—I appear every bit as good as the girls who call me a loser.

But I still pin my hair up and tuck it inside my black knit cap. More out of habit than anything. Collin still hasn't seen my hair.

I dab a bit of eye makeup and lip color on my face. Then tug on black tights since it's still a bit nippy outside. I ride my bike to the back alley behind the bookshop.

Collin meets me at the back door with an enthusiastic grin. "You look great."

Heat crawls up my neck. I'm suddenly hot under my knit cap.

"Closed the shop for today," he says, eyeing me appreciatively.

I love how he looks at me.

"I'm looking forward to this. Haven't been to Avoca since last year around this time," I say, folding myself into the passenger seat of his gray Volkswagen Golf.

"You only visit once a year? It's only twenty minutes away."

Collin buckles himself in and shifts the car into gear.

Shite!

I revealed too much, and I back pedal.

"I don't—I don't drive that much. Ride my bike instead," I say casually, hoping he won't press.

He doesn't. The more time I spend with Collin, the more relaxed I am with him. He's easy to talk to but doesn't need to know I avoid

19

going to Avoca because of unpleasant memories. It's hard enough to for my annual obligatory visit.

Collin glances at me. "I know we've not known each other long, but it's like I've known you all my life."

"I feel the same," I say shyly.

It's time for me to set boundaries. "But please don't ask me about myself. There's nothing to tell."

His manly profile tingles me when he nods at the windshield.

"Okay. But I'm afraid I have to know what kind of beer you like."

"I don't drink beer," I tell him. "I drink tea mostly."

His brows lift. "You won't want to go to Fitzgerald's Pub, then? Made famous by the *Ballykissangel* TV show?"

I laugh, which is rare. I find I laugh more when I'm with Collin.

"Of course, I want to go. Pubs have the best food."

Collin chuckles. "This one sure does. We'll go there for the best stew you've ever had, along with some fruit drinks."

I smile at him because he's irresistible and looks dashing behind the wheel of his car.

I pull out my pack of Ultra chewing gum, an exclusive Irish brand. Cinnamon is my favorite.

"Care for a stick of cinnamon?"

He flashes me an adoring look that melts the gum in my mouth.

"That's my favorite! Yours too?"

I unwrap it for him since he's driving. He turns his head and opens his mouth.

"Pop it in."

My insides squish as I tear it in half and pop both pieces into his lovely mouth.

"Thanks, lass." His tone drops on the last word, a magnetic tug on my heart.

The drive ends too soon—I enjoy being alone with Collin. He pulls into a gravel parking lot in front of a quaint, white-washed building with a wooden water wheel attached to it.

"Here we are, at the legendary Avoca Mill. Ireland's oldest weaving mill," Collin announces, climbing out of the car.

He rounds the front, swings my door open, and extends his hand.

I grasp it as his eyes rake over me, down, then up again.

"You should get rid of that stocking cap and lose the clunky boots. From what I can see of your legs, they're killer."

I startle at his word choice. My legs aren't the only thing that's killer. Ha, if he only knew. I suppress a laugh and hesitate.

Oh, what the hell.

I tug off my stocking cap, letting my burgundy-colored hair fall past my shoulders.

Collin gapes at me, slack jawed as I comb it with my fingers.

"Cripes. You're a frigging beauty. Don't put that hat back on. Not around me, anyway."

His tone sounds different, and his pupils dilate. I'm not sure how to interpret it, so I don't. Like sarcasm...I can't tell if people are serious or whether they're joking. I find sarcasm irritating.

"I've always loved this water wheel against the white building and the pretty lawn and gardens surrounding it," I comment as we step inside.

"I like how colorful this place is," says Collin, lifting his daypack over his shoulder as we take in the array of color, with pillows, throws, and every woven thing imaginable.

"Browse around while I talk to the manager."

Collin disappears into the manager's office, and I wander over to finger the colorful woven scarves and throws. I choose a bright pink flecked scarf and a blue-green throw for myself and pay with cash.

After a bit, Collin emerges and comes toward me. My pulse quickens, same as it always does when I see him.

"Time for lunch," he says, and takes my hand.

I don't pull away, loving the feel of him. I can't remember the last time someone held my hand. My mum, maybe, when I was little.

Collin takes me to lunch at the landmark pub, a prominent blue and yellow building on Avoca's main street. As we settle in at our table, he orders two beers.

"You'll like these." His mischievous wink sends a delicious feeling down low.

"My uncles say that drink is a curse—makes you fight with your neighbor, shoot at your landlord, and makes you miss him."

Collin chortled. "My mum used to say that too."

I drink a beer with raspberry in it, and it percolates my brain with giddy bubbles. I giggle, loving the tingly feeling.

We share a second beer that tastes like oranges.

"This is what you mean by healthy fruit drinks? Raspberry and orange beer?" I chirp, downing the rest.

The timing of when I should say things has never been my strong suit.

"Is this where I say, 'I want you', like they do in the movies?" I blurt innocently.

Collin leans back and gapes at me. "You get right to the point, don't you?"

"Jaysus, I said it wrong," I lament, nonplussed, judging what I said. "I'm too blunt. Not good with the small talk."

"I like blunt. I hate beating around the bush."

He studies me, and I fidget under his scrutiny. The corners of his mouth lift, and I spot a dimple on his right cheek. I want to lose my finger in it.

"Are you joking, or do you mean it?" His candor warms me.

"I don't joke. Yes, I mean it." I flick my gaze to his, then drop it to my empty glass.

"I want you, Collin Stedman."

He's the first guy I've ever wanted to have sex with, and the first person I've ever said this to; maybe because my insides shift whenever I'm in his presence. I think I can trust him.

If I watch what I say, I think I can trust him.

I can do this...can't I?

He leans in, sending a giddy current galloping through me.

"This is where I say, 'I want you' right back. And I'm relieved you said it first."

"Seriously?" Here's a grand opportunity to find out what all the sex hype is about. I'm keen to take advantage of it.

"If you're serious, I know a place down by the river," he says quietly, smiling with his eyes.

I contemplate this. "Like on the ground? Next to the river?"

He throws his head back and laughs. His laugh is warm cocoa to me; it makes me happy.

"I adore your innocence," he says softly, dissolving my insides into goo.

"Let's go," I say breathlessly, excited for this new experience.

We push away from the table, bumping it in our haste to leave. Our glasses fall and roll to the edge. We both snap our hands out, each catching one before they crash to the floor.

His brows lift. "Whoa, good save, lass. A woman after me own wee heart."

His impish Irish cadence works on me in a big way.

Never mind we both have super-fast reflexes, like two star-nosed moles.

I grab hold of him and tug him out the door, laughing.

Chapter 8

Collin closes the bedroom door inside the Riverview Bed and Breakfast. He turns to me.

"How do you want to do this?"

I give him a blank look. "I—em—figured you'd know. You seem like a worldly guy."

"Why would you say that?"

"You're more cultured than other guys I know around here—not that I know that many. Your Donegal accent mingles with American. You've spent time in the States. Am I right?"

His brows shoot up, and his mouth hangs open.

"Keen observation. I'm impressed."

"That's not all I've observed."

Now I stare into his hypnotic blue pools without looking away.

"Tell me what else you've observed."

He moves to me, and a shiver speeds up my spine when he rests his hands on my shoulders.

I resist my instinct to step back.

"You're precise and meticulous—never late." I lift my gaze and tilt my head. "Your hair—sometimes it's mahogany, but mostly it's a glimmery copper, depending on how the sun highlights it. You stay in shape, and you're graceful because of it. You are kind but you have an inner strength."

I peer up at him and don't know why I say the next thing.

"You have a secret life. There are things you don't say—can't say. Things you hold close to your chest. Almost like you're a—" I stop, alarmed I've said too much.

His expression changes and his brow furrows.

"Like I'm a what? How do you know all that?"

Not wanting to divulge that I spied on him long before I met him—I inwardly panic.

24

"Don't worry, I'm not a psychic. It's something I've sensed about you." I swallow hard.

"I've not met anyone like you," he says, lifting my chin.

His kiss is soft and gentle. He seems to sense I'm skittish, like a starling. I close my eyes while he eases his tongue along my lip line, and keep my mouth closed until I realize he wants to French kiss me.

When he lifts away, my eyes stay closed, as does my mouth.

"You're a virgin, aren't you?"

His words cause my eyelids to flutter open. I stare at him, not knowing how to respond—embarrassed to say yes.

"It's that obvious?" I say, a tinge of desperation in my voice.

"I—sensed it."

He slides his palm up and down my arm. "Hey, we don't have to do this."

Collin brushes my hair back and looks into my soul.

"Have you—had a virgin lately?" I ask timidly.

His brows lift as he shakes his head slowly, eyes penetrating mine.

"Are you sure you want me to—be the one?"

"Why would I want anyone else?" I angle my face to his. "Kiss me again."

"Slow or fast?" he murmurs.

I love that he offers me a choice—makes me want him even more. "Neither. Kiss me intensely."

This time I part my lips, and his tongue eases into my mouth like a polite guest. He explores it and when he pauses, I slide my tongue to meet his. I love how our tongues tangle in an amorous dance.

Collin presses against me, and he's rock hard on my stomach. His hand moves up my leg under my skirt and he grabs my bottom and squeezes. I let him take charge of this operation, since I presume he's done this before, whereas I'm a newcomer.

He backs up and pulls me to the bed, where he sits. I stand before him, trusting him. Trust is not my strong suit.

"I want to undress you."

I'm fully under his spell. He does to me what no one ever has...creates a longing so deep I can't describe it. I watch his smoldering expression as he unsnaps my skirt and tugs it down. He lifts my sweater up over my head.

His eyes darken, giving him a sexy, dangerous vibe.

I stand there in my embarrassingly white, bland bra and black tights. "I look like a penguin."

He laughs. "No. Quite the contrary. You look like a goddess."

He reaches behind me to unclasp my bra. When he pulls it from my shoulders, I gasp. I've never stood topless before a guy. Nervous about having something to do, I push my tights and undies down.

Collin waves my hands away. Instead, he tugs everything down to my ankles. He lifts my foot and meticulously removes one stocking, along with part of my undies. He eases my foot back to the floor and strokes my ankle. Skating his palm up my calf, he caresses my knee.

I rest my hands on his shoulders while he performs the same ritual to my other foot. His gentle movements remind me of how I imagine a husband undressing his wife on their wedding night.

"Can I undress you now?" I ask, watching his face change to want as his gaze rakes me.

"I want to touch you first." Collin rises from the bed and caresses my breasts, planting soft kisses on the side of my neck.

When his tongue tickles my ear, overwhelming need washes over me. I suck in a breath to stem the wave that's about to crush me with fresh, unrestrained urgency.

He roams my body with his lips, stopping to suckle a nipple and massage it with his tongue. I claw at his shirt and lift it up. He reaches up to tug it off, and I unsnap and unzip his snazzy dark gray pants and push them down.

We're both naked. My breathing becomes ragged as he pushes me back and lifts my legs up onto the bed.

I say it again, hoping my timing is better this time. "I want you, Collin." His eyes glint in the subdued afternoon light.

"I'm honored you want me to be your first, Shayla."

"Oh, you say that to all the virgins," I murmur, proud of my newfound sense of humor.

Collin chuckles. "Hardly. I'll try not to hurt you."

He reaches for a packet on the nightstand, rips it open, and unrolls protection onto himself.

"You'll have a little pain on this first go around." His round head pokes at my entrance.

He guides himself in, nice and easy, then backs out. He does this a few times, then on the fourth time he pushes in further. There's a painful pressure when he pushes in all the way.

I don't cry out, as this is supposed to be a grand experience. When he rocks gently back and forth, I keep my arms around his back.

"Concentrate on my kissing you. Not the pain," he says, kissing me hard and deep.

I feel need along with the thwarting pain, and this confuses me.

I thought it was supposed to feel heavenly.

He stiffens and grunts hard.

"Shayla," he says in a long exhale, and relaxes on top of me.

There is more to this than the act of our physically joining together—I feel something for this charismatic, handsome Irishman. More than I've ever felt for anyone.

Alarm bells sound off inside my brain, screaming at my heart.

No, too risky! You can't have a love relationship. With anyone. Ever.

But I love how he says my name. And I love that Collin Stedman is my first.

Chapter 9

The next morning, I go to the Celtic Sea Bookshop at my usual time when it opens. I no longer spy on Collin, and I miss those days. But I prefer my intimacy with him much better than peeping at him through binoculars.

I lock up my bike in the back alley and knock on the back door fifteen minutes before opening time. Now that we're intimate, I'm paranoid that some random customer might notice me go in the front door.

The door opens. Collin tugs me inside and lays a kiss on me that would melt Antarctica. He yanks my stocking cap off and fists my hair.

We make out in a wild frenzy, like we're on the Titanic as she points down to the deep.

I breathe heavily and so does he when the front doorbell tinkles.

I laugh into his mouth. "You have a customer."

I give him a fast, sloppy kiss and squeeze his tush. Two days ago, I never would have dreamed of placing my hand on his luscious arse.

"Browse some books. Don't go anywhere."

He playfully points at me and clicks his tongue.

I beam at him because I don't remember ever being this happy.

On my way out to the bookshop, something catches my eye. Collin's red bike leans against a wall, and there's red paint on the wall behind it. I swipe at the paint with my finger, and it's tacky. I inspect his electric motor and compare it with mine.

He has a souped-up version, and his lithium battery has higher voltage than mine.

The handlebar has a large gash, as the red paint hasn't completely dried. Curious, I scrape it with my fingernail, revealing flat black paint underneath. I scrape the red paint on the rear fender, revealing more black paint.

Collin must have painted it yesterday before we drove to Avoca...or early this morning.

But why would he do that? First his bike is red, then black, now it's red again?

My eyes drift to the tires, and my stomach falls to the floor.

I squat for a closer look, praying to God I don't find what I suspect is there...light tan gravel chunks stuck between the treads. Same as the gravel I'd plucked from my bike tires the night of my botched operation—when the thief interrupted things and took off—on a black bicycle with an electric motor.

The realization hits me like a gunshot as I recall the news headline: 'Precious jewels stolen!'

Collin is the jewel thief? No, there must be some mistake!

I back up, my breath coming up short. The attack comes on fast, severe enough for a pill-popping event. I snatch my daypack from the floor and paw through it for my clonazepam.

Shaking, I fumble with the child-proof top, hating these mother effing hard-to-open lids.

I stumble into the jacks and sink onto the toilet. Wrestling the stubborn lid, it flies off and pills bounce to the floor. I pluck two, pop them in my mouth, then turn on the faucet. Cupping my hands, I fill them with water and slurp enough to swallow the pills.

The room spins. I wait for the clonazepam to take effect and calm me the feck down.

It's not working fast enough. The room spins faster.

My heart thunders as usual, and I pray I don't have a heart attack. I hear my name and then...

Nothing.

I rouse myself from my fainting spell to persistent knocking. I stumble to the door and fling it open.

Collin stands there, with an alarmed expression.

I glance at the bike, leaned against the wall, remembering.

"I'm feeling unwell," I choke out.

Turning on my heel, I exit the back entrance of the bookstore. Then hop on my bike and gun the motor at top speed all the way home.

"Shayla!" Collin calls after me, but instead of turning back, tears run down my cheeks.

Collin Stedman is a fecking jewelry thief.

I should have known he was too good to be true. Didn't know what I'd expected; but certainly not his being a random thief.

Who am I to talk? I kill people for a living.

Chapter 10

"**S**hayla! Wake up!" Early the next morning, Uncle Casen's voice booms outside my bedroom door as he pounds on it. He never comes upstairs. My heart quickens.

I spring from my bed and peek around my door.

"We have an urgent situation. A new contract, but a rat of a different hole. The Holden family's youngest son has been stolen. Kidnappers snatched him while they shopped in Dublin. The boy is only six."

Uncle Casen rubs a chubby hand over his stubble. "Prepare for the worst, Shaylee. Bring your nighttime arsenal, including your long and short-range weapons. See you downstairs."

I'm in shock. The Holdens have been friends with our family in Avoca since my parents were kids. I hurry to get dressed. I cross the hall to my supply room and stuff both firearms in a duffle, along with everything I may need.

When I arrive downstairs, Cousin Declan sits at the dining room table, hunched over his laptop, with our Shamrock Cleaners cousins flanking him. His brown hair drops over his forehead and his dimples show, despite his not smiling.

"We've known about a ring that's been doing kidnappings all around Ireland," Declan says, glancing at my black leggings and form fitting t-shirt.

He used to tease that if we weren't related, he would have married me in a Dublin second.

"Word is, there's a holdout kidnappers use across the Irish Sea near the Isle of Anglesey, in Holyhead. They hole up in an old place on Kingsland Road near the Irish Ferries to wait for their ransom. When they collect, they don't return the kids...they sell them."

His words tear my insides. I move to his laptop, peering at the screen.

"Do we know who they are? Are they Irish?"

Declan shakes his head. "Not this group. My sources say they're limeys from Liverpool. They have a sophisticated Internet-based network and move before anyone can get to them."

He glances up at me. "They've been at this for a while."

Keen to do my part to makes things right, I turn to the Uncles.

"I take it we're sailing to Wales?"

"Good thing we had the *Stormbird* overhauled," responds Uncle Brodie, exchanging a somber look with Uncle Casen.

I glance around the room. "When do we leave?"

"Soon as we can. It's four hours across the Irish Sea to the Port of Holyhead. We'll need to fuel up when we get there for the trip back to Arklow. Marine forecast is so-so, give or take a patch of rough seas on the way back late tonight."

I gulp, not being a fan of rough water. I like my seawater flat, like a skating rink.

And I like my operations controlled and uncomplicated.

Chapter 11

Declan rents a car under one of his aliases and drives me to an abandoned stone home down one long road, then another. My two cousins from Shamrock Cleaners rent an enclosed van and hang back to wait for our call. I remind them of our motto: NBLB—no bodies left behind.

Declan breaks a window to get us inside the abandoned house, and I assume my watch at the window facing another stone home a short distance away. The Uncles wait on the *Stormbird*.

They mumble some bullshit to the Holyhead harbormaster about the boat parts they'd ordered.

I know what I must do, and I track it in my head. Declan stays quiet, knowing I demand silence to focus when on a job. The abandoned home stinks of mildew. I try not to throw up, and the mask I brought helps.

I suit up in my usual black spandex, head to toe.

I don't have the luxury of time to scope the situation. Time is critical. I'm nervous about more unknowns than knowns, but when a child is at risk, I shove that from my head.

We wait for darkness. I nibble a biscuit but toss it behind me. I can't eat during an operation.

There isn't time to see how many marks occupy the house. It's a disadvantage, but nothing I can't handle. What I know is, one person moves around outside and sits on the front porch.

The lookout. That one will be easy.

My primary concern waits inside.

For this job, I brought my 9mm semi-auto Ruger pistol and double-hulled, tactical suppressor, to quiet the discharge and prevent a gun flash. The Uncles instructed me to use subsonic bullets to quiet my weapon, so I don't need earphones.

"Will be tricky to nail the limey without him seeing you first."

Declan peeks out the window as we wait in the dark.

"We have the advantage." I squint up at the overcast skies. "No lights, no moon. I'll get in close. Not a problem."

I expertly shove the magazine into the pistol with exactly ten rounds—so I can easily count them. The barrel has the suppressor on it.

I'm ready.

The front door is where I train my binoculars. It opens, and a man ambles out, gets in a car, and drives off. Good. One less threat.

"It's time," I say to Declan, tugging the black ski mask over my head and face. I double-check my pistol and ease it into my padded chest pouch.

Declan talks through my action plan. "One, hit your marks. Two, get the kid. Three, get the hell out. I'll be ready when I see you come out."

I nod and exit the back door of the putrid-smelling abandoned house, positioning my night vision goggles over my eyes. I study the targeted house.

A man sits on a chair on the front porch, smoking a cig. I work my way a short distance behind the house, stepping through overgrown, brown grass to make a wide berth as I close in on the kidnapper's lair. Lights are on, and I twist my lenses to zoom in.

A woman sits at a table with a small boy. Another man stands at a kitchen sink. I wait to see if other marks move into my view.

No one does.

The grass quiets my footsteps, and I move swiftly to the back of the house. I hear voices arguing. Good, they're distracted.

This must be quick. I sneak up to the house and edge along it. I duck below the windows and reach the front. With my back against the wall and pistol pointed up. Quiet as possible, I rack the slide, peeking around the corner.

The man talks on a mobile phone.

Hang up, loser.

JEALOUSY

I don't need anyone else knowing shit has gone wrong. Finally, he ends the call and lights another cig.

Enjoy your smoke, arsehole. It's the last ciggie you'll ever have.

In a flash, I'm around the corner, my red-dot laser locked onto my target. I pump two in rapid succession into his temple. His body slumps in the chair, and I shove my night-vision specs up onto my head, eyeing the door.

I quietly turn the door handle and inch it open. Seeing no one, I creep forward, my arms in a V, gripping my pistol. Living room is empty. *Clear.*

I swing my weapon in a semi-circle in case an unexpected mark pops up out of nowhere.

Voices echo in the bare-bones kitchen. I move steadily toward it, tense with adrenaline.

I'm banking on the child still sitting at the end of the table, near the wall. The man stands in the middle of the kitchen sucking down a beer, pistol tucked in his pants. He is sideways to me as I quietly creep to the doorway and my red dot helps me aim two clean shots at his temple.

He drops as the woman jumps to her feet and aims her weapon.

I empty three into her, my peripheral on the little boy, now huddled in the corner, crying.

There are four shots left. Hopefully, no more marks.

I pull out my burner phone and text Declan: *Completed. Send cleaners.*

Expecting the other man's return, I flip on my safety and jam my weapon into my chest pouch.

After witnessing what I had done, the last thing the Holden boy wants is to come with me. He's too young to understand why I shot the people in the room with him. I have no time to explain. I don't even know how to start.

He cowers in a corner, knees drawn to his chest, his face contorting as he sobs.

Oh God. What do I do? What do I say?

My heart pounds harder than when I entered this awful place. I squat and hold my hand out, hoping the boy takes it. My hand trembles and I can't control it.

"No! Get away from me!" he screams, darting a glance at the blood pooling on the floor next to the woman whose life I ended.

What have I fecking done to this poor kid? He'll never forget this as long as he lives!

My breaths come up short as my brain explodes. "Stay here, don't move. Please God, don't move!" I say, voice shaking.

I scramble to my feet and run down the hallway out the front door, scanning for Declan's car, eyes darting like a frightened animal.

Rescuing a child is not part of my deal.

I don't do the saving—I only do the cessations.

Like Michael the Archangel, Declan swoops in with the car.

I run to the driver's side and fling the door open. "Help me, Dec! You've got to go in and get the Holden boy. He—he saw me do the hits and won't come with me. He thinks I'll shoot him or something. Please, come get him!"

The panic in my voice disturbs me and therefore disturbs my cousin, who has never known me to lose my shit on a job.

Declan leaps from the car and hurries into the house.

I place my palms on the car to brace myself and stave off an attack. *Inhale, one-two-three-four-five. Exhale, one-two-three-four-five.*

I attempt to suck in a lungful of chilly, salty air, every cell in my body on red alert. Can't seem to open my throat enough to do it.

Declan sprints from the stone house, carrying the frightened little boy. I scurry around the car to open the rear door. Declan settles the boy inside and buckles his seat belt.

He sees me laboring to get air and squeezes my shoulder.

"You okay, Cuz?"

I give him a brisk nod and climb into the front passenger seat. When I turn around and attempt to calm the Holden boy, he shrieks with terror. Meanwhile, the Shamrock Cleaners move briskly inside the house. Declan follows to help our cousins zip bodies inside black plastic bags. In a flash, they emerge with the first one to load into their rental van. Same with the remaining two.

Within five minutes, we complete our operation and vacate. I've managed to calm my breathing.

As Declan speeds to the Port, I attempt to reassure the child.

"You're okay now. No one is going to hurt you."

He pulls back, terrified. A thought flashes—how in God's name will I ever be a mother if I terrorize young children? Our practices are violent, but that's the nature of this business.

Sadly, I realize—it can't be helped. Not while evil roams the earth.

The Uncles wave us aboard the *Stormbird*. There's no chaos; everyone knows their jobs. The Shamrock Cleaner boys and Declan load the three body bags in the cloak of darkness.

The boy huddles in the back seat. His arms hug his knees, and he presses his forehead to them. Declan opens the rear door and lifts out the boy, who buries his face on Declan's shoulder.

Declan soothes the child. "We're taking you home, to your mum and dad."

His tone reminds me of when he's done the same with me, when my world fragments after completing my hits.

A spate of jealousy stabs me. Declan would make a tremendous father, while I've destroyed my chances of ever becoming a mother.

Who wants a cessation specialist for a mother?

Declan kneels and reassures the boy I won't shoot him. "She's one of the good people," he says, with an urgency that tells me to say something to the kid.

I paste on a fake smile and hold out my hand.

"I'm here to make sure you're safe."

The boy looks at Declan, who nods, then the kid gives me a wary look. He takes my hand, allowing me to lead him onboard. I talk to him about a chess set he can play with—or anything else I can think of that might interest a young boy in the belly of a boat.

I want to give him something to occupy his mind until we reach the Port of Arklow.

Declan's buddies show up to collect the rental cars and return them. We wave goodbye as Uncle Brodie throttles up the Volvo inboard and backs out of the temporary slip.

I retreat below decks with the child, where Declan sits me down in the galley and feeds me tea, a biscuit, and Clonazepam after he settles the boy into a bunk in the aft. The boy falls instantly to sleep.

Cousin Declan is the calming force in my tumultuous maelstroms. Too bad we're related. I could take him for a lover. Instead, we're close friends and work well together. The vessel's power builds, and the vibration travels from my feet up to my head. My teeth chatter, and I can't tell if it's from my post-cessation anxiety attack, or the powerful motor's resolve to get us across the Irish Sea.

Declan squeezes my shoulder and mumbles about crossing heavy seas in the black of night to Arklow. Along the way, Uncle Casen and the Shamrock Cleaners do their waste disposal thing on the top decks; weighting the bodies and dumping them overboard for the marine life to feast on.

This is the way it has always been done. The Uncles run a tight ship; our family is a well-oiled machine.

But this is the most intensity I've ever experienced during an operation, with a young life hanging in the balance.

When we dock in Arklow, Declan takes the Holden boy to his family.

There's much I want to say before Declan takes him away...*sorry you saw me kill those people.*

Instead, I'm incapable of giving parting sentiments. Now I must live with my personal hell—plus, the worry the poor boy will talk about what he witnessed tonight. Though his family is aware of our operation, I've compromised it by allowing the boy to see me.

I may have to leave town for a wee bit. Thinking about how I'll accomplish that sickens me. I've never stayed away from home. I'll talk the Uncles into letting me hole up in Bramble Hill Castle.

Overwhelmed and trembling, I grip the gunwale and heave my stomach contents overboard into the Irish Sea, where it will mix with the detritus of the evil we deposited.

Even that was too good for the low down, child-stealing scum.

Chapter 12

The Uncles drop me off for my annual pilgrimage to Castlemacadam Cemetery, outside of Avoca. I wave goodbye as they roll off toward town to claim a bar stool at Fitzgerald's Pub and nurse a Guinness or three.

It rains softly as I open the tall wrought-iron gate and step inside, making my way on the soft grass to the middle aisles. I stop at two gravesites, marked 'Byrne.'

I'm not surprised to see the generous flower bouquets on each grave. They've mysteriously appeared each year for as long as I can remember. I stand at the end of my parents' graves side-by-side, staring at the headstones as I do each year on this dreadful anniversary, when our car crashed twenty years ago.

I was the only survivor of the accident on the road to Arklow—a three-year-old in a coma for weeks with a serious concussion. As a result, I've grown up with memory lapses, and my head feels funny sometimes.

I take my meds and deal with it.

"Hello, Shayla Byrne. My, how you've grown." The voice startles me.

I whirl around to see an exquisitely dressed woman seated on the stone bench behind me, wearing designer sunglasses and holding a black umbrella. She has perfectly coiffed silver hair and a handsome face.

My eyes rove the woman from top to bottom. I note her black patent-leather stilettos from an expensive designer. She's out of place in this quaint country cemetery. I envision her striding along a Paris fashion runway, sporting Gucci or Louis Vuitton.

I, on the other hand, am back in my dreary brown fashions and clunky boots, with my black knit cap pulled low over my head.

"Who are you and how do you know my name?"

I'm wary, as I should be. Few wear shades on a rainy day.

I stand still as the gravestones behind me, scrutinizing her.

The woman pats the stone bench. "Come sit with me."

I hesitate, my imagination swirling. Is this related to our recent operation? Is this a set-up to capture me? My heart thunks as we stare at each other.

She smiles, nodding at me to come forward.

Not knowing what to expect, my stomach tightens as I move to sit next to her on the damp stone. She smells good.

She pulls back, removing her sunglasses. "You have the same sea-green eyes as your mother."

I swallow hard. "How did you know her?"

She shares her umbrella with me. "Have you heard of the Sisters of Sin?"

"Who are you?" I erupt in a demanding voice.

"Call me Mother."

"I have a mother," I snap, setting my jaw.

"Not one like me," she says sagely, wiping raindrops from her glasses. "Your Uncles contacted me."

"Why?" I stave off a rising wave of anxiety.

"You have a unique skill set I can put to good use."

Apprehensive heat climbs up my neck, warming my cheeks. "And what skills are you referring to?" I know damn well what she means.

How could the Uncles sell me out like this?

"Our Sisters of Sin is an organization where the best of the best do honorable work—eradicating the scum who maim, torture, and destroy the lives of innocents. Where justice prevails in ways that society wishes it would."

Mother lifts her chin in the same patrician way I've observed the royals do on TV.

"In other words, you're cessation specialists."

She gives me an odd look. "We say assassins for simplicity."

I stare back at her. "Why are you called the Sisters of Sin?"

"Code names of the seven deadly sins. An age-old tradition. Each woman in the organization works to her strengths—and we train each how to use weaknesses to her advantage." Mother shifts the umbrella to her other hand and leans toward me.

"Our objective—our code—is to maintain balance in the world. When a wrong is committed, we right it. When someone takes lives, we take theirs." Mother sits up straight and stares at my parents' graves. "A simple concept, really."

This is rather intense for an uncodified rural Irish girl.

"Why are you talking to *me*?"

Mother smiles. "Your mum, Clara Byrne, was an exceptional Sister in our organization. I miss her fearless, resolute style. She was our Jealousy girl." Mother's words fell on my ears like a nuclear bomb.

My brow furrows as I work hard to comprehend. "You are mistaken. My mother was a stay-at-home parent and hand-weaver at the Avoca Mill."

I try to hide the alarm in my tone.

"Your mother saved countless lives by terminating others. Her tiny stature was under-estimated, which made her effective."

"No! That's impossible!" I fly off the bench and stumble back, horrified.

"You are lying! Why would you say that?"

"Because it's true," the woman says dismissively, opening a compact and wiping a lipstick smudge from the corner of her mouth.

"The Uncles never mentioned my mother was an assassin." Water pools in my eyes, blurring this woman and her absurdities.

Mother lifts her brows. "And why would they tell you such a thing?"

"Because—it's our family business. They would have mentioned it."

"My dear, you wouldn't have been able to deal with that twist of information. Just as you have difficulty dealing with it now. Only difference is, now you are old enough, having followed in your mother's footsteps."

She snaps her compact closed and drops it in her massive Gucci purse.

"This business operates on a need-to-know basis. You didn't need to know—until now. I want to hire you into the Sisters of Sin as my next Jealousy operative. Think of it as Jealousy 2.0. We'll train you mentally, physically, and...sexually."

I sputter. "Sexually?"

"Your Uncles tell me you're still a virgin. You'll be seducing people, men mostly, in some missions. Unless you prefer your same gender, or both."

Horrified at the Uncles telling this woman such an intimate thing, I guffaw.

"I'm not a virgin!" It's out of my mouth before I can stop it.

Mother's brows lift. "All the better. Frankly, it's none of my business. I hope the young man was worthy of you." Her expression is serious, and I see she means it.

"He was—is." It occurs to me I shouldn't refer to Collin in the past tense. I shouldn't hold it against him that he's a thief. After all, I hadn't shared my lovely specialty with him either.

When we live a life of lies, it's hard to know what's true and what isn't.

I swipe at my cheeks and heave out a sigh, leaning back on the wet, hard bench.

"How grand...like mother, like daughter." I stroke the Celtic cross on my mother's necklace the Uncles gave me for my twenty-first birthday.

"Casen and Brodie summoned me. We've known each other for ages—worked together—off and on through the years. You come highly recommended. They explained what you did in your recent job. I'm impressed. And I don't impress easily. Your uncles think you should leave town for a while because of the situation with the Holden boy."

I snap to attention. "You know about that?"

Mother chuckles. "I know everything about you. I don't hire anyone without thoroughly vetting. What pleases me most is, you're nowhere online. A superhuman feat in today's narcissistic world."

I narrow my eyes. "Have the Uncles told you I'm autistic? I must have things a certain way, or I get panic attacks. Things must be clean. Orderly. I've always relied on the Uncles for structure in my life."

"Yes, they relayed you're on the spectrum. They explained your advanced cognitive skills, how educated you are, and your proclivity for memorizing data and numbers. All skills we can use. And you'll be well compensated." She gives me an up-and-down assessment.

"Along with a new wardrobe."

Mother puts on her designer shades, fringed with gold. "And if you need structure, we'll provide that, too, in addition to improving your communication skills."

I chuckle. "All of us are on the spectrum in some form." I don't delve into the substantial amount of reading and research I've done about autism.

"So, what'll it be?" Mother waits patiently for my response, holding her umbrella over both of us.

As hard as it might be to leave my carefully controlled environment, this could be an opportunity to get out of town for a while—until the dust settles from the Holden boy kidnapping.

Mother waits patiently as I process everything she'd proposed. I arrive at a decision.

"All right. I'll be your Jealousy 2.0 operative, provided you tell me about my mum. And my dad." I stare at their graves, then look up at her.

"Agreed." Mother's elegant chin dips into an affirmation. "Excellent decision. I'm glad you'll be joining us." She rises from the bench and extends her black-gloved hand.

I shake her hand, and she squeezes mine.

"Good. Now go home and pack, and we'll fly to Rome."

"Can we wait until tomorrow? There's someone I must see first. A bookshop owner."

"Ah, your virginity man." Mother turns to me. "He won't be a problem, will he? I discourage romance relationships with my employees. Things get complicated."

I hesitate before I respond. "No. He won't be a problem."

"Tell him you'll be working for a Rome-based jewelry design business. We have several faux companies as fronts for our Sisters. We don't exactly advertise what we do," Mother says drily, shifting her umbrella to her other hand.

I nod, feeling naked and vulnerable to this woman who knows everything about me.

First, I want to explain to Collin why I rushed out of the bookshop that day. And I want to say goodbye.

Chapter 13

Fifteen minutes before the Celtic Sea Bookshop opens, I wait for Collin one last time on my old perch up on the hill in the cemetery, behind the O'Toole gravestone. I want to observe him first while he doesn't know I'm watching; like old times when the mere sight of him spiraled me into the throes of erotic desire.

I don't gratify myself sexually, but when I see him, I'm tempted.

Precisely on time, Collin motors uphill on his e-bike and unlocks the store. The sun glints his hair auburn, and he disappears inside. I marvel at his appearance—more delectable than the last time I saw him.

I pick my way downhill in the back of the cemetery and walk my bike across the street to the bookshop. This time, I enter the front door, welcoming the familiar bell that announces my entrance.

Collin arranges jewelry in the display case as I approach. He doesn't look up.

"You're ignoring me," I say softly as I step toward him.

There are new pieces in the display case. His sticky-fingered acquisitions, no doubt.

Collin continues with what he's doing. "Tell me why I shouldn't."

He glances at me, his usual smile absent. His somber expression twinges my chest.

"I'm sorry for leaving in a hurry the other day," I say. "I've been busy with work—with things I had to..." I trail off, hoping he won't ask me the real reason I had bailed from the bookshop.

He takes care to arrange the sparkling designs in his jewelry case. "I wondered why you haven't been in." He straightens and looks at me. "I pounded on the bathroom door that day, and when you finally opened it, you took off like a racehorse. No explanation, nothing."

"I know. I'm sorry." I apologize again, because isn't that what people do when they're desperate for someone to like them?

Do I tell him I know he's a jewelry thief? If I do, he'll know I was there that night at the horse farm—and he'll want to know why.

"I'm leaving Arklow," I blurt, not knowing how else to break the news.

His eyes dart up to me. "For good?"

I stare down at my feet. "I don't know. For a while, anyway. I'm going to Rome."

"Why?" He steadies his gaze on me.

I swallow. "I'm going to work for—em—a—company my uncles have arranged." Mother had instructed me to use my jewelry design experience as my cover. She would make sure I had business cards, brochures, and a professional website, all with an alias.

It was only a half lie. Then again, Collin and I have never been forthright with each other. We're a pair of deceitful twins in lockstep with our dishonesty.

"Which company?"

I shrug, regretting I've said too much. "A jewelry design business. They're only getting started," I say dismissively.

"Oh." His brows lift. "When do you leave?"

"Tomorrow." I search his face. For what, I don't know. Am I seeking reassurance? A hint that he still cares for me?

If he *ever* did.

"Come to dinner at my place tonight?" There's the infectious smile I've longed for since the last time we were together.

My heart lifts. I light up like New Year's fireworks. "Tell me where you live."

When he does, I'm shocked to learn it's near our cottage on the edge of town.

Chapter 14

I stand naked in the modest bedroom of the first man I've ever desired. The one who'd relieved me of my virginity—an aberrant curse at my age. The first who genuinely understands me, despite not knowing much about me.

He accepts me. And I appreciate him for it.

Possibly even...*love him for it?*

I berate myself. No, I can't love him. Not when I'm about to do God-knows-what in God-knows-where for a decades-old entity in Rome that I pray welcomes me with open arms.

Collin doesn't ask what I do besides making Celtic designs, and I don't ask why he steals jewelry from horse breeder magnates.

I figure that makes us even.

Throughout the dinner he'd prepared for me with candlelight, mellow music, and a crackling fire, we'd picked up where we left off. We talked about biology, books, movies, and the history of Rome—carefully avoiding the twin elephants in the room.

Sharp pangs poke my chest, and I question my decision to leave.

Maybe I shouldn't go. If I stay, Collin and I could get married.

I envision what I'd say on our honeymoon. "Oh, sweetheart, by the way...I forgot to mention I'm a cessation specialist—you know, someone who ends lives for money."

Then he'd confess he's a professional jewelry thief, and we'd live happily ever after in wedded bliss—in an underworld of our choosing.

Cruel reality slaps me as I realize this is the end of the road for us.

Actually, there is no 'us'. And I don't have the guts to say it.

But when Collin asks me to stay the night, I don't hesitate. This is our last time together.

He switches off the bedroom light and moves to me, kissing me with ferocious intensity, the way he did the first time. I want his hands on me—and I don't care where, as long as he touches me—holds me.

"I'll miss you." His voice is guttural as he slides his lips down my neck and up again.

"I'll come back to visit." My words are empty—I haven't the foggiest whether I will—but I'm compelled to say it. I don't want Collin to visit me in Rome. Not sure where I'll be living or staying, but wherever it is, civilians will not be privy to my location.

That much I know.

I help Collin shed his clothes and bend to kiss his chest and stomach. I continue lower, wanting to give him a parting gift...one he'll remember.

When I slide my lips down low, he stops me. Cradling my cheeks, he lifts my face to his.

"Look at me, Shayla."

I do as he says, and glue my gaze to his, painfully aware I'll miss drowning myself in his pools of blue.

"Yes?"

"I don't want to lose you. Do you really have to go?"

I'm not sure what to say because I don't know what the future holds. I take a stab at it, anyway. "I have to do this. But I can't promise you won't lose me."

I kiss him, and we fall onto the bed, where he makes love to me. This time without virginity pain, and it's spectacular. When we wake after drifting off, he makes love to me. I can't get enough of him.

A pain stabs me, knowing I probably won't see him again.

I finally understand all the commotion about sex—especially when you care about someone.

I kiss his cheek. "Thanks for being my friend—and part-time lover." But I have much more to thank him for...like gifting me with endless possibility.

I now understand and appreciate the passion and want of another—the tenderness of intimacy with another human being.

Truth be told, Collin had lit a spark in my soul, melting the jealousies of others I'd carried far too long. I'm grateful to him for unchaining me from the shadows—I'm no longer invisible. Not to Collin, anyway.

He nibbles my ear and murmurs, "Come find me when you return."

"I will," I say, wishing I could mean it with all my heart—knowing that I can't.

When we live a life of lies, what we wish for and what we say are...meaningless.

PART TWO
JEALOUSY
The Assassin

You are still worldly.
For since there is jealousy and quarreling among you, are you not
worldly?
Are you not acting like mere humans? —Corinthians 3:3

Chapter 15
Dominika Gagolin

C ode Name: *Aggravate.*
    London, England.

The Italian woman couldn't keep her mouth shut. I knew she'd squeal like a pig. It had to be her—saw her peeking out the door of her flat next door to Armand Adante's flat as I left—after I'd squeezed his neck like an orange until his eyeballs bulged, and his heart stopped.

What was her name again? Ah yes, Aida Russo. I'll make sure she doesn't tell anyone she had seen me. Another loose end to take care of.

I'm used to being alone in this screwed-up mess of a world. And I'm alone now, except for the loyal ones I've recruited to help me reach my goal.

Trusting Jeff Lynsey had been a grave mistake.

Loser.

All men cast women aside when their use for them ends. Why did I think he'd be any different?

Americans— never trust them.

Should have known better. Mother Russia would surely spit on me for thinking anything would come of getting involved. And I'd spit back at her, for betraying me.

Lynsey had awarded me with the code name Aggravate. Probably because I get wicked joy from agitating those who have wronged me.

I'm sick of cleaning house, but it must be done. I must do something about Mother, aka Elizabeth Danvers, who is no more mother to me than my own poor mother was. She tried to be, but I won't allow guilt or my past friendship to get in my way.

If Mother didn't know before, then she sure knows it now.

I'm systematically removing all the men who had a hand in destroying my family. Leaving me an orphan. One. By. One.

JEALOUSY

The bomb that had killed the Conexus kingmakers has liberated me. I'd dented the ancient tradition of these men who think they are gods, deciding who lives and who dies.

Eliminating the ex-Mossad agent, David Adelman, was the most rewarding act of personal vengeance for causing my father's death. Adelman had used him to gain intelligence on the USSR, then abandoned him when the KGB declared him an enemy of the state. Adelman had done nothing when the authorities arrested my father and sent him to a Siberian labor camp. I enjoyed stalking him first, my favorite part of being a killer for hire—best in the world, I might add.

My reputation is known everywhere. Heads of state fear me, and other assassins avoid me. I leave an unequaled trail of carnage in my wake.

The unsuspecting prey has no clue what hell and damnation are about to rain down on them. Because when one must choose between cowardice and violence, I've chosen violence.

And that's how I've survived.

As the most beautiful assassin in the world, I amass power over the weak. The ones who desire a sexual conquest. I let them think they will until I squeeze the lifeblood from them. Some call me Black Widow Assassin for killing when I finish toying with my prey.

Then there's the tetchy matter of the Sisters, who used to be allies. But as we all know, assassins betray one another. Mother has turned them against me. And she will pay. I needed the Sisters but didn't go to Pride's supercilious get together. I figured it was a trap.

I've slipped under the radar for self-preservation and to regroup, plan the rest of my eliminations to get what I want: The Sisters of Sin. Only then will I be the Queenmaker.

Mother will no longer be hearing from me as a Sister of Sin. Not until I decide what to do with her. I'm irritated that some of the Sisters have been poking into my financial affairs. That is the one thing they better not be messing with. That is crossing the line.

Those two new little witches, all cocky and thinking they are good at what they do—they won't know what hit when I come after them. My people tell me, Jealousy, the gutless mouse, is Mother's new puppet to sniff my trail.

When I'm done with Elizabeth Danvers, she won't be sniffing anything.

So, Jealousy and Lust...watch out, girls. I'll enjoy ending you like I've ended others who don't deserve to live. Your ridiculous disguises aren't working. I know who you are, and I'm coming for you. I didn't catch Greed, but I will certainly catch you.

Count on it.

With my boot pressed to my Sisters' necks, they'll be calling *me* Mother when the final bell tolls. Mother blames me for wreaking havoc—I know, because I bugged her phone and listened to conversations with the other pathetic American loser, Finn Rogers—and the other Sisters.

I must implement my plan before Mother comes after me. But she's weak. I know where she's vulnerable. This will be fun. I've assembled a loyal group of followers to do my bidding. I'm a natural, ruthless leader and always knew I was destined for greatness—like Catherine the Great, Russian empress—the longest-ruling female leader and overthrower of men.

They'll never know how many millions I've pilfered from Conexus. I'm clever to disguise moving their money. I stay one step ahead—creating distractions with one hand in their pocket.

I'll drain everything. Their money. Their investments. Their families.

Their lives.

Conexus and the Sisters of Sin will regret ever having heard of the greatest assassin who ever lived. And like the city of my birth, I do not indulge in tears.

Tears are for the weak.

Chapter 16
Shayla

C ode Name: Jealousy.
Bratislava, Slovakia.

When the wheels touch down in Vienna, I take a train to Bratislava under a fake name. I want to view the countryside on the ground, since this is my first foray to Eastern Europe. Trains relax me, unlike hurtling through the air in a metal sausage tube that could fall out of the sky at any given moment.

It gives me time to prepare for my first official assignment with the Sisters of Sin and review a few Slovak phrases I'd practiced. I settle into a comfortable seat in the dining car and place my dinner order. Brushing back strands of my blunt-cut red wig, I resist the temptation to scratch my itchy scalp. I hate wearing these wigs and miss my trusty black knit cap I wore in Ireland.

Mother has made it clear I'm to do a better job of keeping up my appearance, especially for situations like this job I'm on now. I'm anxious about working more in the open; I miss the dark blanket of night where appearance wasn't the major concern in our family's operation back home.

My appearance wasn't high on my priority list until Collin Stedman swept me off my feet—and swept my virginity along with them. I wonder what he's doing right now. I miss how easy I am with him. He accepts me as I am without bombarding me with questions about my past.

Unlike our family operation back home, Mother wants us to know who our marks are and why we remove them. She had assigned Vanity to brief me about this job before I left headquarters in Rome. Vanity's specialty was dealing with the traffickers. She'd explained that my target is a powerhouse in the human trafficking industry that snatches young girls and women from Eastern Europe and traffics them to Western Europe.

I sit up in my seat and open my tablet to read the encrypted email from SOS intel, then I scroll down to the photos section. The bald, middle-aged man with an ever-so-charming smile and expensive suit emulates a successful CEO on the cover of a business magazine.

How quaint.

I move my finger down to note the name of his front company: EuroComm. I frown at the subheading. *The leading edge of Europe's 5G wireless network.*

Not true. Declan says China has now usurped that desirable distinction.

My eyes narrow. It makes sense this guy would run his trafficking business solely by digital means. Cousin Declan had explained how cybercrime investigation bureaus had hacked into encrypted email between the man in this photo and other 'independent contractors' to trace sources and IP addresses. The bureaus had followed his pathway through dozens of servers around the world.

But this sleaze runs a sophisticated network, staying ten steps ahead of everyone.

Until now.

Apparently, someone had become fed up with Mr. Sleaze's operation and relayed his intel to Conexus board member, Jeff Lynsey. In the name of humanity, he had directed Mother to assign this trafficker as a prioritized hit.

Thanks to Cousin Declan—who taught me well—my affinity for navigating the dark web, hacking into mobile phones and email has come in handy. I'd traced the most recent online IP address to Bratislava, and turned it over to Finn Rogers, Mother's right-hand man. He and his staff oversee all things technical, and they'd flushed out the details of where and when the mark would be most accessible.

JEALOUSY

I'm not crazy about doing this hit in an up close and personal proximity. As part of my apprenticeship, Mother is evaluating my ability to execute close contact hits when situations require it.

My reasoning to accomplish this job from a sniper's distance fell on deaf ears. Mother wanted me out of my comfort zone to 'become more flexible.' She didn't realize what she was asking of someone with an autistic obsessive-compulsive brain—I refuse to invoke the word 'disorder.' I don't have a disorder—I just interpret information differently.

The Uncles call it my extra special gift.

Collin told me I'm not disordered. He made it sound I was more normal than normal people. And all my life I'd thought of myself as defective.

I let out a shaky breath, wishing this hit wasn't my first SOS assignment.

There is more than enough potential for me to mess this up.

Chapter 17
Shayla

The breeze teases my face as I sit on a plush bench seat on the starboard side of a catamaran, admiring the beauty of the Danube River, as the chartered boat departs from the Bratislava passenger port. I'm delighted to experience this river for myself after a lifetime of the Uncles playing Johann Strauss's famous waltz.

My mark charters this private cruise each month to attend symphonies in Vienna, spending his profits from the dark web orchestration of buying and selling human beings. These cruises are invitation only, and Mother made sure I have one.

No other guests are onboard. SOS intel informed me Mr. Sleaze enjoys a grand fuck on the way, with the beauty-of-the-month who catches his eye.

Tonight, that beauty is me.

The heavy makeup I've applied feels like Kevlar on my face. My head swirls with the tips and tricks to seduce men Vanity and Pride had schooled me on.

Sitting in the stern, I gauge my position and scrutinize the time, which is critical on this two-hour cruise.

I'd flirted with the captain upon boarding, asking him how long to the intermediary stop halfway to Vienna, where he refuels for much cheaper than in the city. Finn had mined this little tidbit by sending staff to flush out every aspect of this cruise.

He also found out only two security people are onboard. They stay in the front, while Mr. Sleaze frolics in the stern.

I marvel at how omniscient Finn and Mother are, seeming to know everything about everyone.

JEALOUSY

A myriad of sunset colors reflects off the water, as I pretend to sip from my flute of champagne—the taste is bitter, and the bubbles sting my nose. I run my tongue along my lower lip, professing to enjoy it.

I cross my legs in an elegant model pose, making sure the slit in my reversible, silver lamé dress exposes my leg to the hip. I dangle the hook by making it obvious I have nothing on underneath.

The low-life shark takes the bait and I slowly reel him in. He moves toward me in his tux, flute in hand—a predator with a radar lock on his prey. I give him a come-do-me smile, knowing who the real predator is.

The sun drops below the forested hills in the distance as the boat separates the calm waters. Night falls fast as we leave the city lights behind.

"I understand you write smut," he says, in his thick Slovak accent, taking a seat beside me. "I had you checked out."

"We refer to it as erotica." Mother had a fake web page created under a pen name with erotica titles. I don't know how she pulled that off with IDs to match, but God bless her.

He smirks at me. "Something tells me you're good at it."

The way he says it tells me everything; he plans to be inside me in the next ten minutes.

I let him think that.

"It's a living." I hate small talk and pretty much suck at it. I angle toward him so he can see more of what he thinks he's getting.

"Care to show me what you write about?" He sets his flute on the table.

"I'm not into voyeurism," I say flatly, motioning at his bodyguard who's stepped out from the sleek cabin. He stands, watching us, like he plans to get in on an orgy porn adventure. The other bodyguard is in the bow, talking to the captain.

This bodyguard had security-checked me upon boarding to ensure I was clean. He'd also been handsy when frisking me for weapons.

I'd gritted my teeth with a fake smile, focused on completing my assignment.

The mark barks in Slovak to the dark-suited gorilla. "*Nechajte nás, prosím.*"

Yes, please leave us, I say to myself. I want to get rid of this sleazeball and go home.

The man strips me with his eyes. "Lose the dress."

"Mmm, no time for such nonsense," I purr, careful with my own practiced Slovak accent. I can't remove my dress and accomplish my mission; a naked woman strolling down the street after a hit might be a bit of a red flag.

"Then lift it."

I can see he commands his world, and I wonder how many times he's ordered young innocent women to remove their clothes. The thought sickens me, but what makes me feel better—he won't say it ever again.

To anyone.

I scoot to the edge of the cushioned bench and hike my dress high on my thighs.

He eyes his target and licks his lips like a ravenous hyena. As he comes toward me, he says something about my sparkly necklace.

If he only knew.

He tugs the spaghetti strap off my shoulder and traces the top of my breast with his bejeweled forefinger.

I want to recoil when he touches me. Eyeing the dark water surrounding us, I force myself to open my legs to tease. I make a mental note to thank Vanity for imparting this handy tip.

"Come here," I say, tugging him down to where I sit.

He kneels to give me a repulsive, sloppy kiss, hands plunging down the inside of my dress. As disgusting as this is, it's right where I want him.

I reach up and deftly loosen the clasp on my necklace. I lift it up over my wig and loop one end over the other, the same as the rabbit snares I used to set as a kid.

I wrap one end around my fist.

When Mr. Sleaze gropes the insides of my thighs and bends his head down, I strike, lassoing my wire-snare necklace over his head. I yank the end hard, and the snare tightens around his neck, cutting off his air and blood flow.

His eyeballs bulge. He hasn't a clue what's hit him. I spring to my feet, tugging the end of the snare up and taut. I slip behind him as he struggles.

He claws at his neck, but I've garroted him, and his efforts won't earn him any traction.

It's a wonder Interpol hasn't tracked me down with my internet searches—three to four minutes and thirty-three pounds of pressure causes suffocation and brain death.

The time feels like an eternity.

Before this mark collapses, I wrestle his weight onto the bench seat, keeping the snare wire snug until he stops moving. I act quickly—panting and cussing—making a mental note to tell Mother no more close contact hits.

I loosen the wire necklace around his neck and lift it off him. Careful not to drip blood on me, I fling it into the river, repeating our family mantra, "No bodies left behind, no bodies left behind..."

Finn and I had locked horns about my no-bodies-left-behind policy. We'd argued long and hard, until he elevated our gridlock to Mother. She'd rolled her eyes and instructed him to do it.

So, Finn had sent an agent to stash a heavy weight inside the stern compartment. The Shamrock Cleaners and the Uncles weren't here to do body disposal. Bratislava and Vienna were a bit out of their way for the *Stormbird*.

I glance around at the encompassing darkness, thankful for the quiet hum of the motor as the boat slices through the water. I open the stern compartment to remove the rope tied to the portable anchor that Finn had assured me would be there.

The rope wraps easily around the body's ankles, and I tie it off, then unlatch the door in the transom.

Sitting on the deck, I push the anchor overboard with my feet, grunting like a weightlifter. It plunks in, and the hungry water gobbles the rope, then the body follows, as if an underwater monster summons it to the deep.

Everything disappears under the calm black water, like our waste disposal back home in the Irish Sea.

I close the transom door and latch it, then grab my beaded evening purse. I tug the dress strap onto my shoulder and smooth my wig, as the boat maneuvers to the dock and idles.

Perfect timing.

The second the boat stops, I hike up my dress and hoist myself over the side of the stern. Seeing no one around, I slide onto the dock and walk briskly away without a backward glance. I stride up the ramp to the street, where Finn has a car waiting to take me to the Vienna airport.

Once inside the vehicle, I attempt to control my breathing. Declan isn't here to help me through my post-cessation anxiety. Focusing on the city lights zipping past, I'm nauseated by the smell of Mr. Sleaze's repulsive cologne that has rubbed off on me.

I paw through my beaded purse for a moist towelette and rip it open with my teeth. I remove the wet wipe and vigorously wipe everywhere the slimeball had touched me.

The driver glimpses me in his rearview mirror. I avoid his gaze and snap my focus to the night lights of Vienna, while Declan's voice plays in my head...one-two-three, breathe...one-to-three, breathe.

Declan, I wish you were here to help me through this.

JEALOUSY

At the airport, I retrieve the daypack I'd stashed in my locker and duck into the women's restroom. I reverse my dress to the blue side and raise it to knee-length, belting it. I toss the red wig into the garbage bin, then tug on the short white wig and position my librarian style, horn-rimmed glasses on my nose.

Taking a children's book from my daypack, I tuck it under my arm.

Finn figured I'd easily pull off an elementary school teacher look with my built-in nerdiness. Was that a compliment or a put-down?

I don't know, nor do I care.

Thankful to have this over with, I exit the restroom and take a seat, thumbing through *Sally's Happy Unicorn,* waiting for my flight to board.

No one would guess this nerdy teacher is returning from a weekend of killing a human trafficker who was part of an international organized crime ring that sold women and children into slavery.

At least there is one less force of evil roaming the earth.

I wonder how many lives I've saved by eliminating him. The scum viewed trafficking victims as a commodity for financial profit—with a total disregard for human rights and dignity. Tossing him into the river was too good for him.

I should have cut him into pieces, as the Uncles would have done.

One thing is for sure...I refuse to do body disposal again. Why had I insisted on it?

Because that's what I'd learned in our family business—bodies are evidence—leaving them is sloppy practice.

I also want to impress my new employer.

The burner phone Finn supplied me pings a notification: *Call Mother ASAP.*

Oh cripes! Are the Austrian Federal Police after me?

I shoot a nervous glance down both airport corridors and rise, moving to a private corner, tapping the number. It rings once. Mother answers. She knows it's me.

"Jealousy? Why haven't you reported in yet? Wanted to know how your first assignment went." I can barely hear Mother's voice against the overhead speaker announcing my flight to Rome.

"When you get to Rome, report to headquarters. We have additional assignments for you." Mother lets out a heavy sigh.

The old anxieties kick in, pounding my heart. "Not more up close and persona ones, I hope?"

"We'll see about that when you get here."

Oh no, I wonder what she means by that.

"Do I have a choice?" My voice wiggles as I hurry to my gate.

"No," says Mother. "You don't."

"Boarding now. Good-bye Mo—I mean see you in Rome." Code name or not, I stop myself from calling this woman Mother to her face. I had a mother.

I end the call.

My carry-on catches on the door and I yank it loose and scurry along the jetway. I scoot onto the plane, and sink into my first-class leather seat, relieved to be onboard—hurtling metal tube be damned.

I hadn't been with the Sisters of Sin organization very long when Mother said Greed suspected Dominika Gagolin—one of our SOS sisters—had blown Conexus to bits. My stomach turns over as I wonder how the Sisters of Sin organization will move forward, given this information.

In an uncharacteristic maneuver, I accept the wine the flight attendant offers. My hand trembles as I down the whole thing. I grimace at the woman next to me, who shoots me a disgusted look.

Then I ask for another.

What the bollocks did I get myself into?

Chapter 18
Collin

Collin Stedman watched the door close behind his last customer of the day at the Celtic Sea Bookshop. He closed the business accounting program he'd been working on and yawned.

He'd just returned from his trip across the pond to America. It had been a while since he'd visited his parents, who had retired and left Ireland to live—in all places—Anchorage, Alaska.

As always when he visited, he'd played the role of angelic son, smiling as his parents bragged about their bookseller child, who traveled the world on book-buying sprees.

His mother had tried to match him up with a couple of strong and independent Alaskan beauties. Out of politeness, he'd taken a couple to dinner, but when the last one reminded him of a certain Irish lass, he'd lost interest.

Collin sat back and sighed.

It was time to get back to work, doing what he did best—wheel and deal with those wanting to hire him to steal expensive things—and who paid handsome prices to acquire them.

These days he was choosy about the jobs he accepted. With cam surveillance everywhere, and increased worldwide sensor technology, it was an ever-increasing challenge to lift a rare artifact or steal art pieces.

He'd worked around laser technology and hacked into security systems with the best of them, but that technology was old school now, compared to facial recognition, retinal scans, and advanced sensory systems.

He'd learned to adapt by upping his technical skills. Unfortunately, there were no training classes to take, other than informative discussions on the dark web by those who prided themselves in besting the latest technologies. Their good old-fashioned narcissism and need to brag served Collin well in his quest to stay on top of the latest security systems.

Collin pulled his laptop toward him on top of the jewelry counter, and inadvertently glanced through the glass. One of Shayla's unique filigree designs caught his eye—the Celtic cross with the peridot gem on the apex. She had agreed to let him sell the necklace on consignment.

Several people had shown interest, but he'd raised the price.

Deep down he wanted to keep it.

But why hang onto something from a woman I can't have—who I may never see again?

"I'll take the necklace home. If I happen to see Shayla in the future, I'll pay her for it," he mumbled, fishing out his keys and unlocking the back slider to remove the necklace.

He picked up his jeweler's loupe, removed the cover, and slid it back, holding the magnifier to his eye. Shayla did fine work. He especially liked the subtle Victorian touches she applied to her designs. She was a romantic at heart but would never admit it.

She hadn't admitted to much of anything on the occasions they'd spent time together.

Collin thought about it. If he kept her necklace, in all fairness, he'd have to pay her. And to pay her, he'd have to track her down. If he ever went to Rome, that would be a good excuse to look her up.

Shayla had always cloaked her family in secrecy, and Collin wouldn't poke her uncles for information. He knew better than to inquire as to her whereabouts.

No matter. He had ways of finding people.

He carefully set the necklace into a long, rectangular gift box and inserted it into his daypack for the bike ride home. He'd sold Shayla's other jewelry designs and planned to pay her for her share of the sales. It wasn't much. Maybe five hundred euros.

Collin may have been one of the world's finest professional thieves, but he prized honesty.

Now for the next order of business. He rose to make sure he had locked and secured the front and back doors, then sat down and pulled his laptop close.

He tapped the keys to access the VPN he'd purchased with a department store gift card he'd gotten in Dublin. Then typed the fifteen-character username and twenty-character password he kept in his head. Never would he write these down anywhere. Couldn't risk it.

Not in his line of business.

Up popped the chat screen. He changed his handle and site address each week. Sometimes he changed it two or three times a week, depending on site activity. Those who brokered the next-to-impossible jobs had access to this site—not one for amateurs—only a select few knew it even existed.

Collin exercised caution with all things in cyberspace, lest a Garda or an Interpol agent be lurking to snag criminals. He didn't consider himself a criminal. He was a professional thief for hire. But Interpol, the International Criminal Police Organization—with one hundred ninety-five member countries—didn't see it that way.

He clicked several messages and deleted them if they didn't contain enough zeros. Curious, he moved his cursor down to click on the one without zeros—and smiled at the scorpion icon.

This was a handler he'd dealt with before, though he hadn't met him in person. He'd negotiated a deal with Collin to steal a piece of rare art, then the dealers had backed out. The handler had sent him a few thousand as a compensation apology—a good will gesture to assure future deals. Though rare in this business, it was good form. The man knew protocol for dangling carrots to keep the Collin Stedmans' of the world willing to collaborate with him.

Collin clicked his personal key to decrypt the message with the scorpion icon. He sipped his now cold tea and grimaced at it, waiting for the ciphertext to convert into plain text.

A message from Scorpio, the handler. *Have a lucrative job offer.*

Collin typed. *How many zeros?*

Scorpio: *Must meet in person. A ticket will be waiting at the airport of your choice.*

"Yeah right," muttered Collin. *Prove you're legit first.*

Scorpio: *Brokered the deal for your Paris boost a year ago. When my dealer backed out, I compensated you for your trouble.*

"Okay buddy, let's volley," Collin said to his screen, fingers tapping. *Thanks for that, btw. Intrigued. Regretfully, I'm just the business manager. My client needs inspiration.*

Scorpio: *Will look good on your resume.*

"Ha!" erupted Collin. *Not that kind of inspiration. Where am I going?*

Scorpio: *You'll find out, day after tomorrow. Name your airline.*

Collin bit into his apple, chewing loudly. *Emirates. First class.*

Scorpio: *Suppose you want a Maserati as well?*

Collin grinned at the screen. *Just some inspiration deposited into my account.*

Scorpio: *Let's see what my dealer says.*

Collin waited, envisioning the person on the other end making a sandwich and cracking open a beer instead of contacting anyone.

A gif appeared with euro bills scattering everywhere.

Scorpio: *Will send 10k for your trouble and cover your airfare.*

Collin raised his brows. He'd fly anywhere for ten grand.

He typed. *Send to the Moneytree account I specify.*

He sent Scorpio an email address, then pulled up his account. Ten thousand in USD appeared like magic. This must have been a complex heist if they're willing to part with a hefty cash sum just to fly him to a meeting.

Scorpio: *Look for a sign that says John Smith.*

"Seriously?" muttered Collin. *At least tell me where I'm going.*

Smiley face emojis appeared with an Italian flag. Collin chuckled.

"Looks like I'm going to Italy. I like this guy."

The messages dissolved, supposedly showing they'd disappeared from cyberspace. Though he wasn't a computer expert, Collin had his doubts. For all he knew, once he tapped 'send' his message could wander the Milky Way until a black hole sucked it into another dimension.

Not everything came without risk.

Time to head home. It was late, and he needed sleep.

Chapter 19
Shayla

Construction is ongoing at Conexus, to restore the main floor. The incessant hammering gives me a headache. Directly above the underground Sisters of Sin headquarters, workers are doing their level best to breathe life back into our ancient limestone building. Most of the rebuilding is complete, and workers are doing the finishing touches.

Despite the windows being blown out and black soot covering the limestone, the damage hadn't seemed too bad from the outside. The explosion had spared our underground SOS operation, so we still meet here. It was mainly the Conexus board room on the main floor that had taken the brunt of the explosion.

It was a miracle three of the seven Conexus board members had survived. Mother found them and had them rushed to their own private medical facility. She'd kept it quiet the three were still alive and had placed security guards outside their rooms while they recovered. Whoever planned the explosion had ensured the blast happened during a Conexus board meeting.

After the medical facility had discharged the three survivors—Jeff Lynsey and two others—they'd remained in an undisclosed location. Mother was the only SOS person in touch with them. We Sisters remained in the dark as to their whereabouts, which was fine by me.

Mother crosses her arms and leans on the imposing oak desk in her lavish office suite. Finn Rogers stands next to her, as her right-hand man. I've noticed Finn has a thing for Mother, judging from his adoring expression whenever she speaks.

The only other people in the room are two of my Sisters, Vanity and Pride. Everyone else is out on assignment. I'm still getting used to my code name, Jealousy, after being Shayla for so long.

JEALOUSY

Mother leads our briefing. "I've summoned all of you here for an update on our current status." She nods at my Sisters, seated on my left.

"I've asked Vanity and Pride to brief you on what we know so far about the bombing."

I exchange looks with them, and Pride winks—she's such a wild child.

Vanity had helped with my apprenticeship training, teaching me how to work with the close contact targets. After my first assignment in Bratislava, I remembered to thank her for sharing her seduction tips to distract marks.

"As you know, our parent company, Conexus, suffered a setback after losing four of our board members," continued Mother. "The bomb demolished the ground floor, but luckily, the blast wasn't strong enough to damage our underground operation—including our weapons lab." She glances at Finn, who agrees.

"Now that would be some fireworks," says Pride, with her Aussie inflection.

"As we've informed all of you before, our accounting department had identified a shortfall in the Conexus coffers—the funding for our SOS operation," says Finn.

"What was the reason for the shortfall?" I ask.

Finn shrugs. "We suspect it was Dominika, but we'll need your help to verify it."

Mother interjects. "This is just a heads up. First, I have two quick assignments for you, Jealousy. I'll brief you later on those."

I flick my eyes up at Finn. "Not to change the subject, but did you get the weapon I'd asked you to get before the bombing? The 9mm Ruger with tactical suppressor?"

Finn heaves out a sigh. I'm his least favorite Sister. From the second I first entered his weapons lab, we'd argued. I can't help it if I'm particular. I must have things a certain way.

"Yes, Jealousy," says Finn. "I've procured two semi-autos. New ones, not used—as you specified."

"Thanks." I breathe a sigh of relief. At least there was some sense of reliability in this chaotic environment that has been in upheaval since the bombing.

I like Finn's New York accent. It reminds me of Collin, the way he mixes his Irish and American speech. Americans have so many distinct accents. I long to hear Collin's voice, but that's impossible—not while I work for the SOS.

Mother gives me a direct look. "I need to update all of you about Dominika."

Pride and Vanity shift in their chairs.

I wait expectantly, sensing this won't be unicorns farting rainbows with glitter.

"We're well aware that Dominika's best interests are not the same as ours," says Vanity, drily.

"Deffo a woman with issues," says Pride.

Mother paces. "Jealousy, I need your help to find intel about Dominika, since we suspect she was behind the bombing."

"And you want me to do—what?"

"We know where she is, but I want you to locate where she's staying. And obtain what other info you can."

"Where is she?" I ask.

"CCTV has established she's currently in London. At least for the time being. She moves around, so she could be gone by the time you get there," answers Mother. She hesitates.

"We think she's planning further destruction." There is worry in Mother's tone, and I see it in her eyes.

I shrug. "Why me? I've not been with the SOS that long."

"Exactly that reason. Your short tenure with the SOS is an advantage. Dominika doesn't know you. You're too new, plus you're the youngest. She'd assume you're not up to speed."

"Are you sure about that?" I ask slowly, a prickle inching up my spine.

"I'll wager you've not yet landed in her crosshairs." Mother stops, placing both hands on her desk. "The three remaining Conexus board members put out an order to remove Dominika."

Vanity and Pride regard me with solemn faces.

"Eliminate one of our own?" I stutter. "But that doesn't make any sense."

"None of this makes sense." Mother's expression changes.

I can tell by Mother's tone that this has become personal.

Vanity passes me a file. "Greed found out the bomber's name. It's Arman Adante."

She gives me a solemn look. "But we can't tell you how we know, or we'll have to kill you."

My eyes grow large as my spectrum brain considers whether she's teasing or serious.

"Stop scaring the new Sister," snickers Pride. She shoots me a wicked grin. "No worries. Vanity's just messing with you."

"Ah," I say, heat creeping up my neck. Damn my literal interpretation.

Vanity leans toward me. "Get this. Lynsey saved Dominika's ass by getting her out of Russia—brought her here, gave her a job, a place to live, and saw to her overall needs. Mother saw to her needs after that."

Vanity folds her arms and looks at Mother. "I can't believe Dominika bit the hand that fed her."

Mother nods with a rueful smile. "In the beginning, she was like a daughter to me."

"Do you believe Dominika tried to kill you?" I ask.

"Hard to say." Mother wears a pained expression. "But I can't rule it out."

She steps to a credenza and lifts a half-full glass carafe of Scotch to pour herself a drink. She turns to us, swirling brown liquid in her glass. "I have my theory about who she was really targeting. Jeff Lynsey."

Mother purses her lips. "They had a tryst, and she's a scorned woman."

"Dominika told me not to trust you, Mother," says Vanity. "She said *you* were the one who'd gone rogue. I know she killed Arman Adante. I'd stake my life on it. She was afraid he'd squeal that she hired him to make the bomb. Who else would have murdered him?"

"Right now, all evidence points to Dominika," says Mother. "She tried to kill Greed and Nick Walker, an MI6 agent. Greed's identity had been compromised when she fell onto Interpol's radar. I advised Greed to leave the SOS and go into hiding."

"I hear she disappeared with that MI6 agent, and that he was quite a looker," I venture.

Mother purses her lips. "At least there's happy endings somewhere in the world."

She turns her attention to Finn, standing next to her with crossed arms.

"Dominika once again hacked into our phones and security systems. What's your progress in getting things changed?"

"We've switched things up several times since the bombing," Finn volunteers. "First, to get things up and running. Then again, upon finding Dominika had hacked into our systems soon after."

Too many questions rattle my brain. "Is Dominika after the Sisters, as well as Conexus?"

"Hard to say." Mother shrugged. "She could target any of us if she thinks we're close to sniffing out her trail. Right now, there's no way of knowing for sure. She doesn't respond to my phone calls, emails, or texts. There's a definitive silence on her end."

"However." Mother picks up a file and positions her diamond-studded cheaters on her nose. "We have new intel that could be a lead. We found a contact associated with the deceased bomb maker. An Italian woman by the name of Aida Russo. I'm sure it's an alias."

She shoots me a piercing look. "We need to pay her a visit."

"We? As in all of us? Isn't this wee bit below your pay grade?" I smile up at her.

Mother removes her glasses. "Yes, we as in you, me, and Finn. Sometimes I like to get back in the field to hone my skills. Lord knows Finn could use a brush-up on his field skills."

Finn flashes Mother a disconcerting look.

"Besides—I have a personal stake in this." Her voice drops low at the end. I can see that Dominika's actions bother her.

Mother nods at Vanity and Pride. "These two have other assignments."

My heart stutters at the thought of having to interrogate someone with my faulty communication skills. "You'll do the talking?"

"Jealousy, you and Finn will handle the physical persuasion aspects. And, yes, I'll do the talking. How are your persuasion skills?"

All eyes are on me.

"I can hold my own," I say slowly, knowing what she's really asking.

I glance at my Sisters. Is this where I act the tough, ruthless badass the Sisters of Sin expect me to be? So many have died. And many will follow if we don't find out who instigated the bombing—and who wants us dead.

I include myself in that equation because I'm a cessation specialist for this organization—I mean problem solver—I still can't get used to calling myself an assassin. I have trouble embracing a word with two asses in it. I prefer cessation. 'Cess,' as in a cesspool, where our targets dwell.

According to the dictionary and the Sisters of Sin, I'm a hired assassin. It's time I face the music and admit that is what I truly am.

As my mother before me.

Chapter 20

Collin

C ollin was delighted to learn he was flying to Rome. He'd only
carried a daypack onboard the plane, and it felt good to stretch
his legs as he headed down to transportation pickup at Da Vinci
International Airport.

He had tugged on a baseball cap and hoodie to blend with the
mostly American tourists, along with sunglasses and tacked on a gray
mustache and grizzled beard over his own.

He scanned the line-up of signs people held up, finally spotting
one with 'John Smith' scribbled on it. He eyed the person holding it
and nearly laughed outright at the guy's resemblance to a mobster, a
fancy fedora dipped low over his sunglasses. Collin's eyes drifted to the
Hawaiian shirt, which clashed with the dangerous mob vibe.

Collin made a quick scan of the over-sized shirt, assuming the guy
was carrying. He didn't travel with blades or firearms. Too much of a
hassle, and his work frankly didn't warrant it.

But others carried, and Collin presumed this handler did, too.

He gave Mob Man a curt nod and followed him outside to a
waiting cab. Collin scoped out the situation. Had the vehicle been a
private one, he wouldn't have climbed in. Not that a cab was any safer;
it could be an Interpol trap.

"Don't worry, *signore*. We won't turn you over to the authorities,"
the man growled in a heavy Italian accent, as he opened the rear door
and motioned Collin to the back.

"I'm not Scorpio, only the errand boy. My instructions are to escort
you to the destination of your choosing. I'll tell Scorpio where to meet
you."

Collin climbed into the vehicle. "In that case, go to the Colosseum. Tell him I'll meet him on the Arena Floor level and to fast-track his ticket. I'll do the same." He tapped his phone to place his ticket order.

When the cab stopped one block from the Colosseum, the driver motioned out the windshield. "Scorpio wears a hat like mine."

"Thanks." Collin exited the cab and stepped around the buffer zone to the Colosseum entrance. He scanned the ticket with his mobile phone and stood in line to get through security and the x-ray scan.

Once through, he made his way down to the Arena Floor overlook with a tour group and leaned back against a metal rail. He crossed his arms in an unimpressed tourist maneuver, casually watching people move around the circle to view the Arena Floor.

Collin's thoughts drifted to Shayla, and he wondered where she worked in the city. He planned to poke around after finishing his business, to see if he could track her down.

Something caught his eye to his left. A guy in a fedora with a pot belly—and a Hawaiian shirt. Mob Man 2.0. Was this their standard business attire?

Collin chuckled and lifted a hand in greeting

"Follow me," said Mob Man 2.0, aka Scorpio.

Collin fell in step beside him as they worked their way along the narrow stone walkway that encircled the arena. Whenever he glanced down, he shivered, envisioning the countless deaths that had occurred below them.

Rows of worn travertine limestone interspersed with green strips of ground cover changed from every angle as the two men sauntered.

Collin waited for Scorpio to lead off so he could concentrate on ditching his Irish lilt.

"Smart of you to choose a place with x-ray scans. Since I'm not armed, and you're not armed, we can have a cozy little chat." Scorpio shrugged like he was telling a joke.

"Cain't be too careful," said Collin in a slow Texas drawl, mimicking his former college buddy from Houston.

"I should have known you were an American. Is that where you flew from?"

Collin plucked a toothpick from his pocket and stuck it in his mouth, gnawing on it. "I represent the professional thief you're fixin' to hire. What's the boost?"

Scorpio paused and headed to an area with fewer people. He waited for a family of four to take photos and move on. "A painting. And a necklace."

Collin stared straight ahead. "The usual boring fare. Show me."

Scorpio angled his phone toward Collin. The bright sun made it difficult to view the image. Collin leaned in, squinting. His brows shot up.

"Y'all cain't be serious."

Collin stared at the *Rokeby Venus,* by Diego Velazquez, on display at the National Gallery in London. The famous painting where Venus lay naked on a bed looking at a mirror held by a young Cupid.

Not to be confused with the other painting, *Venus With a Mirror,* by Titian, in the National Gallery of Art in Washington, D.C. Neither was easier to steal than the other. Both paintings featured Cupid holding a mirror for Venus, although Collin's favorite was the Rokeby, after studying Velazquez as an art history major years ago at Texas A&M University.

Scorpio grunted. "Dead serious. If you can't handle it, I'll find someone who can."

"I can do it," Collin said quickly, inwardly groaning at the Trafalgar Square location. Jaysus, it was the busiest part of London.

Then again, that could work in my favor.

"My dealer has a buyer who collects Diego Velazquez paintings," said Scorpio.

"The *David* statue would be easier to steal," mumbled Collin, impatiently motioning at the man's phone. "Let's see the other."

Scorpio swiped his phone. "A private collector owns the Angel Fire. Local billionaire. Keeps it in his private compound under impossible security."

The most beautiful necklace Collin had ever seen leaped into view. He'd read about this piece. Gemstone appraisers consider Angel Fire the world's most expensive emerald and pigeon blood ruby necklace. Christy's in Hong Kong established the appraised value at nine hundred million.

That was three years ago. An adrenaline rush shot through Collin's veins, causing his wee heart to flutter like faerie wings.

Collin yawned, feigning boredom. "My client typically requires twenty-five percent of the total value. Half now, half on delivery. However—" He stopped when Scorpio turned his back to text his dealer.

He turned back to Collin. "They agree."

"I didn't finish," said Collin. "The necklace and the painting require extraordinary measures. My client requires forty percent for each boost. Twenty percent deposit now."

Scorpio shook his head. "Forty percent each? No way. My dealer won't go for that."

Collin shrugged. "Then I'm outta here, partner. Sorry, but y'all's offer must inspire my client. Other dealers will gladly pay forty percent."

Grimacing at his phone, Scorpio worked his thumbs like a chimp on speed. He glanced up. "Thirty-five percent for the Rokeby, thirty for the necklace."

"Nope. We're done here." Collin tapped his cap in farewell. "See y'all later."

Collin pushed off the railing and walked away. Of course, he'd consider Scorpio's offer. But when there was a chance for more zeros, he'd play hard ball. These boosts were no joke; despite the excitement of the challenge, he'd still be taking one hell of a risk.

"Wait!" Scorpio hollered after him. He caught up to Collin and spoke in a low tone. "My dealer respects your work as a proven professional."

"Tell you what. I'll take thirty-eight percent for the Venus, but the necklace stays at forty." Collin straightened to full height, slanting a serious look down at the rotund handler.

"Thirty-four and thirty-nine," countered Scorpio.

Collin snorted. "This ain't no flea market. Forty for both, or no deal. Half now, half on delivery. Them's the terms." In classic Texan style, Collin rolled his toothpick to the other side of his mouth. "First, make the deposit for the necklace. When that delivery is complete and we've made the transfer, then we'll arrange for the Venus boost."

Scorpio held up a wait-a-minute finger and moved off to talk on the phone. He gesticulated wildly with his free hand, then moved back to Collin.

"My client accepts."

Collin gave Scorpio his email address for the deposit into Collin's Moneytree account, then logged in with his phone to confirm the transaction. He waited while Scorpio worked his magic.

The welcome sound of a ringing cash register pinged Collin's phone. The Moneytree app had dutifully emailed him the deposit receipt.

"I love the sound of money in the afternoon." Collin dipped a nod and grinned. "Much obliged."

All was right with the world.

Collin confirmed the amount, then logged off and zipped his phone into an inside jacket pocket. He was curious to know who Scorpio's dealer was. Who would pay this exorbitant amount for the Angel Fire heist?

"Keep me informed." Scorpio hastily shoved his phone into his back pants pocket, drawing Collin's eye. A good thief doesn't miss a trick.

I could lift Scorpio's phone in a Dublin second and be gone—to find out who the dealer was.

Collin thought better of it. Patience was an asset in this business, and he'd find out eventually.

"Good doing business. Later, alligator." Collin shot Scorpio a smug smile and moved briskly down the stone steps to exit the Colosseum.

He ducked around a corner to an outdoor men's toilet. Once there, he removed the dark hoodie and tied it around his waist. He yanked the gray beard and mustache from his real ones and winced. He replaced his baseball cap with a red beret, stuck on dorky eyeglasses, and stuffed everything in his daypack.

Exiting the restroom, he blended with the crowd and made his way to a taxi stand.

The last person he'd trust would be a handler for billionaire art dealers who'd rather steal than purchase pieces for their collections. Since the Angel Fire job was close to Rome, Collin had reconnaissance work to do before he flew back to Dublin.

First, he'd rent a car, then see if he could locate Shayla. She'd mentioned a jewelry business but was dodgy about the name. He knew many of the major businesses in Rome and was confident he could track her down.

He tapped his phone to change his return flight. Two days here ought to do it. Scorpio and his dealer could wait.

He had more important work to do.

Like find the woman who'd stolen his heart back in Arklow.

Chapter 21
Shayla

It is time for me to request a meeting with Mother.

When she recruited me back in Arklow, she said she'd transform me into an efficient human weapon, though I already was when she'd enlisted me.

But that isn't the problem.

I take a seat in her comfortable wing chair in her luxuriously furnished office suite, and help myself to a piece of dark chocolate, unwrapping the foil.

"Don't worry, my chocolates aren't laced with anything," says Mother as she bursts into her office, startling me.

"After what happened here, you should have Finn's people check anything you leave out like this," I suggest.

Mother concurs. "We have much more security now, but I suppose it couldn't hurt."

I stare at the piece of chocolate, then I carefully wrap it back up in the foil and set it on the table. "Doesn't hurt to be cautious." I give her a lop-sided grin.

"What's on your mind?" says Mother, taking up her usual post and leaning on her desk.

"After I briefed you about my first hit assignment in Bratislava, I'd left out a minor detail."

"Such as?" Mother gives me a plaintive look.

"Close contact jobs aren't my thing." I wait for my words to settle.

"I see." Mother folds one arm with one hand under her chin. "But you accomplished your mission."

"Yes, I did." I haughtily reply. "I'm a professional."

Mother smooths her skirt. "Remember this. A good assassin kills without leaving a trace, like she was never there. A great assassin is when people believe the mark dies from illness or natural cause—more challenging to accomplish from a distance. Sometimes, close is the only option."

I protest. "I don't like the marks touching me. I don't like anyone touching me, except—" I stop short of saying Collin Stedman.

TMI—Mother doesn't need this information.

I rush to explain. "The other Sisters are good at the seduction game, but I find it stressful and excruciating. I hate dirtbags touching me."

Mother gives me a slow wink. "We'll work on that one. Unfortunately, not all situations are under our control."

• • • •

Finn's technology lab is the wonder of the SOS. I can't get over how much it must cost to run and maintain these sophisticated systems. I've seen similar set-ups in television films, but this is for real. I'm awed by this operation. Declan would salivate over it.

I sit at a desktop computer with my hair in a messy bun munching an apple, noting the rows of desktop computers and laptops. Others in the room occasionally glance at me like I shouldn't be here.

Finn had informed me few Sisters spent time in the tech lab doing online research. I argued with Finn about this. But when I showed him my expertise at hacking into various systems, he'd raised his brows and left me alone.

One wall has floor to ceiling monitors. Four lab people sit at desktop systems, scrutinizing the wall of monitors, showing video cams of key areas around Rome...the Via della Conciliazione where the Conexus and Sisters of Sin headquarters is located; Via del Corso with the People's Square; and Piazza Navona, to mention a few. Finn says they can access cams in cities all over the world.

Finn bends over one operator, peering at her desk monitor.

"This is like the CCTV system in London, where five hundred thousand cameras watch every corner of the city," I say. "You can spot a gnat landing on a pigeon in the dead of night."

Finn glances up. "Have you been to London?"

"Not exactly."

"Either you have, or you haven't," he snips.

I'm tempted to throw my apple core at him. He's persistently combative with me. I obviously bring out the worst in him—quite the opposite of Mother—who brings out the best. I clamp my mouth shut, stopping short of disclosing that Cousin Declan taught me to hack into the CCTV system.

"Not been to London. I watch BBC, so am familiar." I wave my apple core dismissively.

Finn hands me a file folder. "These are captures of Dominika, the day of our headquarters bombing, just before the explosion."

I thumb through the stills and read the attached notes.

Finn reviews the file with me. "Dominika staged a hit not ordered by Conexus. One that she did on her own—a David Adelman—an Israeli ex-Mossad agent."

"Why did she go after an ex-Mossad agent? They're merciless. When they sight a bead on a target, that's the end of it." I say drily, my Irish cadence sneaking out.

Finn gives me a grim look. "Dominika blamed Adelman for the death of her parents in Russia, which then was the Soviet Union."

"Oh." I examine the file, seeing a dated photo of Dominika's parents. "I can relate to that. I have suspicions about how my own parents died—if it really was an accident."

Finn stares at me. He clears his throat and continues.

"Dominika has killed others outside of SOS ordered hits. Some we know about, others we don't. We can only speculate."

I flip to the photo of Dominika perched on the side of a building some distance from our headquarters building—the day of the bombing.

"She's obviously waiting for something to happen," I say, handing back the file on Dominika.

Finn motions me to keep it. "It seems she's gone rogue. Hang onto this file for background information. You may be getting an assignment pertaining to this."

Mother breezes in, dressed in classy workout gear. She stands next to me, balancing an open laptop with one arm.

"I have an assignment for you. This one must appear as a natural cause. We can't afford an investigation." She lowers her laptop to show me the location.

"It's local, five kilometers from the city. And this is confidential. Not a word to anyone except me and Finn. Got that?"

"Why is this different from any other?" I ask.

Mother narrows her eyes. "Never question a hit. Just do your job. I'll transmit the encrypted info through our intranet."

"I'll scope it out tonight," I say, ignoring Mother's testiness.

"I'll leave it up to you how to execute the operation. You're a quick study, so dazzle me." Mother pivots. "First things first. We have an errand to run. Jealousy, Finn, follow me." She breezes back out.

Finn and I follow Mother out the door and down the corridor to the weapons lab.

"Finn, get Jealousy set up with what she needs. Fix her up with some fine blades and that pistol she goes on about. We're paying Aida Russo a visit. Meet you in the car park. Drive that beater of yours."

She points at me. "Go see Asia in wardrobe, to change up your look."

I shrug at Finn and head to the wardrobe room, where a woman with blue hair greets me.

"Hallo, I'm Asia," she says with an American sway, I guess to be Californian. "Mother told me to change you up. What would you like?"

She gestures to rows and rows of wigs in all lengths and colors.

The OCD part of me screams a hell-no to the wig action, and I go deer in the headlights. All I can think of are head lice or other vile creatures lurking under the heaps of hair, waiting to infest my defenseless scalp.

I won't wear a wig that has lived on someone's else's head. Plain and simple.

I blow out air, wandering up and down the rows of hairpieces in every cut and color imaginable. My eyes dart around for something—anything—in a sealed package.

Bullseye! I spot a long black wig in a sealed plastic package and point.

"That one. I'm not comfortable wearing community wigs others have cavorted around in. God knows *where* they've been."

Asia considers, then breaks into an understanding smile.

"What statement are you shooting for? If you don't mind the pun?"

"Statement?" My mind gropes, wondering what she means. "How do you dress for torturing someone, so they spill their wee guts?"

Asia doesn't flinch. Instead, she thinks a moment. "Basic black, for that impeccable intimidation vibe. And bold accessories."

I scan a rack of glittery evening gowns—maybe if I was torturing a prom date.

"Nothing complicated, please."

I browse the racks and don't see my normal cessation fashions. "Actually—do you have a black spandex catsuit and ski mask? Mine are back at the apartment."

Asia's face lights up. "For that starfighter ninja look? I'm Japanese American, so I'm totally into the whole ninja thing."

"Yes. Me too," I say, with a pleased grin.

"Hold on, be right back."

She hurries to the next room and emerges holding my grand intimidator outfit. The ski mask is brand new, store tags still on. I double check to make sure.

"Are you sure no one has worn this?" I inspect it within an inch of its life.

"Quite sure." Asia motions at the tags, and I note her weird expression.

I'm used to these expressions now after my co-worker Sisters, Mother, and Finn discovered my obsessive-compulsive tendencies; especially after my discussion with Mother about me doing cleanup and body disposal.

I figured I could handle those once I came onboard the SOS. I'd shrugged to myself...how hard could it be? I know one thing: I'll never take for granted what The Uncles and the Shamrock Cleaners did after our cessation ops.

"Thank you." I make a mental note to keep one or two of my own outfits here at headquarters for those occasions where I don't have time to change at the apartment that Mother had arranged for me when I first arrived in Rome.

It occurs to me I'm about to accompany Mother and Finn on an assignment when I'm used to working alone.

This will be interesting.

Chapter 22

Collin

Collin's first order of business was to rent a car. He had to get around the city, plus do the reconnaissance on the billionaire's compound.

He wasn't worried about the necklace. Boosting it was a cut and dry job. He'd done similar ones. The painting was another story. That one would take extra planning and require a trip to London ahead of time.

He wondered who wanted this painting badly enough to part with so much cash to get it. Whoever it was, they must be billionaires with private collections. It went against his grain to remove it from an art gallery; he didn't like when popular works of art were hidden away in private collections, where the public couldn't enjoy them.

Well, hypocrite that he was, he hadn't blinked when he accepted the job, had he?

It wasn't that he couldn't figure out how to do it; that was the simple part. The hard part was getting away with it in Trafalgar Square, one of the busiest parts of London.

When Collin stepped off the bus at a Rome rental car office, his tablet pinged a notification from the dark web message site.

He tapped his codes, turning away for privacy. Up popped a pulsating scorpion, and he opened Scorpio's message.

This one made him blink.

Tell your client the last thief my dealer hired on a different job brought us an expertly crafted replica. The dealer shot him upon delivery.

Collin's brows raised. He knew people who painted replicas, and there was a lucrative industry built around imitating originals on the black market. If these dealers had the money to pay a professional thief to steal them, they had the money to hire art or gemstone appraisers who could easily identify whether pieces were originals or replicas.

After acknowledging and sending a reply, Collin closed his tablet and put it in his daypack.

He rented a dark red Alfa Romeo Giulia and drove to a hotel in the middle of the ancient Roman goldsmith district between the Pantheon and Piazza Navona, where most jewelers were clustered. He parked his car and moved around on foot. He was familiar with the district after doing business here over the years.

Now, his reputation as a professional outmoded all that work. He figured after the painting and necklace heists, he'd retire and run his bookstore business back in Arklow. Maybe pen a novel, *How to Become a Professional Thief.*

Arklow—reminded him of Shayla. He had to get busy searching for her.

He checked the first shop; no luck there. He proceeded to the next. And the next. Everyone shook their heads when he lifted his phone and showed them the one and only photo he'd taken when they'd been in Avoca all those months ago.

After making the rounds of most of the high-profile design businesses, it dawned on Collin that Shayla may not have been truthful—that she had come to Rome for other reasons. He wondered if it was a guy. He doubted it; she didn't seem the type to string guys along.

After all, she'd lost her virginity to *him.*

Dejected, he headed back to the hotel for a bite. He had friends and associates here in Rome who might find her. He still had his reconnaissance to do at the billionaire's estate outside of Rome—to scope out for the necklace.

Time to get to work. Scorpio had sent a blueprint to the mansion and marked the location where the necklace resided. Now, all Collin had to do was to work through the intricacies of obtaining it.

Without being caught.

Chapter 23
Shayla

Later in the morning, Finn drives Mother and me to pay Aida Russo a visit in Tor Bella Monaca. It's called the Black Hole of Rome, where the dark underbelly of drugs and violence is said to dominate. It's one of the most dangerous neighborhoods in Rome.

We're in a beat-up hatchback pile-of-shite Finn keeps on hand for such errands.

I see why as we pass dilapidated buildings, walls decorated with colorful graffiti and black soot. I wish we were conducting this little soiree under cover of night. But Mother is in a hurry. She wants answers about the bombing and says every second counts.

I have my pistol and magazines on the ready in my chest holster, under my light jacket. Finn has guns stashed on himself as well, and Mother—well, apparently, Mother depends on us to protect her.

Not only am I a problem solver, I'm also a tormentor *and* a bodyguard. Well, today anyway. When I came to work for the Sisters of Sin, Mother hadn't given me a written job description. The torture and bodyguard capacities fall into the category of other duties as assigned.

Mother sits in the front seat with Finn, eyeing the building numbers as we cruise along a street with broken glass and cans littering the gutters.

A scrappy-looking man slumps in a shabby lawn chair, hunched over his mobile phone. He glowers at us as we drive past.

Despite Mother's protests, I'd tugged off my long black wig and instead replaced it with my trusty black knit cap. Mother and Finn had rolled their eyes when I raised a stink about wearing wigs from the wardrobe department. I made a mental note to buy my own.

Finn pulls up to a six-story rectangular apartment building with laundry strung across the balconies. He swerves around garbage piled on the sidewalk and parks halfway up on the cracked concrete, same as the other parked cars.

When he switches off the ignition and I exit the back seat, I'm overcome with a stench that causes me to gag. I trade my knit cap for a black ski mask I stretch over my head and face.

Mother opens the car door and quickly closes it. "Bloody hell. Another garbage strike."

We all suit up; Finn stretches a black ski mask like mine over his head, while Mother pulls on a curly, shoulder-length red wig and bug-eyed sunglasses.

We could be mistaken for Maureen O'Hara and her two ninjas.

I hold back a laugh.

Finn and Mother move along together, and I follow, checking out our surroundings as we approach the building. Finn opens the door to a dirty stairwell that smells of urine.

"Unit thirty-four on the third floor."

He stops and gets in my personal space. "Give me some stink-eye."

I back up, giving him a blank look. "Stink what?"

"Stink-eye." He grasps my shoulders and glowers, as if all the evil in the world has assembled on his face.

I pull back. His stink-eye scares the bejaysus out of me.

"I showed you mine. Now you show me yours," he says in his no-nonsense, American manner.

Heaving a sigh, I summon my inner badass by narrowing my eyes and curling my lip.

Finn grimaces. "Too serial killer. Make me afraid. Fear and intimidation are the name of this game. From the second we walk in, wear your stink-eye. Then do as you're told."

My eyes widen at his stern command, but I nod obediently. This is no time for yet another debate with our boy, Finn. I'll pick an argument over his Irish slam later.

Mother had briefed us on what to do if Aida Russo doesn't let us in. I'm prepared.

She knocks on the door.

A woman's voice speaks through the door in Italian, wanting to know who it is.

"I'm with the electric company and we need to talk to you," Mother calls out in English, lifting a clipboard to the peephole.

"Go away!" the woman responds.

Finn is on one side of Mother, me on the other.

"Then we'll turn off your electricity," Mother says through the door.

A brief silence, then the door opens a crack.

Mother smiles, showing her the clipboard. "May I come in?"

"Identification," the woman demands.

Mother complies, showing her a fake utility company ID.

The door swings open, but when the woman sees Finn and me with our badass stink-eye, she tries to slam the door. Mother wedges herself in and shoves the door open.

The three of us rush at the woman. Finn grabs her wrists and holds them behind her back.

I check each room in the tiny apartment to make sure no one else is home. Mother had mentioned the woman lives alone but clearing a mark's space is a standard operating procedure.

"All clear. She's alone," I relay to Mother and Finn, upon returning to the small living room, which sits in quiet disarray.

"Aida Russo, we need some information," says Mother, affecting her Italian accent.

"Who are you?" The woman gapes at Mother and me as she tries to wriggle loose from Finn's grasp. "Let go of me!"

Mother dips her chin at me, and I pull my semi-auto pistol from its chest holster, rack the slide, and point it at the woman.

"No! Who are you people?" she yells.

"Don't scream, or it won't end well for you," says Finn calmly releasing her wrists. He leads her to a chair. "Sit."

She gives him a defiant sneer.

"I said sit!" he snaps, in a tone I've not heard him use. Our Yank, Finn, is full of surprises. Besides being a computer geek, his job description must also be an assassin-of-all-trades, like me. What diverse resumes we have.

When the woman sinks into her seat, Mother drags a ramshackle chair close to hers and sits. She leans into the woman's face.

"Miss Russo, we can do this the uncomplicated way or the unpleasant way. Personally, I prefer the former."

Finn leans on a table behind Russo in his imposing all-black ensemble, reminding me of a funeral director.

Mother gets to the point. "Who hired Arman Adante to make the bomb to blow up Conexus?"

"Are you Interpol?" The woman leaps to her feet to flee.

"Oh no, you don't." Finn beats her to the door and flips the lock to prevent anyone from entering.

He grabs the woman's arms, zip-ties her wrists, and duct-tapes her ankles. I'm amazed at his speed and efficiency.

"No, dear. Not Interpol." Mother shoots me a look. "Show Miss Russo we mean business."

I reach inside my jacket and produce the tactical suppressor. I point my pistol at the ceiling while I leisurely screw the suppressor onto the muzzle with my black-gloved hand. Russo's eyes follow my every move.

Ramping up my not-a-serial-killer stink-eye, I train my gaze on her. Without blinking, I point my weapon at her, then slowly lower it to her left foot. I make a straight-armed V with my arms, hands on my pistol as I ready my stance to shoot. All for show, hopefully.

I don't want to blow off this woman's pinky toe.

"All right!" Russo cries out, dark eyes full of fear. "The Russian woman. She's the one."

Finn and Mother swap glances as I continue to hold my weapon steady. Russo glares at the gun, then at me. All she sees are my eyes and mouth. Same with Finn. Who knows what she makes of Maureen O'Hara with her perfected Italian?

"We need a name," says Mother, casually brushing lint from her pant leg with the back of her fingertips.

Russo doesn't speak.

I move closer and point my weapon at Russo's thigh. Finn dips into a nod of approval.

"I don't know her name!" hisses Russo, swiveling her head toward me.

She looks as though she'll spit at me. Bacteria and microbes are not in my wheelhouse. I'll come undone with a fecking panic attack if she lobs a loogie in my direction. Finn will grab my gun and shoot me, and we'll wind up with a fecking bloody mess.

Don't spit on me, lady.

Finn clears his throat, and I glance up, noting his lopsided smile. I must be giving Russo good stink-eye.

"Think, Miss Russo!" Mother's eruption startles me, and I almost blow my fear and intimidation vibe.

I press the muzzle against the woman's thigh.

Russo's eyes flash with terror. "I don't know! All I know is she's Russian and has long black hair and wears tall shiny boots."

"Is there anything else you can tell us? Anything at all!" Mother practically yells. She's losing patience, as am I.

"She'll kill me if I tell anyone anything. Arman told me so," confesses Russo.

Mother lifts her chin. "I'll see to it you're protected. But you'll have to leave here."

Russo flicks her gaze at Mother. "She will find me. She finds everyone."

Mother's eyes narrow. "How do you know this?"

"I overheard things at Arman's—when she came there. Arman told me to hide in another room. He said she'd kill me if I was there." Russo's face contorts, and tears fall.

"He was my good friend. I know she's the one who came back and killed him."

"That's why we need to find her, Aida. Please—is there anything else you can tell me?"

Russo acts like she suddenly remembers something.

I don't buy it; she plainly didn't want to tell us.

"One thing. I heard her tell Arman she's stealing money from someone called Conexus. She has an accountant in Zurich that takes care of it."

Mother perks up at this news, and she and Finn's eyes meet.

"I suspected that's where the deficits went," muttered Finn, shaking his head.

Russo broke down, sobbing. "Please, don't let her know I told this to you. She'll kill me. That one is vicious—ruthless—she has a black heart." Russo lifts her cuffed wrists, pleading.

"We'll keep you safe. Don't worry," says Mother in a soothing tone. "Did Arman ever say her name? Was it Dominika Gagolin?"

Russo's head snaps up. "Yes. Dominika. But no last name."

Mother motions at Finn, then me. "Remove the restraints. Stow your weapon."

Finn bends to cut the duct tape with a box cutter. He removes the zip tie, and Russo swipes at her cheeks. I do what Mother instructs and shove my pistol into my chest holster. Good, I didn't want to shoot this distressed woman's leg.

"One last thing. Did Dominika say any other names? Please think."

We all wait while Russo closes her eyes in a pretense to think. After a moment, she snaps them open.

"She mentioned her accountant sent Arman the funds to pay for the bomb device he made for her. Someone named Leon Schelling. I remember, because Arman wrote it down."

"Thank you, Aida," says Mother, smiling in that elegant way of hers. "I apologize for putting you through this. I know Arman was your friend. But I suggest you make friends with people who don't make bombs."

I admire her coolness. Me? Not so much. I'm not a fan of this fecking intimidation thing.

Mother rises. "Pack your things. A car will come for you and take you to a safe place where Dominika can't find you."

Russo pushes to her feet. "What is your name? I don't know who you people are."

"It's in everyone's best interests to keep it that way. And, it is in your best interest not to breathe a word about this discussion. Or that we were here." Mother pauses. "Because if you do, there will be consequences."

Mother jerks her head at Finn and me, and we head for the door.

"Get packed. A car will arrive shortly." Mother pivots and exits the apartment in her authoritative fashion, reminding all present who commands this operation.

Finn and I follow, like the good little ninja minions that we are.

On the way to the car, Mother calls over her shoulder.

"Jealousy! Time to prepare for your next assignment."

"I'm on it."

I tick through my mental checklist of what I'll need for my scoping mission tonight.

Chapter 24
Collin

All Collin had to do was snatch a nine-hundred-million-dollar necklace from the current owner who lived outside the city on a billion-dollar estate, surrounded by an army of security, dogs, cameras, and enough firepower to light up Rome.

Just before sunset, he'd perched on a nearby hill to assess. Only a few kilometers from the city, the mansion was a prominent fixture on the landscape—hard to miss—which came with its own challenges.

"It's not like I haven't had a challenge before," he mumbled to himself as he lay prone on his belly—dressed in black—steadying his binoculars as he glassed the compound. A two-meter-tall stone wall surrounded the whole thing, reminding him of ancient Irish castles with partially crumbling, stone walls.

Collin had arrived before dark to get the lay of the land for his operation. He pulled his portable laptop from the daypack and powered it on, switching the display to a dark setting so it wouldn't be noticed.

A 3D model of the imposing mansion rotated on his screen, and he lined it up with his angle. He homed in on the real deal, to see where the Angel Fire necklace resided at one end of the building. Windows? Yes, but for the life of him, he couldn't figure why.

This guy must have faith in his security systems.

Outbuildings sat behind the mansion where the house and grounds workers stayed, along with bodyguards and security guards. A horse paddock—no doubt thoroughbreds—was on the other side of the grounds.

Collin thought back to the burglary he'd done at the horse breeder back in Arklow. He hadn't enjoyed working in his own backyard but did that job as a favor to a friend whom the thoroughbred owner had screwed over in a breeding contract.

He'd spend tomorrow observing work routines on the grounds and would take as much time as he needed; stealing a nine-hundred-million-dollar piece of jewelry was no walk in the park.

Except maybe for *him*. He smiled to himself.

Scorpio had messaged intel that made Collin's job easier. The target's name was Antonio Vittorio. He'd hired someone to lift the necklace from Christie's in Hong Kong three years ago. Collin had to admit the heist was an admirable job, and difficult to pull off.

There was a healthy respect between professional thieves. Collin considered himself to be among the best on the planet. He'd worked his way up, starting in college back in the States. Small burglaries to help his parents with medical bills. He had easy access to his Sigma Nu frat brothers' wealthy families, doing some ballsy heists from their homes.

Back then, he'd taken on a Robin Hood mentality, stealing for noble causes. When he'd sell his loot, he'd take half the money and invest it to support himself. The other half he donated to medical facilities for children with cancer.

His younger sister, Bridget, had died of brain cancer when she was seven. He'd think of her before every heist—dedicating his actions to her.

Scorpio had sent Collin the precise location of Angel Fire. The necklace lived in its own display case at one end of the mansion, designated a private art gallery. Scorpio had also sent the codes to turn off the lasers, and the alarm attached to the display case.

Easy pickings—if Collin could trust Scorpio's intel.

Scorpio had mentioned an ex-employee had been paid handsomely for the info. Hopefully, he or she would keep their mouth shut. In this business, there was no trust or reliability. What trust did exist usually evaporated when contracts weren't honored, or Interpol came sniffing around.

Collin waited until night settled, thankful no moon drew attention to his cozy hilltop position. He had all the time in the world to surveil, with plenty of snacks and drinks in his daypack. He'd hidden his Alfa Romeo rental car down the hill in the opposite direction, in an abandoned vineyard grown over with gnarly vines.

Cars and limos came and went all day from the compound. Vittorio had all kinds of things delivered. A wine delivery truck showed up, and people streamed from the service quarters to unload it.

Collin trained his binoculars on the wide circular driveway.

A truck delivery person caught his eye: a petite woman hefting a case of wine. She wore a black knit cap and resembled—*wait a minute—was that Shayla?*

He snapped his head up and squinted. No, can't be her—she wouldn't be a delivery girl. Would she? Jaysus, for all he knew, she might be. Her life was shrouded in such secrecy, he didn't know what to think.

Only that he couldn't get her out of his mind since meeting her back in Arklow.

He pressed the binoculars to his eyes. The driver and another guy climbed into the box truck. The woman was the last to get in. She stood, glancing around as if scanning for something. Then she climbed inside, and the truck rolled away.

He had an impulse to follow it—see if the delivery woman was Shayla. He debated as the truck drove through the tall wrought-iron gates and lumbered down the road back to town. Even if he hoofed it to his car, he wouldn't catch it.

It seems I've been searching for Shayla in the wrong place.

Tomorrow, he'd scour the wine delivery businesses.

Tonight, he'd perform a dry run to make sure all would go as planned with his operation. He'd do the boost tomorrow night, now that he had the codes to intercept the house alarm, the Angel Fire room, and the display case.

Collin waited until activity lessened, still glassing to see how people moved around. He could see inside most windows. In an isolated place like this, no need for window coverings. Vittorio's wife treated him to a full-on view of bare breasts when she changed.

Later, she emerged from the mansion with luggage and got into a limo.

Collin yawned and glanced at his watch. At precisely nine o'clock, Vittorio emerged in his skimpy swimsuit—*God help us*—and dove into the swimming pool. He swam a few sloppy laps, then rang a bell at poolside and a server appeared with a glass of brandy or whiskey.

Nice. The guy is a health nut. Have some fermented cereal grains and fruit mash with your workout, buddy boy.

After the third glass, Vittorio hoisted himself from the shallow end and staggered inside. Once the door slammed shut, no other activity occurred outside.

This was Collin's cue. He stuffed his laptop and binoculars inside his daypack, pulled out his black mask with two eye holes, and stepped down to the portion of wall that Scorpio had pointed out was a video cam blind spot.

As expected, Collin had worked through all the security systems Scorpio had supplied him. Thankfully, there was no facial recognition on his way to or from the display case in the artifact's room. There had been other impressive pieces in there as well: paintings, busts, and small statues.

He recognized a Cupid statue that had been stolen from a French art gallery.

This guy was quite the art aficionado.

"These things should be in a museum gallery," he'd muttered, glancing around. His impulsive side tempted him to lift Angel Fire tonight; but it was late, and he was too knackered, having taken more time than he'd expected with his dress rehearsal.

On his way out, he helped himself to a butler outfit from a service closet and stuffed it into his knapsack.

As Collin swung his rappel hook over the stone wall, which he noted had begun to crumble—as all the old stones had in Rome—he thought he saw something flash.

He put his hands on his hips and hesitated.

Had someone spotted him despite his stealth and code busting? Now wasn't the time to think about it. He gave the rope a yank to make sure it held, then pulled himself up the rope with the balls of his feet, pushing him upward.

When he crested the top of the thick stone wall, he saw it again—a red flash—from the hill he'd just perched on.

Someone was up there in the dark.

Quickly, he rappelled down the other side to the ground. He snapped his rope to undo the hooks, stashed it in his daypack, and took out his night vision goggles so he could see his way up the hill and down the other side to his car.

Another flash. *What the hell?*

He glanced at the hilltop, seeing a tiny red light. Was he in someone's crosshairs? He'd made sure no one saw him earlier. He'd been careful.

He couldn't afford to have anyone screw up his operation.

A red dot danced on his chest. *What the feck?*

Collin gave chase, breaking into an all-out run. He sprinted from tree to bush, zigzagging his way up the hill, hoping he wouldn't take a bullet.

He trained his night vision specs on a figure who stood watching him.

By the time Collin reached the top, the person had disappeared down the other side.

Dammit!

He scanned the ground for clues and snatched a wadded gum wrapper. He stuffed it in his pocket as he sped down the other side of the hill, tripping over rocks, nearly losing his balance.

He reached the road to his dark red Alfa Romeo in the abandoned vineyard. This was the only road back to the city, so the person he pursued would be up ahead.

The moon came out, gloriously lighting the pavement. His night vision goggles were an annoyance when he ran. He removed them and carried them in his hand.

He noted movement straight ahead on the pavement.

If he kicked serious ass, he could catch the guy.

Collin reached his car, tossed his daypack in, and fired up the motor. He switched on the headlights and pulled onto the left side of the paved road. He defaulted to the UK side of the road, then corrected and veered into the right lane. Not a good time for a head-on.

He strained to see movement, noting the city lights up ahead. Once he reached the city, it would be easier to see, but harder to spot the person he was after.

There! He caught sight of a blue Vespa motor scooter zipping effortlessly away from him.

"Ha, I'll catch you," he said through gritted teeth. "I have the faster vehicle, my friend."

The sparse night traffic helped him gain on the Vespa. He had to slow when he hit the narrow city streets. The scooter turned right, onto an alleyway. With luck, it would dead end and he'd catch the man who'd interrupted his recon.

Unfortunately, the rider swung left, veering around a stack of wood crates blocking the right side. Collin hit his brakes to inch the car through the narrow passageway.

When he emerged, he'd lost sight of the motor scooter.

Dammit!

He sped down a straight alley and the corner of his eye caught the blue Vespa on a narrow street to his left. He cranked the wheel, almost hitting a man next to a stack of garbage containers.

Collin squinted, trying to get a good look at the rider up ahead.

Was that a mother effing woman dressed in black on that scooter?

If so, she expertly milked the maximum speed from her maneuverable Vespa.

He'd gained on the scooter when an oversized truck pulled out in front of his speeding Alfa.

"Mother fecker!" He slammed his brakes, screeching his tires.

Collin braced for a t-bone impact.

Chapter 25
Shayla

Accelerating like a wild woman, I put distance between me and the man who chases me. Who is he? I'm furious. My scoping mission got interrupted by this unexpected loser who popped up at my mark's compound.

I don't do well with interruption; I must complete my tasks.

No time for my usual anxiety attacks—I can't let him catch me.

I steal a peek over my shoulder and glimpse a truck pulling out in front of the dark red car pursuing me. I speed up, hoping to lose it. My tires bump over cobblestones at a speed that jiggles me like a rocket when its afterburners kick in.

Bejaysus, the wee bastard is behind me again! I know my way around Rome, but I'm still learning the back streets. I never know when I'll turn and run into a dead-end.

I can't lead my pursuer to SOS headquarters or my apartment—I have no choice but to lose him. Otherwise, Plan B is to ditch my scooter and flee on foot.

A narrow stone bridge looms ahead and I go over it. Traffic has picked up during the early morning commute. At least I have the advantage of weaving through vehicles while his fancy-assed car gets stuck in Rome's snarled traffic.

As luck would have it, all goes silent when my motor quits. *No! Don't die on me now!*

I attempt to restart it. It won't kick over.

The dark red car closes in on me. A driveway juts to the right after the bridge. I jerk my handlebars to the right, sideswiping a tall metal streetlamp. I kick it away and coast down a steep, winding driveway. Dang cobblestones rattle my teeth as I try to restart my motor.

The girls that live on my chest are sore from all the high-speed jiggling.

Neat rows of olive trees lead off the driveway. I'm in an olive orchard.

I break free from the curves to see a courtyard with a wide expanse of marble steps leading to a sprawling rectangular building—fronted with dark windows—and a sign, *Rome Olive Oil Imports*.

"Oh, shit!" I brake hard and my scooter skids to a stop, attracting unwanted attention. Early morning workers gape as they walk from an adjacent car park to the building.

I'm still dressed like a ninja.

I whip my head around in time to see a dark red Alfa Romeo swing around the last curve. I jump off my Vespa and ditch it behind a clump of dense bushes. Then I scramble up the steps, two at a time, and enter the building.

The air conditioning feels wonderful. My eyes dart around for a place to change into the clothes I'd stuffed into my daypack.

I glance behind me, and through the dark glass, I see the Alfa Romeo stop.

I tug off my black ski mask.

A cleaning woman buffs the marble floor and I casually approach her. "Toilet?" I ask.

She points upstairs.

"*Grazie.*" I dip my chin and spring up the staircase and beeline to the 'Toilet' sign. I push open the door, and the first thing I search for is a window to escape through once I change.

Yes! And it's open! Thank you, God.

It occurs to me I'm on the second floor, but that's the least of my worries right now.

Quickly, I tug off my black spandex. I pull out a short blue skirt and white turtleneck from my daypack and put them on. I also take out my purchase of a short blonde wig, along with a pair of oversized designer sunglasses.

I stick them on and stuff my other sweaty clothes in the garbage bin.

If Alfa Romeo Guy catches me, it'll be easier to deny I was the one he was chasing. Someone left their *Olive Oil Imports* name tag on the sink. Sure, I can be 'Maria' for the moment. I pin it to my turtleneck, then stick on my flat Mary Jane shoes, toss my others in the trash, and retrieve my lipstick.

Heels click on tile and the door opens. A woman with dark hair enters, angling her head.

"Have you seen a lady in black?" the woman asks in broken English. "Cutie out here looking for his girlfriend."

I freeze with the lipstick tube and shrug. "Sorry. No one else in here."

Have no idea which accent I used, but it sure as shite wasn't Italian, much less Irish. Summoning an indifferent expression, I catch my reflection in the mirror and steady my hand to apply lipstick.

"*Grazie.*" The woman's eyes dart a quick up and down, then she exits.

I let out a breath I didn't know I was holding and rush to the door, pressing my ear against it.

"She's not in there, sir. Someone else is," says the woman.

A male voice responds. "*Grazie.*"

Damn! I want to get a look at him, but I don't dare open this door.

The woman's heels click away, but I don't hear Alfa Romeo Guy walk off. I wait with bated breath, listening for his footsteps to leave the hallway.

Silence.

That can't be good. He knows someone is in here and he's waiting for me to come out. He'll lose patience, if he hasn't already.

JEALOUSY

Wasting no time, I scramble up onto the heat register and hoist myself up to the open window, praying I don't break something when I jump.

I balance on the windowsill and take a leap of faith—muffling a scream on the way down.

Chapter 26
Collin

Collin moved to the end of the wide hallway on the second floor of the busy olive oil distribution center, pretending to wait for someone.

He wanted to check the women's toilet to see who was still in there—but figured employees might not appreciate a random guy waltzing into the women's jacks.

After parking his rental car, he'd taken off his black pullover and put on an obnoxious Ireland t-shirt, to seem like a clueless tourist. He'd entered the building, and when the dark-haired woman had approached him in her Versace business suit, he knew he had to act the part.

He'd shamelessly flirted—turned on his dimples, along with his charming Irish brogue and five o'clock shadow. Versace Woman had fallen for it as she hurried to help him find his 'girlfriend'.

He glanced at his watch, then back at the women's toilet. No one had come out, but the woman had indicated someone was in there—but not the person he'd asked her to search for.

Something wasn't right.

He casually made his way to the door. Turning his head both ways to ensure no one saw, he ducked inside to find it empty. His eyes lifted immediately to the open window.

Damn, she escaped. Who the devil was she?

Now she'd gotten away—and it disturbed him that he wouldn't know who'd been watching him at the Vittorio estate. He hurried from the building and tapped his way down the stairs when something to the left caught his eye.

A blue Vespa sped like a race car between two rows of olive trees.

He dashed to his vehicle. This time he wouldn't be stupid and let her know he was following. He drove slowly down the driveway and waited behind some hedges. His eye caught the motorized scooter heading back to the main road.

Collin's patience had paid off. The Vespa rider was no longer speeding to get away from her pursuer. In fact, she was taking her sweet time weaving through downtown Rome to the *Via della Conciliazione* area. Her blue Vespa was easier to see now that the sun shone.

Traffic barely crawled in this congested part of the city. Collin lucked out, finding a parking spot when a car pulled away from the curb. In this section, pedestrians gained faster distances than traffic.

At a busy intersection, the Vespa rider stopped, and she put her foot down on the cobblestone. He figured her motor had quit as her left foot repeatedly pumped the kick-starter.

Collin smiled. *Good. This will be easy.*

To his dismay, he noted a puff of exhaust when the Vespa motor restarted.

The woman had changed her appearance. He raised his brows, tapping a burst of photos with his phone, hoping she'd turn around.

He wanted to see her face.

When the Vespa moved again, he maintained his distance, making sure she wouldn't see him following her. He watched until she disappeared to the left.

Collin jogged to where she'd turned, seeing a narrow side street too tight for vehicles. He peeked around the corner of a brick building—just in time to see her lift the scooter and wrestle it inside of an apartment building, while a doorman held the door open for her.

Not bad digs if she lived in this upscale neighborhood. His curiosity ate at him.

Now he *had* to know who she was. There were a million and one ways he could play this. Yep, this grand encounter would be fun.

Some good, old-fashioned *craic* was in order.

Chapter 27
Shayla

I settle in for an evening of relaxation. The previous night has left me knackered, especially after being chased through the streets of Rome. All I yearn for is to curl up and watch a good film in my penthouse apartment on top of the building Mother had set me up in.

A buzzer from the building comm has me growling with annoyance. I told them I wasn't to be disturbed for any reason.

I press the comm button and the doorman tells me I have a food delivery from an upscale *ristorante*, and should she send him up? I haven't ordered anything, but I'm so hungry I could eat a small planet after my high-speed, early morning getaway.

My suspicious nature kicks in. I ask the doorman who is delivering. If it's a delivery mistake, sure, I'll take the food. Long as it's not poisoned or tampered with. On second thought, maybe I shouldn't.

The doorman replies in his thick Italian accent. "A nicely dressed man from Cacciatore Grill. Says his name is Mickey O'Shea."

An Irishman in the middle of Rome? My curiosity gets the best of me. I wouldn't mind talking to someone from my homeland.

"Send him up."

When the doorbell chimes, I squint through the peephole and press the comm.

"Yes?"

A tall, bearded guy with the signature fedora, and *Cacciatore* across the headband stands in a white tailored shirt and slim pants. His sleek sunglasses cover his eyes.

He lifts two food boxes. "*Consegna del cibo*, food delivery!" he sings out.

I unlock the door, annoyed that he'd interrupted my cartoon film. I won't admit to anyone I watch films about puppets who wish to be real boys—or romantic comedies where people only kill each other with love and laughter.

They help me counterbalance what I do for a living.

My pistol is on the ready as I swing the door open. Delivery Guy holds out the food boxes. "Where would you like me to set these, *signora?*"

He may have an Irish name, but he has a lovely Italian accent.

"I'll take them, but please remove your hat and shades. I want to see who is offering me food that I haven't ordered."

His jaw drops. He freezes as if I'd transformed him into a pillar of salt.

I take the food boxes and wait. God, it smells good. I don't care who this guy is—I want to dive into Cacciatore's homemade pasta.

"Bollocks! Shayla Byrne?" Now he's talking like a full-blown Irishman. I know this voice. Collin Stedman smiles in all his steal-my-heart splendiferous glory, standing in my doorway.

In Rome.

A trillion rockets launch inside my chest as he lifts his hat and removes his shades. I gawk at his glacial blues and can't speak.

I'm gob smacked, and step back, my mouth hanging open.

"Are you going to invite me in?"

"Well, that depends, Mickey O'Shea." Now I'm befuddled. "Why did you disguise yourself?"

"I honest to God didn't know you lived here. But now that I know, let's enjoy this food together."

I gape at him. "Wait—I didn't order these dinners. Who are they for? Who did you think lived here?"

"May I?"

Collin takes the food boxes, moves past me, and sets them on my square marble coffee table.

They smell delicious, and I'm ravenous—but more importantly, *Collin Stedman is here.*

In Rome. At my apartment.

"Collin—what are you doing here? How did you find me?"

"So many questions." He holds up his hand.

"First, I didn't know I was bringing dinner to you, specifically. Second, how the devil do you afford this swanky place?" His eyes dart around, wonder plastered on his gorgeous face.

I'm at a loss for words upon seeing the one person on God's green earth that I've longed for since leaving Ireland. Despite our mutual shock, it's good to hear another Irish brogue.

I'm suddenly homesick.

He gives me an up-and-down appraisal. "Damn, Shayla. You look good."

Is he mother fecking blind?

My sweat-dried hair is stuffed into a freakish ponytail bun and one side of my frayed, distressed t-shirt hangs off my shoulder. I'm not sure why, but I tug it back up.

He's hot and rugged as ever, with an exciting edge I've not seen before. His dark cropped beard and mustache command a steamy testosterone vibe. No wonder I didn't recognize him.

I close and lock the door. I'm guarded as I cross my living room, where we face off.

"How did you find me?" I ask cautiously.

"That blue Vespa led me here." He motions at my scooter leaning against the wall, that I lugged up here on the lift. "Funny thing, though. Didn't know it belonged to *you*. You do realize it needs a tune-up."

I follow his gaze and connect the dots; realization prickles my spine. My fast intake of breath gives me away. My chest squeezes.

Holy mother of God. Collin is the mother-effing Alfa Romeo guy?

I wait for him to say it first. He doesn't. Instead, he sends a 'gotcha' smile down to me like he's holding a royal flush in a poker game.

"Well, lass—this is quite the coincidence."

"I—em, told you I was working at a jewelry design— "

He cuts me off. "Funny you should mention that. Happened to be in town for a job, and thought I'd look you up. I checked those places." He shrugs. "No one's heard of Shayla Byrne."

"That's because—"

I can't tell him I'm now Jealousy—can't breach my NDA with the Sisters of Sin. My heart sputters and wobbles around like it always has in Collin's presence.

"Because what?"

I drink in his broad shoulders and beautifully outlined top half in his tailored shirt—tucked into fitted trousers—he still takes my breath away. I'm careful to keep my eyeballs from drifting south to his lean hips—and other manly things.

There's more to Collin than meets the eye. I'd sensed his worldliness before.

And here I stand, completely manky. I aim for casual.

"I travel all over—working with different companies."

His eyes narrow, and he folds his arms. "Tell me about it."

There are so many elephants stuffed into this room it feels like the frigging Savanna. My nose grows as I spin my web of lies.

"I travel all over, selling our company designs— "

He interrupts. "What's the company's name?"

I stoop to open a drawer in my coffee table and snatch a business card that Mother had whipped out of fairy dust for me. "Victorian Designs. With an Italian flair."

I push out a smile, hoping to satisfy his curiosity.

Collin studies my card, then levels his gaze as he flips it onto the table.

So much for satisfied curiosity.

"It must be lucrative." He scrutinizes my luxury apartment I'd had decorated Victorian style—only because I liked that era in history.

"What else you got in your drawer of surprises?" He steps over to peek into my open drawer.

I race him there and slam it shut. "Don't know what you mean."

Collin reaches into the pocket of his trousers. He produces a crinkled gum wrapper. Unfurling it, he holds it up to me.

"If I'm not mistaken, this is your favorite flavor."

I stare at the Ultra cinnamon gum wrapper between his thumb and forefinger, and suck in a breath.

"Uh-huh." I flick my eyes up at him. "What about it?"

"Let's cut the shit, shall we?" He breaks into that panty-stealing smile that drew me to him in the first place.

"Let's discuss what you were doing last night next to the Vittorio compound."

His words slap me as I piece our puzzle together. I stall by conjuring cluelessness. "Compound?"

"We both know it does you no good to lie." He places his hands on his hips. "You had a red dot on my chest. Were you planning to shoot me?"

"It was a penlight!" I correct him, closing in on his personal space with my Finn-tutored stink-eye. "And what were you doing there, Mister Chase-Me-Around-Rome? Explain why *your* bloody arse leaped over the wall like a Cromwell castle marauder or a wannabe superhero."

His heat this close to me is kryptonite—*I'm* the weakened superhero. But I can't let my guard down. Not as a Sister of Sin. That would be bad.

"You're in Rome to steal something from Vittorio, aren't you?"

"Why are you so sure I'm here to steal?" he challenges.

"Oh, for fuck's sake, Collin!"

My temper percolates as I step toward him and poke his chest.

"Because this is the second time I've caught you sneaking off after a burglary. You popped into my crosshairs in Arklow, and you did it again last night!"

My cheeks heat—I haven't been this spun up since my Bratislava job.

"Crosshairs? You handle guns?" His voice rises.

We've landed onto a different playing field. Suddenly, we aren't Shayla and Collin—we've morphed into Jealousy the cessation specialist, and Collin, professional thief—or Mickey O'Shea—or whatever his name is.

Since actions speak louder than words, I decide to show him, rather than explain. It's easier. Plus, I'll enjoy the shock value.

"Have a seat. There, on my sofa," I say coolly, motioning toward it.

He does as I say. I wish everyone did that. He drops onto the middle of my sofa and leans back with outstretched arms.

I take a deep breath and cross to where I stash my pistol. I pick it up, and with the muzzle pointed down, I casually sit next to him. Avoiding Collin's unwavering gaze, I quickly and efficiently dismantle my pistol like the true professional that I am.

The only sound in the room is metal clicking on metal as I demonstrate my prowess.

I arrange my components neatly on the coffee table, as if I'm in a military training exercise. My peripheral vision catches Collin watching my every move with stunned amazement. Smug as Jesus, Mary, and Joseph, I assemble the Ruger at lightning speed, then rest the unloaded weapon on the table.

As a grand finale, I set the loaded magazine next to it and give it a tap to show I'm finished. I sit back and fold my hands in my lap.

"You could say I know my way around a weapon."

Collin lets out a slow whistle. "Holy shit, woman. What else don't I know about you, Shayla Byrne?" he says, with a slow, measured reverence.

I rise to return the pistol inside the bookcase next to my door. I amble over and stand in front of him, relishing his astonished face. He isn't the only one who is worldly these days.

"All I ask is that you don't breathe a word of this. Please don't judge. And please don't hate me."

He lets out a sigh and rests an ankle on his knee.

"I think it's time you and I had a talk."

I stay where I am. If I get close to his heat, God only knows what I'll say or do next.

"I've known you were a professional thief since that night in Arklow at the horse breeder's mansion. I was positioned outside the house that night when I saw you slinking along the roof. Then you jumped down and rode off on your electric bike."

"Slinking?" His brow rises, but he admits nothing. Instead, he sits watching me.

"At the bookshop—you'd painted your bike red, but it rubbed off, showing the black paint underneath."

He purses his lips. "Why didn't you say something?"

I narrow my eyes and drill him with my stare. "Why do you think?"

He stares down at his lap, then looks at me.

"I don't know—maybe because—you kill people for a living?" His words, though true, pierce my ears like a gun report.

Now he knows.

I'm quick to correct. "Cessation. I'm a cessation specialist—a problem solver."

I've outed myself. Now I must do damage control.

"Collin?" I search his face for any hint that he won't rush out the door in disgust and I'll never see him again. "I've been doing this a long time, and I'm good at it. But I only do it to the ones who deserve it and who get away with their injustices of destroying other people's lives."

His solemn expression worries me, and I brace for the inevitable.

He's going to walk out that door.

I rush to explain. "I save innocents. When I accept an assignment, I take it on faith that what I'm doing is right. By killing one, we save hundreds—thousands, in some cases. That's—that's our code—our compass."

I stop to take a breath, studying him for signs of disgust and disapproval.

I don't see either.

"Please—say you understand. I'm not a cold-blooded killer—I'm a gladiator for those who can't protect themselves. I consider myself morally righteous, that I'm justified. Yes, I kill people—but for all the right reasons."

My words plummet to the floor like cannon balls. I want to say more but further explanation sticks in my throat. The SOS pays me to solve problems—but I still struggle with the word assassin—but I'm also a woman with feelings.

Collin doesn't speak.

In a final desperate attempt, I put myself out there—more than I ever have.

"Collin, I'm still Shayla...the introverted geek on the autism spectrum. I can't change how my brain is wired, but I've learned to adapt and make it work for me."

I've never said this to anyone—never have I parted with any revelation of myself—not even to Mother or my Sisters.

"Come here, lass," he says quietly. Unblinking, he pats the space next to him.

I move to the sofa and lower myself to sit.

Collin takes my hand. "I figured something was going on from the way you didn't talk about things back in Ireland."

He rubs my hand with his thumb, a twinkle in his eye.

"You're hard to catch on that motor scooter of yours. You have a turbo on that thing?"

I smile because it's Collin Stedman and we're easy together. "Only the best."

"Did you hurt yourself jumping out that second story bathroom window?"

I do a double take. "Why didn't you come in after me?"

"All the employees were watching me. I still didn't know it was you. You'd gone by the time I barged in. There were only two ways out of that olive oil place. When I saw your scooter, I hung back and followed you."

He spreads his arms. "And now...here I am. Lo-and-behold, in Shayla Byrnes' lair."

I replay it in my head. I got careless in my haste to escape. *That won't happen again.* But in this case, I'm glad it did.

I mean, it's Collin fecking Stedman.

"I won't ask who you work for. I know you can't tell me." He flicks his eyes at me. "Just as I can't tell you who I work for."

"Makes us even, then." I'm relieved all of this is finally in the open between us.

"Except I don't end people's lives," he said.

Ow. That one stings.

"No, Mister Self-Righteous, you just steal from them."

Collin pulls back, defensive.

"Hey, I have moral standards!" He jabs a thumb at himself. "In the world of professional boosting, I consider myself honest and reliable, with an elevated level of integrity. I keep my clients happy. And how I know this is, they give me outstanding reviews. If I had a Yelp or a Better Business review page, you'd see those attributes listed."

I guffaw as my own defenses jump to the forefront.

"Well, my own Yelp and Better Business reviews would list those same attributes. I, too, am honest and reliable, with bucket-loads of integrity!"

I see where this stand-off is going as we one-up each other in our haste to justify ourselves.

But I still must say it. Give him an out if he wants it. It's only fair.

"If you choose to walk away and never want to see me again, I'll understand." I give him a definitive look and let out a shaky breath. "But I don't want you to. I honest-to-God don't want you to."

"How about this?" He tosses me a side-eye. "I won't judge you, and you won't judge me."

"I can live with that." An anvil lifts from my shoulders. I'm lighter. Happier. Much, much happier. "Pinky promise?" I cover his slender hand with my smaller one, loving the feel of him. I snake my little finger around his.

"Seriously? This isn't very assassin-like." Collin feigns a dramatic eyeroll, but he squeezes.

"You want me to hold you at gunpoint instead?"

"Hmm, that might turn me on, actually," quips Collin.

I ignore his comment. To me, this is serious business.

"Now that we have that wrangled, we have things to discuss," I say, wanting desperately to pick up where we'd left off back in Arklow. "Are you in Rome for a job? Is that what you call your targets?"

Collin chuckles, and it warms me. "Yep, targets. Same as you."

"Technically, in my business we say marks," I casually clarify, though semantics is the last thing on my mind right now.

"You know what the beauty of this is? We're the perfect match—since we won't narc on each other—there's no trust issues."

His logic warms me. "I like the way you think."

Collin knowing *what* I do is an unbelievable relief—but he can't know *who* I do it for. I want to leap over the Leaning Tower of Pisa that he finally knows.

"Have to say, Miss Byrne, feels damn good to be with you again." His sexy Irish candor spins my heart. "Okay, I'll come clean—I accepted a job in Rome, hoping I'd find you."

I want to fling my arms around his neck. Instead, I say, "What a strange coincidence we have the same target."

Collin draws back. "And why is that do you suppose?"

We stare at each other, openmouthed at our lineup of bizarre circumstances.

"I don't know. But I intend to find out."

The whole thing baffles me, but I shove it aside—because of the way Collin looks at me in this exact moment.

His mahogany hair has grown, giving him a wild vibe. The back of it tickles his collar. Dark lines frame his glacial eyes, like someone outlined his eyeballs with a fine point marker.

Collin's entire package goobers up my brain, not to mention my woman parts.

"Yes, we'll find out," he says. He strokes my cheek. "But first, I have other priorities. I've missed you, Shayla."

I tingle as he pushes my frayed t-shirt back off my shoulder. He rubs my bare skin—leans in, kisses it. Unprepared for the sensation it delivers, I suck in air—willing every cell in my body to flow freely to him.

"I'm completely onboard with your priorities right now, but shouldn't we eat first?" I whisper, our past and present mingling into one shared moment, ours for the taking.

Collin fastens his gaze to my mouth. "The food can wait."

He knows what he wants.

And so do I.

Chapter 28
Collin

Collin brushed her lips tentatively with his. Kissing Shayla was like a quenching rain after a thirsty drought. Her mouth waited for him—a gift he couldn't wait to unwrap.

"Collin." She drew his forehead to hers with glassy eyes. The way she said his name undid him. They were kindred souls, apart far too long, for reasons he no longer cared to understand.

He'd found her and wasn't about to let her go.

Not this time. The world was too damn uncertain.

He didn't give a rat's blarney arse what she did for a living. She could have been a post hole digger, for all he cared. He couldn't wait for the next cocktail party, like the ones he'd attended in his American fraternity days:

How do you do? I'd like to introduce my girlfriend, she's an assassin, thank you very much.

Well, he did care that she was an assassin, but he sure as shite wouldn't judge her for it.

No, he wouldn't judge, lest he point the finger at himself. Her revelation had genuinely liberated him. He was free to cherish her, maybe even love her if the world allowed. How different they both were, yet so much the same.

Collin slid his arms around her in a tight embrace. He recalled when they'd made love that first time in Avoca, in that quaint and peaceful bed and breakfast next to the river, where she'd offered her virginity to him.

He didn't take such things lightly. And he remembered it because he remembered everything.

Her body was the same as he'd pinned to his memory, silky and solid—her lips warm and pliant. He slowly lifted away, stroking her wine-colored hair and worshiping the fullness of her lips.

He wanted to devour them.

His breath grew heavy as he drank her in, like a fine Irish whiskey. He fumbled with the hair tie holding her ponytail and tugged it off.

"Want to lose myself in your hair," he murmured, as it tumbled down. He brushed it back and kissed her neck. Her hair drove him mad, like a comfy blanket he'd wanted to lose himself in.

She held back when he covered her mouth with his. He softened his take, and when she offered to give, raw desire engulfed him. Her tongue in his mouth was a haven he'd longed for since she'd left him in Arklow. His own tongue stroked hers with a tenderness he found sensual.

She squeaked a high-pitched moan and broke the kiss, her hands cradling his face.

He saw his reflection in her emerald pools.

"Is there love among thieves?" she asked, nibbling his lips.

"Depends," he breathed. "Is there love among assassins?"

"Let's find out." She fell back on the sofa with outstretched arms. "And it's not assassins, it's—"

"I know, I know, cessation specialists," he groaned out, his voice husky.

She reached for him. "I want you, Mickey O'Shea."

His mind reeled and heat waved through him as he gazed down at her lying there.

Waiting for him.

It doesn't get any better than this.

"Which is it? Do I call you Mickey or Collin?" she purred, in a lyrical Irish tone. Her eyes glinted, speeding his pulse.

"I stole the Mickey name tag." He bent to tug her black yoga pants and undies down from her shapely hips. He removed his own, freeing himself. He didn't bother with his shirt. She didn't bother with hers either.

Her arms reached for him, and he pressed his body to hers, kissing her.

"Can't believe that is someone's actual name," she panted, helping to guide him inside of her.

"You seem more experienced. Have you been with anyone since me?"

"No," she gasped as he entered her. "You were a wonderful sex-ed teacher. Still are..." She trailed off and moaned, kissing him as he began moving inside of her.

He wanted—no he needed—her on this elemental level...show her he'd surrendered to her, accepted whatever she now did in her life. He sought acceptance in return. They both led dangerous lives, and he wouldn't waste a second on minor details.

His claim of her, while impulsive, was important to him. He knew that now.

If someone would have told him that the woman he'd chased through Rome—who'd put a red dot on his chest—would result in his making love to her, he would have thought them two ravioli short of a food box.

He buried himself in her hair as he gently took her, each intense push easing her toward the body shattering orgasm he wanted for her.

She writhed under him, but she was so petite he took care not to hurt her. He remembered when he'd made love to her the first time and how the virginity pain had deprived her of pleasure. The last thing he wanted was to cause Shayla Byrne pain.

And God help anyone who even considered hurting her.

Because now they'll have me to deal with.

He wasn't a killer and not prone to violence. So far in his business, he'd avoided such entanglements. But if push came to shove? He could kill if he had to, every human was capable of it. Collin didn't care if Shayla could shoot circles around him.

He would do whatever it took to protect her.

Chapter 29
Shayla

I grip the arm rest of my seat as the plane dips and rises over the Swiss Alps. My stomach somersaults with each pitch of the airliner as I eyeball the rugged snow-capped peaks on my hour and a half flight to Zurich.

A flight attendant offers me a basket of snacks and I politely decline. We're bouncing around so much I can't even focus on the packaged biscuits. Instead, I rest my head back and squeeze my eyes shut, so I won't see us plunge into the Matterhorn.

I envision Collin naked, standing before me, as he did last night.

What calms me is, imagining what I do to him as he stands there, with those killer pecs and delicious bumps on that glistening abdomen.

Now I'm sweating.

I steer my thoughts back to my fact-finding mission, to find out what I can from Dominika's accountant, Leon Schelling. Mother wants me to meet with him, since it was rumored that he trips on his dick whenever a beautiful woman enters his office.

Not that I'm a raving beauty. I've never thought of myself that way, but Asia thought so, after doing my hair and makeup this morning. She'd made sure my tight red dress dipped low enough to flaunt my girls.

Finn had arranged everything for my meeting. Mother wants me to find out as much as I can about the infamous Dominika. The woman reminds me of a catastrophic cyclone, busting everything in her path and disposing of anyone who gets in her way.

Hope I don't land on her radar. The thought sends shivers up my spine.

I'd much rather think about Collin.

He'd stayed the night with me, and we'd talked and made love until orange and pink streaks appeared out my window. I'm running on little sleep, but my soaring heart makes up for it. Nothing that three demitasse cups of espresso couldn't fix this morning, while I waited to board.

After we made love on the sofa, Collin had lifted me up and onto my vast granite counter in the kitchen—this time naked—then we ate Cacciatore's pasta and admired each other's tats. Collin's was a colorful over-the-shoulder animal design from the Book of Kells.

I'd traced the designs with my tongue. It had driven him insane, leading to another bout of lovemaking, this time on my dining room table. I chuckle, recalling how Collin had bent to kiss the ink on my left hip—a Celtic symbol for my Byrne family, in remembrance of my deceased parents.

He'd slid his lips up my side to my mouth, where we swapped spit, and traded bites of linguine. At first my OCD kicked in when he'd eased a linguine into my mouth with his tongue, and grabbed an end with his teeth. I'd clamped on the other end and we each sucked in the noodle until our lips met for another chewy kiss.

Just like those two cute dogs in the cartoon film.

But when Collin had nibbled my lips and continued to my nipples, licking me, I promptly forgot about staying clean from germs, because it was erotic as hell.

The multiple orgasms may have had something to do with my forgetfulness. When it comes to Collin, my orgasms are like a box of chocolates—I never know what I'm going to get.

Collin made me feel like the most desired woman in the universe. I ache down low, thinking about him.

I shift in my seat, to calm Woman Parts Headquarters.

Since working for SOS and learning more about the world's evils, I'm now questioning my parent's deaths. The Uncles had always been tight-lipped, and when I'd asked Mother, she said she didn't know since it had happened in Ireland.

After these assignments, I plan to go home and chat with the Uncles about what had happened with that fatal car accident. Seeing Collin again had made me long for home.

But first things first; I have work to do.

I couldn't share with him the Sisters of Sin end of things. I'd bit my tongue and focused our talks about Rome, as we used to do back in Ireland.

We'd talked about Vittorio, filling each other in on our individual operations. I told Collin I'd try to find out if we had the same contractor. I'd filled him in on what I'd found on the Internet, that Antonio Vittorio is a high-profile guy who lives large and makes sure the world knows it—and is also a key player in the global oil industry.

When Collin had shown me the Angel Fire necklace he planned to steal, I couldn't believe it. The emeralds and pigeon blood stones were spectacular, framed with sparkling diamonds, unlike anything I'd ever seen.

Collin hadn't mentioned what his take was, and I didn't ask. I told him I didn't know why the hit on Vittorio had been ordered—didn't know who paid for the contract.

It was mostly true.

I could tell Collin had been dying to ask me who I worked for, but I'd made it crystal clear I couldn't reveal that, nor would I in the future. He'd refrained from asking, and I appreciated that.

• • • •

My plane touches down. I gather my bag containing my fake passport and IDs, and I make my way down to a car Finn has ordered. The driver opens the door and helps me settle inside.

Mother had picked out the shoes for me, red and black stilettos that beg admiration. I'm getting used to tall heels, now part of my work uniform. I chuckle.

If the Uncles could see me now.

I've come a long way from my Shabby Shayla days...but I still trip in stilettos.

I arrive at my destination, a Credit Suisse bank in downtown Zurich. I expected a fancy high-rise, but this is in a nondescript, three-story building. I step from the car and assume the role of Susanna Lipinski, Polish bag designer.

As per usual, I practiced my Polish intonation on the way here. I already had experience with the language, after hearing it spoken around Ireland while growing up.

Mother outfitted the faux-designer bag I'm carrying with an elaborate S and L in cursive with a metal logo she found in a secondhand thrift shop in Vatican City.

Schelling won't know the difference.

If and when he does, I'll be gone.

Chapter 30
Shayla

Mother's office is cool with the air conditioning as I sit waiting for our briefing. The door opens and Mother clicks in, followed by Finn. Since the bombing, Finn is the only person Mother trusts, next to the remaining loyal Sisters.

"Good afternoon, Jealousy. How was Zurich?"

"It was worth the trip," I say.

"Good. Let's have your report." Mother sits across from me, and Finn takes up his usual post, one hip balanced on her desk.

"Took some persuading, but as you said, he spilled once I shamelessly flirted. Schelling confirmed Dominika has made regular deposits from money she embezzled from Conexus. She must have hacked into the accounting system," I reply.

"I'd sure like to know where she got her hacking skills. Hopefully not from anyone around here." Finn shoots a side glance at Mother, and she shrugs.

I give Finn a devilish grin. "I didn't have to use your stink-eye on Schelling."

Finn chuckles. "I'll bet he sang like a meadowlark when you walked in."

It appears the Finnster and me have found common ground. Perhaps I've been too hard on the old boy.

Mother lets out a long sigh. "Dominika still hasn't responded to my calls, texts, or emails. It seems she's slid under the radar. Not a good sign."

"Sounds like she's ghosted the SOS." I twist the top off my bottle of water and sip.

"Finn gave you the Dominika file," says Mother. "Here's some additions."

She passes me a several photos. "We found recent captures of Dominika from CCTV in London. As you know, Dominika's SOS code name is Aggravate. Appropriately named."

"Yes, Finn briefed me before." I thumb through the captures. "I take it you want me to go to London?"

"While you were in Zurich, we dug into the Conexus and Sisters of Sin accounting systems." Mother tosses ice cubes in a glass and pours water. "Dominika has been moving money to her account on a monthly basis."

Finn purses his lips. "She's hidden it successfully under fake names substantiated by services rendered to SOS. Payment for weapons, vehicles, corporate jets, and travel expenditures."

Mother shakes her head impatiently. "I don't know why. She has plenty of her own money. Unless she's funding something she's unwilling to pay for. I ordered an audit to identify the aliases she used to compare with Schelling's deposits."

She lifts a sheet of paper. "I have it right here."

"Schelling said Dominika stole the money out of vengeance," I say.

"Oh, really?" Mother's ice cubes tinkle as she empties her glass.

"How much did Dominika steal?" I ask.

Mother's eyes flash. "Twenty million."

I choke on my bottle of water. "Jaysus! What a pile of gobshite!"

"Gobshite is right," says Finn with a grim face. "Conexus can write it off as a loss, but it's still a chunk of change."

Mother lets out an exasperated sigh. "We can't have Sisters stealing from our organization."

"Now what?" I ask.

"First, you'll execute your hit tonight." Mother fixes me with her cool gaze. "Then you'll go to London first thing in the morning. We have leads where Dominika may be staying. I need to know what she's doing."

I stay casual, to get intel for Collin. "Who is it that wants Antonio Vittorio dead?"

Mother's brow furrows. "A long-time associate of Jeff Lynsey's. He won't say who, only that it's someone Vittorio double-crossed in an oil and gas energy deal in Saudi Arabia."

I raise my brows. "Why order the hit for tonight?"

"There's an OPEC meeting the day after tomorrow. The contractor doesn't want Vittorio present."

My wheels spin. I must talk to Collin. This will affect his operation. Once Vittorio is dead, Collin won't have access to the compound. It'll be locked down so tight ants won't get in.

I remember the other reason I'm here to see Mother. Declan had sent me crucial intel about an operation he and the Uncles had been working on back in Ireland.

I clear my throat. "Mother, as you know, my family is active in this same business, back in Ireland. Cousin Declan has gathered intel concerning sophisticated cybercrime cartels. He's identified five key individuals responsible for half of the world's cybercrime. Everything from planning genocides and human trafficking online, to corporate thefts and hacking into military and hospital systems to steal money."

"Go on," said Mother, her hand supporting her chin in her thoughtful stance.

I have Finn's full attention. They both need to hear this.

I continue. "Cybersecurity can't keep up with the malware and ransomware attacks. Cybercrime has skyrocketed out of control on a global level." I take a breath and hold out a USB to Finn.

"Here's the dossiers on the five. These individuals skip through servers like rocks over ponds, but my cousin and his merry band of associates have nailed down who they are—and *where* they are. Eliminating these five would drastically debilitate overall operations and reduce widespread global impact."

Finn takes the USB and inserts it into Mother's desktop system. "Need to scan for viruses and corrupt files first."

Silence governs the room as Finn's sophisticated detection systems run through their paces.

His expression changes to amazement. He lets out a slow whistle. "Here we go. Impressive. Excellent work, Jealousy."

I watch him scan the monitor. Wish I could read that fast, but I'm a slow reader. I linger on every word.

Finn flicks his eyes to mine. "I'll have my staff do further intel and prepare a report for the Conexus board. Ultimately, it will be their decision. I'll let you know when Mother hears." Finn is the perfect assistant—forever deferring to Mother.

It's no secret that he's crazy about her. I think it's cute.

I motion at the computer screen. "Note the locations. Some will surprise you, but one certainly won't." I'm referring to the one in Beijing.

Mother stands behind Finn, peering around him at the screen. "Reykjavík, Oslo, Newcastle in Northern Ireland, and Falmouth in Cornwall, England. Interesting."

Mother turns to me. "What strategy do you recommend?"

"I think we should execute the hits at the same time. At least as close as possible. When word spreads, the other scum will scatter and disappear. Took a while to nail down these five. Declan knows their routines, travel schedules, the works."

Finn moves around Mother's desk. "Jealousy, this is huge. I'm ninety-eight percent sure Conexus will greenlight this. I'll let you know for sure when you return from London."

Mother gives me a thoughtful look. "This will be a hefty payout for you. Good detective work. However." Her eyes flash a gentle but firm warning. "Don't get any ideas. Don't want you migrating over to Interpol or Ireland's Cyber Security Center. Or worse yet, Italy's domestic intelligence agency."

Does Mother doubt my loyalty to the SOS? I've certainly not given her reason to.

"No chance of that. I can't take all the credit. Cousin Declan is the expert in cyberspace. He's taught me hacking and other ways to dig up info, but his tentacles are far-reaching in his own network. He makes good money customizing cyber protection for companies."

Finn flicks his eyes up from the screen. "S'pose he'd come work for us?"

He sports a mischievous grin, but I know he means it.

"You can't afford him." If nothing else, at least I'm truthful.

Collin jumps back into my brain. I must talk to him as soon as possible. My heart speeds as I stand, impatient to get going. "Heading out to prepare for tonight."

"I don't care what time it is. Check in with me on your SOS phone when it's done."

"I will." I exit Mother's office, pressure forcing its way into my temples.

I'm working two ends against the middle, and I'm the middle. No way can my employers find out the man I love—yes, love, I've decided—is involved in this operation, albeit indirectly.

No, that would not go over well.

I've had second thoughts about having joined an organization that someone wants destroyed. After the bombing, I'd worried about signing on with the SOS, wondering what the blue bollocks I had gotten myself into.

I'd talked to the Uncles after the bombing, since they'd heard about it and had contacted Mother. Uncle Casen advised me to lie low and do as Mother says, but not to quit.

One simply doesn't quit an assassin organization.

Uncle Brodie recommended that I stay alert from now on, and not to let down my guard.

For *any* reason.

Mother had only told me about my mum in terms of generalizations when she'd worked for the SOS twenty-five years ago. She refused to tell me about the jobs Mum had been assigned. All she'd said was how well Mum did them and what a wonderful person she was.

I'd left it alone. Some things a daughter doesn't need to know.

I miss my family in Ireland, and it aches me. I also need answers about Mum and Dad's car accident. Declan had alluded long ago he didn't think it was an accident. Now that I work for the SOS, I can easily see how someone would have wanted Mum dead.

I need to talk to Declan and the Uncles. There is much they haven't told me.

It's time I knew the truth.

Chapter 31
Collin

Collin parked outside the trattoria on the corner, at the agreed upon meeting place. A woman with sunglasses, long black hair, and a wispy scarf wrapped around her neck flung open the passenger door.

"*Bonjourno*," she said with a demure smile as she climbed into the Alfa Romeo.

He drew back. "Who the heck are you?" he teased.

Shayla assumed a surly expression. "No one you should mess with. *Capische?*"

Her exotic Mediterranean vibe was an attention-getter. It certainly had *his* attention.

"Ladies and gentlemen, I give you the many personalities of Shayla Byrne," said Collin in a film trailer voice. He turned to her. "You look like Audrey Hepburn."

"*Roman Holiday*," quipped Shayla, positioning her sunglasses. "I used to watch it with the Uncles."

"How are the old boys, anyway?"

"Uncle Casen has a lung disease." She said it matter of fact, but Collin knew it bothered her. She loved her uncles.

"Is it serious?"

"I don't know. I'm going home to see him when I finish these assignments."

"Assignments? As in more than one?" he asked.

She shook her head to dismiss it. "There's some things I have to do."

"From the employer you can't tell me about."

"Yes."

He knew when to shut it, when it came to Shayla. And this was one of those times.

"Hurry up and get us out of the city," she mumbled.

"Embarrassed to be seen with me?" he teased. "I'm taking us to an out of the way place. A quaint *ristorante* nestled in a family vineyard where we can have privacy. Scarce these days," he said drily, hitting the gas to duck in and out of traffic.

They rode in strained silence, tonight weighing heavily on their minds. Collin pulled into a gated driveway and drove to a parking place. He cut the engine, got out, and opened Shayla's door.

She gripped his hand and squeezed. "If you don't kiss me right this minute, I won't tell you what I have to tell you."

Collin tugged her to him and laid a kiss on her that would drop grapes from the vines. He tasted cinnamon and wanted more—but he broke the kiss, loving how she stumbled back, dazed.

"You're a good kisser, Stedman," she murmured, wiping her mouth as an elderly couple smiled at them.

Collin and Shayla moved through the cozy restaurant to an outside alcove, where he guided her to a table for two nestled in a corner surrounded by ivy. He pulled out a chair and waited for her to sit.

She removed her sunglasses and her lashes lifted. "I love your grand, chivalrous nature."

"My mum is death on manners." He smoothed his hair back and seated himself. "Not to change the subject, but have you found out anything about the Vittorio contract?"

"Only that the hit has to be tonight," she said quietly, making sure no one could hear. "Vittorio pissed off some Saudis in an oil deal. They want him gone by tomorrow."

Collin nodded. "That still fits with my plan, provided I boost the necklace before you do your operation."

"This one must look like an accident. My employer doesn't want inquiries." Shayla let out an annoyed sigh. "This hit must be close proximity."

"I sense you don't like cozying up to your targets."

Shayla rolled her eyes. "You sensed correctly."

"Why not do a sniper hit when he's in the pool?" He glanced at the server coming toward him.

They placed their orders and waited for the server to move off.

Shayla leaned forward and spoke in a hushed tone. "Must be close range. No bullets, no blood. My employer doesn't want the Carabinieri, or other police involved."

"You mean you're going inside the mansion?"

"We intercepted Vittorio's email. His wife is gone, and he has ladies over—women from brothels." Shayla wrinkled her nose. "It seems I'm on the menu for tonight."

Collin's eyes grew large. "Shayla, that's too dangerous."

"And you going inside his mansion, isn't?"

"Now that you put it that way." He held up his hand. "I don't need to know the gory details of how you do your job. But for my end of things, I need to know a specific time. I must be in and out before you conduct your operation."

"Each night Vittorio swims around nine p.m. That's when I'll do it. Can you get in and out by then?"

Collin thought for a minute. His earnest eyes sought hers. "If you can keep him distracted, I can. I typically do middle-of-the-night jobs."

He leaned toward her. "Don't let him have sex with you."

"What do you take me for? Jaysus, Collin!"

He hadn't meant to insinuate. "It's just...now that I've found you, I think of you as mine."

Her eyes flashed like summer lightning. "Here's a reminder—no one owns me. Got that?"

Collin regretted the words as soon as they'd slipped out. "That's not what I meant." He back peddled. "I meant to say you're the *Peg O' My Heart*."

He breathed relief when it elicited the soft reaction he wanted.

"Mum sang that to me when I was a wee child." Her eyes glazed over with a remote look, and he knew she played it in her memory. He did the same, except his parents were still alive.

"Oh, before I forget." He leaned to the side to retrieve his wallet and lifted five-hundred euros. "This is yours. From your jewelry sales at the Celtic Sea Bookshop."

Her lovely jaw dropped as he took her palm and placed bills on it. "Oh, Collin, thank you. Honestly, I'd forgotten."

"The Celtic cross peridot necklace was the only piece I didn't sell. I kept it because it reminds me of your eyes." He fixed on those eyes, motioning at the bills. "Paid you for that, too."

"Oh, Collin." Her face softened. "You don't need to pay me for that. Consider it a gift."

Shayla set the bills on the table and closed her hands over his. "You're right. Your best attribute is honesty. I'll note that on your Yelp review page."

Collin chuckled. "That would be grand, lass."

He wished he had a bona fide Yelp page, instead of his professional credentials languishing deep inside the entrails of the Dark Web. Maybe someday, when he'd steal back everything he'd taken in the past, karma would go easy on him and not bite him in the bloody arse.

"Is there any way at all you can find out whether the contractor who ordered the hit also ordered the heist?"

Shayla sipped her water. "Not sure how to do it without raising suspicion and compromising your operation. I'll see what I can find out after tonight."

Collin had considered messaging Scorpio for the information. But if that can of worms opened, carnage might ensue. Not a clever idea.

"Met the handler in person. Goes by Scorpio. A paunchy, middle-aged Italian—or at least he sounded like one," said Collin. "We only talked about the necklace—and the painting. No mention of anything else."

"What painting?" Shayla arched a brow.

"The same dealer wants the Rokeby Venus painting from the National Art Gallery in London."

Shayla nearly choked on her pasta. "The one in Trafalgar Square? Now that's one potato short of a Boxty. They'll lock you up and eat the key."

"I've boosted from galleries before. Once you figure them out, they're a snap."

"A snap?" Her voice rose, and she glanced around, as if someone might overhear. "You're acting the maggot, Collin! What is this guy paying you?"

"I can retire on both heists. For good." He beamed.

Shayla sat back. "I wish for once that you thieves who steal from art galleries and museums would steal them back and return them to where they belong. I hate that one person deprives the entire world of extremely rare pieces of art."

Her words nicked him because he felt the same. "I hear you. I've entertained the thought myself."

The server brought their food, and Collin picked at his pasta. He never could eat before a major job.

Shayla stopped eating and set her napkin on her plate. "Not hungry. Can we go? We need to get back and prepare."

"I'm with you on that score." Collin dropped his napkin on the plate.

They rose, paid for their meals, and stepped out of the restaurant.

Once outside, Shayla took his hand and led him down a stone walkway to a nearby stream. "Let's get our heads in the game before we get into the game."

He liked how she framed things.

Collin had given his second chance relationship with Shayla considerable thought. He'd concluded she was someone he wanted in his life—no matter how abnormal and dangerous each of their lives would be.

When they reached the babbling stream, watching water slosh over rocks, Collin contemplated how to put into words what he should have told Shayla back in Ireland.

As he struggled to put the words together, Shayla tugged off her black wig, removed her sunglasses, and shoved them into her bag. After resting her bag on a bench, she tugged him close and slipped her arms around his waist. Her emerald pools were clear and bright—same as the day he met her.

"You know me from before, Collin. You know how words don't come easy for me. There are things that—there is something I need to..." she trailed off, her eyes searching his.

He sensed what she wanted to say, knowing the risk for the first person who said it.

He welcomed the risk.

Collin cradled her face. "I love you, Shayla. Should have told you, back in Ireland I want you to know that before we—before you, in case...in case..."

"I love you too!" Tears gathered, and he knew she meant every word. "I loved you the second you said two percent of the world population has green eyes. Love doesn't scare me anymore."

"I didn't know it did."

"I've always been too terrified to love anyone or anything. It would have compromised the Uncles and the rest of my family. I talked myself into fearing love."

She flicked her meadowy gaze up to his. "Until you. Once I got past finding out you're a professional thief."

He laughed, recalling the day they'd met at the Celtic Sea Bookshop, when he'd felt the same way. "Why did it take us so long to get here?"

"Because we're both eejits. You men are always slow to say 'I love you.'" Shayla threw her arms around his neck, and he lifted her and pressed her against him—holding her—loving her.

She wrapped her legs around him and gave him a long, probing kiss. They stayed that way until the urgency of his business carped at him. He broke the kiss and set her on her feet.

"I want to do you right here next to this beautiful stream," said Shayla, her gaze locked with his. "Reminds me of the Vale of Avoca and the bungalow you took me to for our first time together."

"I remember it well." Collin blew out air, willing his lower body part to deflate along with his lungs. "We'd better go prepare for tonight."

"Why didn't we become doctors, lawyers, or teachers? Something normal. Instead of this..." Shayla motioned at herself and Collin with a what-the-heck-are-we-doing expression, and they both broke out laughing.

She swiped at her cheeks. "We've got to get ready for work—you know, make sandwiches, memorize access codes, fill the thermos, load our weapons, lay out our clothes..."

Collin cut in. "Pack our tools, get ready for the commute, buy a latte for the boss..." He dissolved into more laughter until tears leaked. When their mirth subsided, Collin wiped his eyes.

"If only we were that normal. Normal people don't know how good they have it." Shayla's lingering merriment made her beautiful, the way her mouth curved up.

"Normal people aren't hired killers or professional thieves." He stood back and observed her burgundy hair shimmering in the noontime sun. Her cheeks flushed, and her full lips begged for him to nibble at them. He bent to do just that.

She palmed his cheek and nibbled him right back.

"Where do we go from here, Mickey O'Shea?" she murmured.

"We do what we each came to Rome to do. Simple as that. And when we complete our jobs, we'll take a vacation. I'll take you anywhere you want to go."

"Anacapri," she said. "On the Island of Capri."

"I can arrange that. Have a friend who has a villa there. Consider it done." He took her hand and led her back to the car park.

They climbed into his Alfa Romeo and sped back to town. Shayla had him stop at a diving equipment store on the way to her place. She wanted him to take something into Vittorio's mansion and position it at the pool tonight.

When they were back in the car with her purchase, she gave him a juicy kiss and topped it off with a nip of his bottom lip. "I enjoy working with you, Irish Dude."

She faced forward and sat tall in her seat, adjusting her sunglasses.

"Now let's go. We have jewelry to steal and people to kill."

Chapter 32
Shayla

A sia whips out a classy dominatrix outfit in the wardrobe room, after Finn informs us that my mark is into BDSM. Finn seems to delight in having discovered this lovely little morsel of intel, bless his heart.

I don't give a flip what my marks do for recreation. Since I'm conducting a proximity hit, Finn thinks it's a good idea. Me, I'm not so sure. If Collin and I weren't coordinating tonight's operation, I would have asked Mother to delegate this hit to Vanity or Pride.

Asia's blue hair shines in the fluorescent lighting, as she equips me with a black strappy teddy, with not much to it. She holds it up to me and assesses.

"Hmm, this gives you a dash of slutty elegance to go with your badass woman vibe," she says, brown eyes sparkling.

"You think?" I take it from her and make a face, fingering crisscross straps that zigzag in random directions. My crave-for-order brain can't figure what goes where.

Asia reaches for a black garter belt and wiggles the hanger.

"Let's get you into these."

"I'll need your help." Once I recover from my bashfulness at stripping down in front of her, Asia sets to work helping me wriggle into the torturous, wee lingerie.

"Honey, I've seen it all," she says, pointing. "Okay, stick your legs in these holes."

"I've got that much figured out," I say, tugging the thing up. "It's the rest that baffles me."

Asia sorts the straps and separates them. "Try this. I think your arms go through here."

The torturous thing twists around me. I resemble a Picasso painting.

Asia barks out a laugh and gets us both giggling, as we attempt every imaginable way to make sense of these bloody wee straps. We laugh until tears roll down our cheeks.

"Shit girl, you ruined all that heavy makeup," she says, swiping at her eyes. "I'll scrape it off and start over. That's what Bob Ross does."

"Who?"

"Never mind—an American artist," she says dismissively.

When my false eyelash falls off, Asia yelps. We laugh even harder.

She recovers first. "You're ready to work at the Purple Velvet Room."

"I'm afraid to ask," I say, attempting to channel my inner badass to get my head in the game.

"It's a popular burlesque show in San Francisco." Asia repairs my heavy makeup and reapplies the derelict eyelash.

"When I move my eyeballs, I see spiders sticking to my lids," I say when she finishes.

Asia shakes her head. "Don't let those lashes get in the way of your job." She hands me a full-length belted raincoat to cover my dominatrix ensemble.

I wonder what Collin will think when he sees me in this get-up. My family would sure get a kick out of it.

What I didn't tell Collin was that Declan had found intel that Antonio Vittorio ran a successful cybercrime operation from Sicily, then had expanded. He'd gotten away with his sophisticated network for years, stealing millions from unsuspecting people from around the world.

Declan had uncovered fraudulent sites and emails where Vittorio and his goons had targeted elderly and other innocent people to hand over credit card numbers and identity information.

I didn't want to ask Finn to do this research—didn't want to raise suspicions why I needed more intel. I don't want him compromised in any way. When I first came onboard with the Sisters of Sin, Mother had discouraged us from having romantic relationships. At the time, I didn't think I'd see Collin again.

Things have certainly changed on that score. Nonetheless, I've decided to keep my relationship with Collin under wraps for the time being.

As a result, I had enlisted Declan to see if he could somehow find a link between my hit and Collin's heist. If anyone can find intel like that, Declan could. His tentacles reach deep inside the bowels of the criminal underground.

He'd not come up with anything yet, but said he'd keep looking.

• • • •

I take an Uber from the city proper out to the Vittorio compound at seven p.m. On the way, I finger the Celtic necklace I'd made that doubles as a snare, in case Plan 'A' fails. I hope it won't come to that, as a kill by other means would spark an investigation and an inquiry by the Carabinieri or the *Polizia di Stato*, the Italian civil national police.

Collin and I had purchased burner phones and traded numbers for texting, to coordinate our moves. We'd discussed contingencies along with our coordination of everything else.

I'm thrilled at the thought of working with Collin. The last thing I ever considered would be that we'd be working together in his badass world and mine.

The car stops at the compound's wrought-iron gates. I tell the driver to wait while I slide the window down and tap the code on the dial pad. The fifteen-foot gates swing open, and we drive through. Inside are acres of beautifully landscaped grounds. Peacocks strut, showing off their plumes. Cultivated flower gardens surrounding fountains dot the landscape.

The car pulls up to the mansion with six columns and a portico. A man in a suit opens my door and helps me from the car. I take a moment to balance on the same stilettos I wore to Zurich. He pats me down and paws through my velvet bag. I'd hidden my flat burner phone on the inside of my garter belt.

Suit Man opens the front door and I enter a high-ceilinged foyer done in crystal, marble, granite, and every other kind of engineered stone known to man. Naked cherubs pee blue water in a sculptured pool in the center.

He leads me through double doors, then up a flight of stairs and down a hallway wide enough to land a spaceship.

Paintings adorn the walls, and sculptures grace the spaces in between. Reminds me of the Vatican hallways when Mother had gotten the Sisters VIP passes to tour it.

Collin and I had synchronized our phones down to the second. It is seven p.m., the exact time he plans to gain entry to the mansion from the service entrance. The day I'd posed as a wine delivery person, I'd gotten the service entrance gate code by downloading the security data onto the electronic collection device Finn had supplied me.

This handy device speedily collects data from laptops, phones, and anything with computer memory, including building security systems.

That day, little did I know I'd be going in as a prostitute through the front door. From wine delivery to hooker to cessation specialist. I would surely impress the Uncles.

I had passed the gate security code to Collin, who drove his Alfa Romeo onto the grounds, posing as a new house employee, during a seven p.m. shift change.

Collin had changed into the butler suit he'd stolen the first time he'd entered the mansion. I'd talked him into staying with me for the rest of his time in Rome. Beholding him in that snazzy butler suit had taken my breath away, causing my mouth to water like he was a juicy dinner steak.

We'd kissed each other good luck. Collin had tugged at the belt on my raincoat, wanting to see what I had on underneath for my so-called date. I'd repeatedly slapped his hand away. He had to stay focused on his operation, not on me—who knows what would have happened had he peeked under my raincoat.

As much as I'd wanted to get Collin out of his dashing butler outfit, we had work to do, so I mentally undressed him. In the old days when I'd mentally undress him, my OCD would kick in and I'd find myself folding his clothes in my mind instead.

I choke back a laugh, loving the new me and how easily I poke fun at myself now.

Suit Man escorts me down another long hallway to a room with a dial pad. He taps the numbers, and the door opens.

"Enter," he says gruffly.

I step inside the ornate suite, and he closes the door behind me. The bolt action locks.

I move through the room into the massive bedroom suite, with its own living room. This one has a bar, floor to ceiling fireplace, and animal heads from Africa adorning the walls.

"Come here. Let me look at you," rumbles a voice from a tall leather chair in front of the fireplace.

"*Buona serata*," I say, moving to where he can see me.

"I asked for an English-speaking girl this time," says Vittorio.

"I speak English." I'm careful to tinge my words with an Italian inflection.

He gestures at my raincoat. "Take that off."

I comply. Because it's showtime.

I slowly undo my belt. Every move I make from now on must be slow, to tease and tantalize. I remove the raincoat and drape it over a nearby chair.

When I get a good look at him, I give myself a start. I expected a short, stout, hairy guy. The photos I'd seen must have been outdated.

This person is hairy and short in stature, but not that bad looking. He has a dark widow's peak—giving him a wee bit of a werewolf vibe.

Too bad he must die.

Chapter 33
Collin

Wheeling a cart of food delicacies, everything from beluga caviar to sumptuous seafood and choice chocolates, Collin made his way to Vittorio's suite to deliver the food. He'd cheerfully volunteered when the servant who normally delivered it had taken sick.

He'd bullshitted his way into the center of activity from inside the service quarters, listening to conversation and noting the activity throughout the mansion. He didn't have much time and had to stay on task.

He stopped at the double doors to Vittorio's private suite and tapped the code on the dial pad. The door opened, and he entered with his cart, a white towel over his forearm. What he beheld when he glanced up nearly undid him.

Shayla stood before a leather sofa, resplendent in a shiny black thong and leather bustier that lifted her breasts—narrow black straps crisscrossing each one—bulging them. Black elbow gloves covered her forearms as she held a brandy bottle.

Her arse cheeks resembled an upside-down heart, with full flesh exposed.

The black patent leather ankle boots with the spike heels looked like weapons. For all he knew, maybe she'd used them on other targets. They made her look badass.

He almost hadn't recognized her with the long blonde tresses and heavy makeup. She looked good enough to eat.

She wears slutty very, very well.

For a split second he wished he was the one on the sofa. A wave of jealousy smacked him. This slime ball ogled the love of his life in all her hot glory. Collin jarred himself back to reality, shaking off his spellbound horniness.

Stay focused, eejit!

Good thing he stood behind the food cart to hide the swell in his pants.

"Thank you. I'll take it from here," Shayla said coolly, as if she were queen of the manor.

Her heated gaze locked with Collin's, detonating his pulse. Her in-charge attitude turned him on, although this new dominatrix vibe had taken him by surprise. What a turnabout from the old Shayla of Arklow.

She's only playing a role...right?

He made a mental note to check that wee tidbit out for himself later, when things were back to normal—whatever the feck normal was.

Vittorio spoke up. "Did you bring the whipped cream?"

"Yes, sir." Collin had indeed noticed a sizeable bowl of whipped cream on a corner of the cart, along with melted chocolate.

Don't tell me this wee bastard is into food sex.

Collin loved food and sex, but not together. He preferred his food *after* sex.

"I'll get us some." Shayla strode over to the cart with her back to Vittorio. With her eyes locked onto Collin's, she slid Vittorio's phone into the cart. His phone controlled the home security system. Shayla slipped a note in with it and gave Collin a sultry wink.

The password for the phone.

Good girl. Collin smiled with his eyes.

"Here's your whipped cream, *signora.*" Collin held up the bowl of whipped cream, exchanging an amused look with Shayla.

"Take the food to the pool, then go," ordered the inebriated Italian, his speech slurred.

Good. Collin dipped a nod at Shayla and wheeled the cart through the wide patio doors to the pool deck.

This made his task easier. He lifted the white linen draped on the sides of the cart and retrieved the items Shayla asked him to place out here. He stooped to shove them under a lounge chair.

Collin headed back inside and stood near Vittorio, still seated in his chair. Shayla was now on his lap, offering him more brandy.

"Is that all, sir?" Collin asked in a cultured servant's tone.

"Yes, go." Vittorio gave Collin a dismissive wave and fixed his undivided attention on Shayla.

• • • •

C ollin exited the suite, plucked the phone and Shayla's note from the cart, and slid them into his jacket pocket. He hurried to the other end of the mansion to the art collections room, noting he only had an hour to get the necklace and get out before Shayla did her hit.

This shitebag better not hurt her, despite Collin knowing Shayla could take care of herself.

What the hell was the man going to do with all that whipped cream?

I know what I would do with it...

Collin ducked into a service closet and retrieved Vittorio's phone. Using Shayla's note, he typed in the password and the screen leaped to life. He tapped a lock icon and a schematic of the house popped into view. Collin tapped the Art Collections room. The room appeared in real time with green lasers at varied angles on the phone screen.

He studied the security menu and tapped the 'off' button. The lasers disappeared from the screen.

Excellent.

Collin emerged from the closet and continued to the end of the hall. He quickly tapped the code. The door opened, and he made sure the security light indicator was off. He'd soon find out. He waved his hand.

Nothing happened. No lasers.

He strode to the Angel Fire display case in the center of the room. It had its own system that he'd figured out how to disable his first time in here. Using Vittorio's phone, he scanned it for another security icon. Nothing that displayed an isolated security for the necklace.

Which icon is it?

He studied the lit display case.

If the light went out, that would indicate the system was off, right?

Most of these systems operated that way, but not always. Sometimes they had two and three separate security systems on these things.

He glanced at the time on the phone. Eight forty-five. Vittorio would go for his nine o'clock swim in fifteen. Shayla would keep him on track by filling him with brandy and entertaining him. She had to, so Vittorio wouldn't miss his phone.

Collin heard a sound outside the door.

Dammit, someone's coming!

A security guard doing the nightly rounds. He'd heard them discussing it when he'd hung around the service area, but no time was specified.

He searched for a place to hide in the vast room.

Holy shit, the lasers!

He had to get them back on. He spotted a window with velvet drapes on each side. The old hide behind the drapes routine he'd seen in a dozen movies.

What other choice did he have? He'd get shot on sight if he didn't. He ducked behind a heavy velvet drape, fumbling with Vittorio's phone.

Where's the fecking laser security button?

He swiped through screens and finally located the icon. He tapped it and heard the distinctive hum of activating lasers.

Collin waited as the lock clicked open, and the laser hum switched off. Footsteps echoed on the marble floor as someone cycled around the edge of the room—then they stopped.

He held his breath. What was the guy doing?

He didn't dare peek out. Instead, he remained still as a stone, hoping no one outside the house would see him standing inside the window.

The footsteps sounded. A phone rang with an old-fashioned bell tone.

"Yeah?" said a man's voice. "Vittorio is still with the *prostituta*. I'll secure the pool area when he's done and takes her to bed."

Takes her to bed? Over my fecking dead body.

The man exited, and Collin let out a relieved stream of air. It was nine p.m.

He was out of time.

Collin had to snatch the necklace and get his bloody arse out of there.

He knew one thing. Antonio Vittorio wouldn't be going to bed with anyone after tonight.

Collin had confidence in Shayla's ability to successfully complete her operation, but the protector side of him wanted to be sure she wasn't harmed.

Chapter 34
Shayla

I get Vittorio drunk, after spreading whipped cream on his chest that he insists I lick off. It is all I can do not to gag. When he isn't looking, I wipe my tongue with an alcohol wipe. He wants whipped cream on other body parts, too, but I escape those pleasantries by pumping booze into him.

I help Vittorio stagger out to the pool after I coax him with the promise of a raucous bout of sex. I laugh and tease and carry on like a good little hooker.

"Have another sip," I say, handing him more brandy. This whole scenario is so far out of my comfort zone it's like an out-of-body experience—like I'm watching someone else act out this whacked pre-cessation seduction.

I keep stifling a laugh after seeing Collin's face when he saw me in this get-up. It was priceless. I couldn't tell if his expression was one of wonder, horror, shock, awe, or amusement. Probably all of those things.

No doubt he'll tease me until the sheep come home.

When Vittorio sits on the edge of the pool, I drag the dive belt and the portable aqualung breathing device from under the lounge chair where I'd told Collin to stash them.

I fasten the dive belt around Vittorios's waist. He's blitzed, and mumbles that I'm outfitting him with something kinky.

"Oh, it's kinky all right." I tug off my long blonde hairpiece and toss it on the pool deck.

After I secure the dive belt on him, I get into the shallow end and tell Vittorio to come and have some fun. He flops into the pool, and I tug him to the deeper water. I grasp the dive belt from the back, insert the breathing device into my mouth, and drag him underwater.

The weighted dive belt sinks him, and I lie on my back five feet down, on the bottom of the pool, holding him. He struggles, and I hold on tight, making sure he stays under. Eventually, he weakens and stops moving as water fills his lungs. It seems to take forever.

Damn these up close and personal jobs. They wear me out.

When I'm certain Vittorio's breathing and heart have stopped, I surface. I unfasten the dive belt from around his waist and heave it up onto the pool deck.

Antonio Vittorio floats face down.

Billionaire gets drunk and drowns.

No guns. No blood. No inquiry. No Carabinieri.

No more ripping off the elderly's retirement accounts with Internet scams, and all the other shady deals he had going on.

Mother and the contractor will be happy. And so will I, when the money for this job deposits into my account.

I hoist myself from the pool and towel off, so I won't leave a wet trail. After retrieving my raincoat, heels, and my bag, I hurry outside and grab the dive belt and portable breather. I stick on flat shoes and let myself out of the pool gate. I circle around to the nearby service parking lot to find Collin's dark red Alfa Romeo.

Everything so far is going according to plan.

Collin should have the necklace by now.

Chapter 35
Collin

B ack at the service quarters, and with the Angel Fire tucked inside a velvet bag, Collin slipped out when no one was paying attention and immediately spotted Shayla sitting in the passenger seat of the Alfa Romeo.

Excellent timing.

Collin opened the driver's door and climbed in. Despite Shayla's drowned rat appearance, she looked hot in that strappy, sexy slut-suit that made her breasts stand at attention as if saluting him.

He couldn't help himself—leaned over and fondled one—then kissed it. "Shall we depart, my lovely?"

"Better fire up those afterburners before they unleash the dragons. When security finds the body and the necklace missing, hell will be upon us." Shayla's eyes sparkled.

Her skin glistened in the moonlight, exciting him. "You sound like a Tolkien novel."

"Do you have the necklace?" she said, breathless.

"Affirmative." Collin passed her the cloth bag containing Angel Fire, then started the engine. He threw it in reverse and drove to the service gate entrance. He slid his window down to tap the code on the dial pad when alarms sounded.

"They found the body—or know the necklace is missing," said Collin, waiting impatiently for the gates to open. His chest clenched. Had they already locked down the compound?

Collin heard shouting. He craned his neck out the window to glance behind them.

"We have to get out of here—tap the code again!" yelled Shayla.

He did as ordered, and to his relief, this time the gates opened.

"Time to suck diesel. Hang on." Collin pressed the accelerator, and the Alfa Romeo shot forward. He eyed the rearview mirror to see the gates close. He gunned it, catching the tires on the gravel shoulder. The car fish-tailed on the loose gravel, until Collin corrected and pulled onto the pavement.

He put on his night vision goggles and sped down the highway, as fast as safety would allow. Along the way, he cut the headlights.

Shayla didn't say a word as he raced through the darkness, zigzagging his route. He turned onto a lane and skidded the car to a stop at an isolated farm, behind a sizeable building.

Collin cut the engine.

They both leaped from the vehicle, peering into the darkness to see if anyone had followed.

"We lost them," muttered Collin, pulling off his night vision goggles and brushing back his hair.

"Good. One less thing." Shayla blew out air and fell back on the front of the Alfa.

Collin gathered the dive belt and tossed it into the boot of the car. He slammed it shut and came around to Shayla.

Her eyes glittered in the dark as she held out the velvet bag. "Can I see Angel Fire?"

Collin took the bag from her. He was eager to make sure it hadn't twisted, and no stones had come loose in all the jostling that couldn't be helped. He eased the bag from Angel Fire and exhaled relief. The necklace still clung to the velvet contour form supporting it. He angled it toward the moonlight to sparkle the gemstones.

Shayla's eyes grew large as she leaned close to examine the necklace. "It's gorgeous."

She swung her gaze to his. "Now what?"

Collin's phone vibrated, and he fished it from his pocket to see a pulsating scorpion. He gave her the necklace to hold while he tapped the encrypted message.

Do you have Angel Fire?

Collin tapped the affirmative with his thumbs.

An immediate response appeared. "Go to London for transfer. Transfer and access codes will be at tomorrow evening's fundraiser for the National Art Gallery. Details to follow." The message dissolved into individual pixels and disappeared.

"Looks like I'm going to London." Collin glanced at Shayla. Things were on track and proceeding as planned. Tomorrow he'd be halfway to his financial goal when he delivered Angel Fire.

"Looks like we're both going to London," she said, eyes glittering as she handed back the necklace.

He stowed it safely back inside the velvet bag and placed it inside the car.

Collin straightened and slanted an appreciative smile at the beauty facing him, her hair still damp from her pool excursion, natural waves gone wild. His gaze drifted down to ogle the woman he loved, drinking in her sexy shape in the strappy barely-there black thing she had on, as she leaned on the front of the Alfa Romeo.

Feverish desire seized him by the balls. "I want you, badly."

"Now?" Shayla's peridot eyes shone bright in the pale light of the moon, searing him.

Collin didn't hesitate. He pressed her gently back onto the car, plunging his tongue into her mouth, running his hands over her. He enjoyed her in this badass outfit, but he wanted her naked.

He broke the kiss. "This strappy thing is still wet. Let's get you out of it, so I can warm you up."

"I am a tad chilly, come to think of it," she murmured into his mouth, shivering.

The clouds parted, and he noticed her goosebumps in the moonlight. He ran his hands over her skin to warm her.

"This'll be easier to take off than it was to put on. Actually, it took two of us," she said, gazing up at him.

Collin's brows shot up. "Sounds kinky. Tell me more."

"And ruin this grand moment?" Shayla's Irish inflection kicked in. "Just don't expect me to lick whipped cream off your tits."

He saw the amusement in her eyes and let out a peal of laughter.

Shayla reached up to remove one of her shoulder straps.

"No." Collin's laugh broke off and he pushed her hand away. "I'll take this off."

He pulled Shayla to her feet, so he could unwrap her.

The spontaneity and freedom of this moment had Shayla as enthusiastic as he was. Not like the old Shayla back in Ireland. The new Shayla offered herself completely, fully trusting him. Trust had always been an issue for her, and he realized what a gift she was offering.

He was humbled by this trust and resolved never to betray it.

They were alone. No one to bother them...for the time being, anyway.

Collin eased his fingers under her shoulder straps and tugged them down.

Her breath hitched and her face angled skyward, offering him unfettered access to her neck.

"Kiss me, Collin. All over. Devour me."

"I'll do more than that," he whispered in her ear.

Like a ravenous wolf, he attached his mouth to her gorgeous throat, tugging the black teddy down to her waist. She disentangled her arms and pressed him into her as he nibbled her delicious skin, gleaming in the moonlight.

He loved how her nipples pebbled like succulent little cherries, and he slid his lips down to lick and suckle them. He tasted remnants of pool water, reminding him of their combined successful mission, which excited him even more.

Shayla moaned, her pleasure evident, and it spurred him on.

Collin grabbed hold of the black teddy on both sides of her waist and yanked the bloody thing down to her ankles, so he could drink in her nude body.

She stepped out of the wet teddy and kicked it aside with her patent leather ankle boots.

He recalled his infusion of heat and incredulity upon seeing her in those boots earlier.

"When I first saw you in those badass boots, I had a stiffy the size of Dublin's Wellington Monument."

She chortled, amused by his disclosure.

"Glad you like them, Mr. Angel Fire."

Her eyes gleamed with want, and he was more than happy to deliver.

Collin drew her close, and she tugged off his butler jacket and tossed it on the car.

Her eyes captured his and he smoldered when she slid her hand between them and undid his butler pants. He finished the task by shoving everything down. Then slipped his fingers down to her center and stroked her.

Shayla moaned louder and backed up to the car, situating Collin's jacket on the bonnet. She hopped up and positioned herself on it, her eyes melting into his.

"Can't lie down on a dirty car."

He nuzzled her ear. "Should have cleaned it off for you."

"It's handled." She reached down and massaged him.

Now it was Collin's turn to moan, but he wanted to taste her. He lifted himself off, but first he stood gazing down at her. He bent to kiss her stomach, slid his lips to pay homage to the tat on her hip, then moved his mouth to her center. She writhed as he lapped and laved, wanting her swathed in ecstasy.

"Fuck's sake, Stedman. Get inside me before I explode," she groaned out, tugging him up to her.

He was happy to accommodate.

Loving her with everything he was capable of, he took Shayla on the bonnet of the Alfa Romeo in the moonlight, enjoying every wave of pleasure that capsized his senses.

When she peaked, she called out his name so long and loud, nearby cows lowed.

And when he released, another cow lowed. They crumpled with laughter, her naked self, and he with his white butler shirt still on...holding tight to each other as they spiraled down.

Thief and assassin.

Collin hadn't felt this much alive in a long, long time.

Nor had he ever been this much in love.

Chapter 36
Shayla

I settle into my hotel room in London, glad for a brief respite to catch my breath. I take a shower and wrap a towel around myself, with one twisted around my hair.

Last night's success had me on a high all day.

I'd never known what it was like to work with someone—someone I cared about, loved. After we had completed our synchronized operation, Collin was as turned on as I was, judging by how he'd enthusiastically taken me on the bonnet of his rented Alfa Romeo.

I'm pretty sure my risqué outfit had something to do with his enthusiasm.

I still feel the car under my hips, Collin's jacket brushing the backs of my calves as he thrust into me, harder with each push. I was afraid we'd set the car in motion...that it would roll onto a cow field with us humping furiously on the bonnet.

Of course, no such thing had happened, but the thought of it made me laugh.

I repeatedly play the scenario in my mind to relive the erotic sensation of arching against the car as he'd drilled into me, my senses overloaded with whiffs of moon-kissed clover and wildflowers, mingling with Collin's scent, cologne mixed with his dried sweat from earlier.

For once I wasn't stressing about my cleanliness, or his. I'd been caught up in the thrill of the moment—our working together and the successful operation for both of us. We'd connected on a level I'd never experienced before with anyone, as if reading each other's thoughts.

I wonder if we'll get to the point where we finish each other's sentences. I've heard that happens with some intimate relationships. This is my first one, so I have nothing to compare this to.

All I know is, I want us to stay together, however that plays out.

And the glorious sex. Jaysus, Mary, and Joseph, I'd never dreamed it could be like this, feel like this. So different from the first time we did it back in Ireland.

Collin has introduced me to all kinds of new and wonderful things. I just hope that we can continue, given our dangerous occupations. I'm a wee bit anxious about Mother finding out about our torrid love affair.

I'd texted Mother to relay I'd successfully executed my operation. She'd responded by reminding me my next order of business was London, to track down Dominika. I didn't mention Collin. Nor did I mention I'd be attending a fundraiser at the Galleria Hotel.

While I'd thrilled Collin with the news I had business in London as well, his delight changed to concern. Every move we make will be tracked by CCTV cams on the streets and inside most buildings. We can't afford anyone to connect our dots.

We pretended not to know each other at the airport or on the flight from Rome to London, so we texted on our burner phones while waiting to board.

Me: *I'm staying at the Blackford Hotel. Know where it is?*

Collin: *Covent Garden district, north of Trafalgar Square and The National Gallery.*

Me: *Whoa, I'm impressed. Where will U B?*

Collin: *Same hotel as National Gallery fundraiser. Get a gown, you're going with me.*

Me: *What about our being seen together?*

Collin: *Disguise yourself.*

Me: *Any preference?*

Collin: *Your long black wig...and that grand strappy black thing you wore last night.*

Me: *Thought you said wear a gown.*

Collin: *Changed my mind. (devil emoji)*

When we'd landed, Collin and I had parted ways. I'd taken a taxi to my hotel, and Collin had rented a car. He texted a photo of a Porsche Panamera 4S luxury sedan, with a note suggesting we make love on the bonnet of this sexy car, too.

After last night's steamy love fest on the Alfa Romeo, I enthusiastically make a mental note to make sure we keep that one on our to do list.

The Blackford Hotel is the five-star hotel Finn had advised I stay at, since the CCTV cams captured Dominika coming and going. Asia had loaded me up with enough wigs and wardrobe changes to outfit the entire cast of *Les Misérables* on the West End of London.

However, she didn't include an evening gown.

Luckily, I'd spotted a sleek, black gown in a boutique shop in the hotel lobby—a wee bit pricey at a few thousand British pounds—but SOS pays me well, and cost was no longer a concern.

A quiet knock on my door has me up and peeking through the peephole. Collin's lanky frame in a baseball cap and sunglasses fills my view as he lifts two food boxes and waggles his brows.

My heart speeds as it always does when I'm about to see him. I swing the door open.

"Delivery for Shayla Byrne." His Irish lilt kicks in, and I want to climb him like a pole.

"You're a lifesaver. I'm ravenous." I usher him in and take the food boxes.

His arms come around me. "Here, let me take care of that towel for you." He dips his head to tug it off with his teeth.

"Oh no, you don't!" Not wanting to, I back away. "We have business to discuss." I set the food on a small table and take a seat. Voracious, I open a box and squeal at seeing the fish and chips. I pop a chip into my mouth.

"Thanks for this," I say with my mouth full.

"You're constantly ravenous. I can't keep you satiated—at least with food." Collin sinks into the chair opposite me and dives into the other box. The room fills with a delicious food aroma.

I swallow and give him a devious look. "But you keep me satiated in other ways."

"Thanks, lass, I'm glad of that." Collin shoots me an appreciative grin. "Here's the latest. I'm to pick up the access codes and where to meet Scorpio for the necklace transfer at tomorrow night's National Gallery fundraiser. He didn't want to message them."

"Where at the fundraiser?"

"There's an Oliver Cromwell statue at one end of the grand ballroom at the Galleria Hotel near Trafalgar Square and the National Art Gallery. Scorpio says the codes and the transfer location will be hidden at the statue."

"Cromwell wasn't exactly a friend of the Irish," I say, wrinkling my face.

"True." Collin chuckles, while crunching a chip.

My protector side kicks in. "Collin, do you have a weapon?"

He gives me an odd look. "Don't need one."

I sit back in my chair. "The man you stole Angel Fire from is dead. I should know, I killed him. Then the necklace goes missing. We both must be careful. Especially you. Can you trust this Scorpio person?"

"There is no trust in this business."

"What if he's setting you up somehow?"

Collin stares at me and I can tell his wheels are spinning. He shakes his head.

"Scorpio won't sell me out. He's too greedy. He needs the Rokeby Venus painting for his dealer, and he'll get a hefty percentage."

Collin chomped on a chip. "Scorpio mentioned that Antonio Vittorio has a twin brother named Lorenzo, who suspects his brother was murdered—and he wants the necklace."

I raise my brows. "There's nothing to connect either of us to Antonio Vittorio."

"I know that, and you know that, but just a matter of time before his brother, Lorenzo figures things out."

"We need to speed things up." I suck in a breath as an idea takes form. "Can you get the painting during the fundraiser? Perfect timing with everyone out of the Gallery except security."

Collin studies me. "Knew there was a reason why I loved you. Talk to me."

I smile at the man across from me who occupies my heart.

"Complete the job before Lorenzo Vittorio catches up with us. Then we'll slip into hiding for a while. In Anacapri."

I give Collin a scorching look that he appreciates, judging from the quick rise of his delicious chest.

Rising from my chair, I move to him.

"I worry about you for this next mission. You need to get the Rokeby Venus, so we can get out of London."

"What about the business you're here to do?" he asks, gazing up at me.

I brush a lock of his hair away from his forehead. "I'll take care of it tomorrow before the fundraiser. What can I do to help you prepare?"

"You're doing it, lass." He twists in his chair to fiddle with my towel. "I work best alone. Don't want you to incur any risk."

The minute he says it, I've already figured out what I have to do.

Because of that, I don't stop Collin from tugging my towel off and letting it drop to the carpet. I also don't stop him from running a hand up the front of me to palm my breast, while sliding his lips down to suckle one.

And I don't stop myself from stripping him bare and tugging him to my bed, where we tenderly explore each other's bodies and spend an hour making slow, lazy love...taking time to relax and enjoy each other.

For who knows what tomorrow will bring?

JEALOUSY

We both know the dangers we face. And because of that, I love Collin as much as humanly possible in case the worst were to happen.

I know what I must do.

I am now Collin Stedman's self-appointed bodyguard.

Chapter 37
Collin

Collin checked into the Galleria Hotel, since it was the location of the gala fundraiser for the National Gallery. Anyone who is anyone would be there to take part in the art gallery's 'Leave a Legacy' program, where the wealthy made hefty contributions—enough to support several small countries.

He'd read about this annual event and the glitz and glamor that followed it; Collin had been tempted to track down and recover a few stolen pieces and return them to the Gallery.

If only galleries and museums paid him to do it.

He wasn't crazy about the idea of lifting the Rokeby Venus painting, since that is where outstanding works of art should remain; but when offered as much as he stood to gain from the Velasquez boost, it was hard to say no.

He placated himself with pie-in-the-sky resolutions to return what he stole from art galleries and museums.

Some day.

His phone pinged with a message from Scorpio:

Transfer location in Cromwell statue at hotel. Bring necklace to fundraiser. Stand by for instructions. Exercise caution.

Collin readied everything he'd need for the heist of the Rokeby Venus painting. He took his essentials—gloves, his packet of compact tools, and his charged burner phone to download the access codes to boost the painting.

He already knew the Rokeby's location in the gallery. The sad thing was, he'd have to cut the canvas out of the frame. This bothered him, knowing the history of a woman called 'Slasher Mary' back in 1914 who'd slashed the painting with a meat cleaver in protest of a fellow suffragette. They had restored the painting soon after.

And there was Collin, planning to cut the painting, roll it up and deliver it to a private dealer. He nudged the guilt out and replaced it with knowing he'd never have to steal again. He also assuaged his guilt with the noble intention that someday he'd steal it back and return it to the National Art Gallery.

Collin dressed in the tuxedo he'd bought for the occasion and trimmed his beard and mustache short. He drove to the Blackford Hotel where Shayla stayed and parked his Porsche in the underground car park.

He texted her and sat back, waiting, mentally ticking through his checklist to make sure he had everything he needed.

With increasingly sophisticated electronic security systems, it was a greater task to hack the art gallery systems to gain access. Professionals of Collin's caliber viewed such jobs as challenges, or so they boasted on the Dark Web chats.

He knew he couldn't pass through security at the fundraiser with the necklace, much less his portable tools packet. That's where Shayla came in.

Although Scorpio had instructed Collin to bring the necklace to the fundraiser to execute the transfer, Collin wouldn't hand it over until his forty percent of Angel Fire's value landed in his Moneytree account.

Transfers were invariably the tricky part, and the most dangerous.

The door opened to the car park, and out strolled the woman of his dreams. Shayla moved toward him in a figure-hugging black gown with a slit up her right leg. Her sexy, strappy heels made her look like a runway model.

Collin wondered how women could walk in those incredibly tall heels, loving that they could.

Shayla's natural-looking wig parted in the middle, both sides pulled tightly back to her long, black ponytail she'd draped down one side to her waist. The strapless dress hugged her shape, and she easily pulled it off.

He knew that because his pants became snug, and he shifted in his seat.

Collin gulped, watching this heavenly, audacious goddess approach his car.

I wouldn't mind a wee quickie before driving to the Galleria Hotel.

He remembered himself, hoping he hadn't drooled on his steering wheel, and scrambled from the driver's seat to open the passenger door.

"Greetings, Mr. Stedman. Don't you look dashing, all cleaned up?" she murmured, kissing his cheek before ducking down to get into the Porsche. She sunk down sideways and swung her legs in, the slit in her gown revealing her leg all the way up.

"Whoa, lass, must concentrate here." His other brain raised a salute as he rounded the car and settled into the driver's seat.

"How is it you're more ravishing than the day before?"

"Ha, ravishing?" Shayla gave him a shy side glance. "No one has ever said that to me."

"Well then, they must have been blind."

He reached behind him for the velvet bag and carefully removed Angel Fire. "You need to wear this. I won't get it through Galleria Hotel's security without a bombardment of questions. I obviously can't wear it."

She smirked, giving him a once over. "Why not? It would accessorize your tux. But won't it be recognized as the Angel Fire?"

"Not likely. We'll hang in the background. You, however, will draw every eye in the room." He twirled his finger. "Turn sideways, and I'll festoon you with the world's most valuable emeralds and rubies."

When she did as he asked, he couldn't resist dipping his head to kiss her sexy, exposed shoulder.

Goosebumps appeared, and she sucked in a breath. "Oh, Collin..." She brought her palm to his cheek and turned to give him a soft kiss.

He lifted the sparkling necklace with one hand and reached around Shayla to grasp both ends. He rested the necklace on her chest and clasped the back, taking diligent care to secure it tight.

Shayla faced forward, and Collin's breath caught at how perfect the intense green emeralds and blood red rubies outlined in diamonds adorned her.

"Angel Fire was created for you. The emeralds match your eyes," he said softly. "The necklace pales, compared to your beauty."

He knew how cheesy it sounded, but it was true. He may be Irish but was the first to admit he wasn't the most eloquent guy. He was no Yeats, that was for sure.

"Oh, come on, you say that to all the girls," she purred.

"I wish you could keep Angel Fire." He hesitated, as the wild thought cycled through his brain. He loved Shayla enough to give up the millions he'd make for stealing it. But no way could he pull it off without endangering both their lives.

He buckled in, started the engine, and drove out of the car park.

"All right, Miss Byrne. Let's review our plan."

Chapter 38
Shayla

I have no problem passing through the x-ray machine, even though Angel Fire triggers a beep.

In my best practiced British, I inform security, "It's the necklace. And it's a bug-a-boo to remove."

I knew no one would slide a hand up the inside of my thigh, where I'd strapped a small pistol to my leg. Security would assume the necklace was causing the x-ray beeping ruckus.

As expected, Angel Fire and a sexy flirtation enable me to pass through the screening.

When one security guy opens my clutch, all he sees is a metal tube of lipstick. I'm relieved when he doesn't lift it out to discover the hidden blade. He snaps it closed, and a uniformed woman waves me through, ignoring the incessant beeping.

I retrieve my clutch on the other side and pivot with style and elegance, waiting for my handsome tuxedoed partner to pass through. I had strapped Collin's tool packet to the back of my other thigh.

Not sure what I would have done had they discovered Collin's portable tools. While they aren't deadly like mine, I can transform any tool into a weapon if a situation calls for it.

I link my arm through Collin's elbow in the formal way others do at these affairs. We hover at the edges of the room. Though some eyes rest on my necklace, no one says anything—at least so far.

As much as I love the beauty of Angel Fire, I want to be rid of this necklace as soon as possible. With this crowd, the possibility that someone might recognize it is higher than in regular social circles.

"Collin, has Scorpio messaged?"

His vibrating phone responds. He glances at it. "Codes are at the statue."

"Is he watching us?" I ask, glancing around.

Collin smirks. "He doesn't know what I look like. I had myself disguised when I met with him. He thinks I'm a Texan."

I arch a brow. "Why?"

Collin whips out his long, tall drawl. "Buh-cause ah talked like this, little lady."

There is no end to Collin's marvelous talents. Tossing my head back, I laugh.

He steals the opportunity to plant a kiss on the side of my neck.

"Follow me, Stedman." When we'd first arrived, I had staked out the Oliver Cromwell statue in a corner at the back of the ballroom.

We edge our way around the crowds to the back.

Aside from a gentleman with his busy hand inside his wife's low-cut gown, no one else is around. Both are too hot and bothered to pay us any mind.

"For cripes' sake, get a room," Collin murmurs under his breath for my benefit.

The couple eventually moves off, and I shock myself with what I say.

"I think it would be fun to do it in public."

He draws back in surprise. "Didn't know you were into exhibitionism."

"I've not thought about it before. But wouldn't it be fun to see what it's like?"

"Why, Shayla Byrne, you never cease to amaze. An exhibitionist assassin. I rather fancy that—along with your dominatrix attributes."

Collin's tone tinges with eroticism.

He clears his throat. "Bollocks—now my Jack O'Grady has a stiffy."

I can rely on Collin to make me laugh at the most inappropriate times—like when I sidle up to Oliver Cromwell and ease myself to the back of the statue. I feel around the base, then run my hand up to the bronzed arse. There's something wedged in a space tucked under the cute suit of armor.

I pluck a USB from the statue and offer it to Collin. "Found this in Cromwell's arse."

"How fitting," says Collin drily. "You hang onto it for now. First, we wrangle the necklace, little lady. Then the painting."

His American drawl amused her.

"Spoken like an Irish Texan," I quip, dropping it into my clutch and snapping it closed.

"Where do we go for the transfer?"

Collin's phone vibrates. He reads the text and turns to me.

"We're meeting upstairs, in the Galleria Mezzanine. I'll go, but I want you to stay here."

I grab Collin's arm. "But I'm the one with Angel Fire. I must go with you."

"First, I want to make sure it's safe. You need to wait here. I'll come back for the necklace."

"No, Collin!" I try to hold back panic from my tone. I don't like that I can't protect him, but don't want to infer he's incapable of protecting himself.

"I need to stay with you," I say firmly.

"Too dangerous. I don't want you involved."

"Too late. I *am* involved," I counter. "However, my job at the mo, is to protect you. I've hired myself as your newly appointed bodyguard."

"What'll *that* cost me?"

"You can pay me later." I give Collin a sultry smile, and shove his hand inside the slit of my dress so he can feel my 9mm pistol.

His eyes widen. "How the bollocks did you get in here with that?"

I shrug. "It's what I do."

He lets out an exasperated sigh and holds up his hand. "Stay here. I know what I'm doing."

Turning my back to the room, I reach inside my dress, retrieve my pistol, and place it in Collin's grip. "Then take this."

He reaches behind himself and shoves it into the waistband of his pants.

"Your bodyguard declaration gave me another stiffy."

"Happy to accommodate your Jack O'Grady." I'm ecstatic I have this effect on him, yet I assume an authoritative tone. "Know how to manage a pistol?"

He rolls his eyes and shoots me an insane look. "Did you seriously ask me that?"

We have a stare down.

I win.

"You're a thief, not a—you know..."

"Cessation specialist?" Collin interrupts with a wily grin.

"Yes, Miss Byrne, I know how to manage a pistol. Unlike you, I don't smuggle guns past x-ray machines." He gestures at the slit in my dress.

His expression turns curious. "By the way, how did you get a gun here in London?"

"My employer ensures we have everything we need..." I trail off, shrugging.

"Right. The employer. You must work for one helluva organization." Collin leans in and narrows his eyes.

"Come on, you can tell me. Do you work for MI6? Or the Americans in the CIA? Who else can afford to supply you with an on-the-spot arsenal wherever you go?"

I shake my head, wishing I could tell him.

"None of those things. I'll tell you one day when the time is right. In the meantime, be careful." I finger the weighty necklace like it'll calm my brittle nerves.

"Not to worry." He hesitates. "But, just in case—if I'm not back in ten minutes, you need to disappear. Fast."

Collin offers me the key fob for the Porsche. "Take the car if it comes to that. But don't go to your hotel. If we need to communicate—like in code for whatever reason—"

He stops, taps his phone, and holds it up. "See this?"

I squint at the small screen displaying the Irish alphabet. "What about it?"

"The old Irish alphabet doesn't contain the letters 'x' 'y' and 'z.' If I text you these letters or say them to you, it means do the opposite."

"The opposite of what?"

"Whatever I tell you."

This cinches my stomach. "You aren't making sense. But okay, thanks for that wee bit of Irish trivia. You'd better get upstairs."

Collin lifts my chin and kisses me.

"Like I said, don't worry about me. Keep your burner handy." He lifts his and jams it into another pocket.

"I'll leave you to it. Be right back."

Collin gives me another fast kiss, then disappears through the door to the Galleria Mezzanine.

My stomach ties in a knot, knowing how things can go wrong.

And they usually do.

Chapter 39
Collin

When Scorpio had informed Collin that Vittorio's brother, Lorenzo was hunting for the thief who stole Angel Fire, he figured this transfer could potentially be dangerous. Because of this, he wanted Shayla to wait until he was sure Scorpio wouldn't double cross him—a standard procedure in this business, regretfully.

Collin strode briskly up the stairs. He'd given Shayla the USB with the Art Gallery access codes in case this necklace transfer headed south.

When he reached the Mezzanine level, Collin moved along the hallway leading to a sizable outside balcony, several stories above the street. Other than a couple at one end, no one else was around.

Collin moved to the edge of the balcony and heard a door close behind him.

He turned to see Scorpio come toward him.

"Lorenzo Vittorio found us! You must go. Give me the necklace!" His hand shot out.

"Deposit my money first." Collin's heart sped. He'd hoped something like this wouldn't happen.

Scorpio's expression became a thundercloud.

"Give me the necklace. *Then* I'll deposit your money."

Rapid footsteps sounded as two men in suits emerged onto the walkway and ran toward the overhanging balcony.

Collin wasn't taking any chances. He speed-dialed Shayla, and she answered right away.

"Get out of here—go *now*! Lorenzo Vittorio found us!" he barked into the phone. Without waiting for her response, he slipped the phone into his pocket.

The two men reached Collin and Scorpio, pistols drawn.

"Hand over the necklace."

Scorpio's arms raised as he whined denial.

"I don't know anything about a necklace!"

The men turned to Collin.

"Unless you give us the Angel Fire, we'll kill you both."

Collin eyed the muzzles of both pistols aimed at him. He toyed with the idea whether to pull a gunslinger move and yank the 9mm from the waistband of his trousers to out-gun these thugs. He was quick, but not that quick. He was no Texas Ranger, as he used to say back in America.

The minute he'd reach behind himself to grab the pistol, he'd take a bullet in the chest.

Bad idea.

Instead, Collin opened his suit jacket and spread it wide to show these goons he had nothing underneath.

"Neither one of us have the necklace."

The bald gorilla raised the pistol, racked the slide, and aimed it at Collin's nose. "Where is it?"

Collin's eyes crossed to focus on the muzzle, his peripheral vision tracking the hairy gorilla holding a gun to Scorpio's forehead.

"Who do you work for? Who's your dealer?"

Scorpio's eyes bulged, and he rocked his head violently. "Don't know what you're talking about."

"Liar!" Beefcake pulled the trigger.

Collin jumped. Blood spurted, as Scorpio dropped to the concrete walkway.

A woman screamed, and Collin tore off running, pulling Shayla's pistol from his waistband. He racked the slide, then twisted and fired several rounds before yanking the door open to re-enter the building.

Collin slammed into a couple, knocking a woman off her feet.

"So sorry, excuse me!" he hollered, sprinting down the long hallway leading back to the grand ballroom. Once he made his way to the middle of the crowd, he'd have a better chance to escape.

He thought wrong.

As he worked his way down the center of the room toward the double door exit leading out of the hotel, shots rang out.

Screams and shouts erupted from the crowd.

Mayhem ensued as women in long gowns and men in tuxes rushed to the exit. Collin couldn't tell if anyone got hit, but he couldn't return fire. He shoved the pistol into his waistband and inserted himself in the middle of the surging mass, streaming toward the doors.

A man behind Collin shoved him forward, pushing him into an elderly woman in front of him. Collin grabbed hold of her and helped the woman out of the ballroom to the rectangular foyer, where a younger woman appeared to assist her.

"Come on, Mum, this way! The young woman hurried her mother to the revolving door leading outside.

Collin inserted himself into the door section as it turned, then broke free and sprinted down the concrete steps to the sidewalk. He bolted to the left, cursing that he'd parked the Porsche in the hotel's underground car park for his sake, but glad that Shayla could use it to make her getaway.

When he reached the corner, a colossal pain penetrated his skull, and the traffic light blurred.

Collin's knees turned to jelly as hands grabbed hold of him. The last thing he remembered were car doors slamming shut and his head falling against a window.

Then he blacked out.

Chapter 40
Shayla

I follow Collin's instruction and scurry along the side of the ballroom, heading for the front foyer and the side door leading to the underground car park.

Pressing my burner to my ear, I bolt down the stairs and across the car park, searching frantically for the silver Porsche. Spotting it, I beep the locks open and dive into the driver's seat and slam the door.

I tap the speaker icon and position the mobile in a holder on the dash, cranking up the volume. Leaning close, I strain to hear muffled conversation.

"Hand over the necklace."

"I don't know anything about a necklace!"

"Unless you give us the Angel Fire, we'll kill you both."

My heart practically stops as I stare at a concrete column through the windshield.

Collin's voice. **"Neither one of us have the necklace."**

"Then where is it?"

A gunshot jumps me out of my mother fecking skin. An agonizing pain stabs my chest.

Frantic, I stage-whisper into the phone.

"Collin! Collin?"

He obviously can't hear me. His phone must be tucked in a pocket. Mind racing, I press my head against the high-backed seat. Think!

Should I follow his location? Dammit, I need my pistols!

I start the Porsche and punch the gas pedal, thanking Collin and Finn for teaching me to drive. I glimpse the exit signs to navigate out of this hella underground maze.

Once on the street, a light rain dots the windshield. Automatic wipers kick in to clear it.

Please God, let Collin be alive.

I know I shouldn't go to my hotel room, but I have to get my SOS phone with my advanced geolocation tracker that Finn had set up for me.

I swing into the outside car park next to my hotel, scramble out, and beep the car locked.

I need to get a grip.

Bolting inside, I head for the elevator, and punch the button for the fifteenth floor. Another woman enters—a woman with long dark hair, thick lips and other familiar features. She presses a button. She shifts her weight from one side to the other in her high-heeled boots, heaving impatient sighs as she thumbs her phone.

I stand holding the burner to my ear, with the sudden realization Dominika Gagolin just got on the elevator with me.

Holy Mother of freaking God.

Thankfully, I still wear my long black wig, hoping she won't recognize me.

After what Mother and the Sisters have said about Dominika's wit and cunning, I'm wary and careful not to assume anything about this woman. I'll have to risk it to get information. If I get off and follow her, she'll suspect something.

One mother fecking crisis at a time, thank you very much.

"Blimey, I broke a nail," I say in my best Cockney voice. "Do you have a file by chance, love?"

Dominika rotates to give me an up-and-down evaluation. The woman is striking, as everyone says, but her eyes have a hard look—one I have no want to screw with—and she's not a woman who smiles easily.

"No." She turns back around.

If I wasn't connected to Collin's burner on the other end, I'd be texting the dickens out of Mother.

"What brings you to town?" I ask casually.

"I'm on holiday," she says with a Brit inflection. How funny; an Irish and a Russian both pretending to be British.

"Wonderful. How long?"

She quirks a brow suspiciously, and her eyes drift to my necklace.

"Long enough."

The elevator doors open, and she holds one side. She turns and pierces me with an icy stare.

"Take care someone doesn't steal that expensive necklace," she says in an ominous tone that curdles my blood.

I'd forgotten about the Angel Fire. My hand flies up to touch it.

I force a sincere smile. "I will. Thanks, love."

My mind is so preoccupied with Collin I don't remember which accent I used.

Feck it, it can't be helped.

Dominika steps out onto the tenth floor and briskly moves to a room at the end of the hotel corridor.

I have no time to follow.

As the elevator continues to my floor, I press the burner to my ear. Nothing. No sound. Collin's phone had ended the call. They must have discovered his phone.

With my burner number on it. And my texts. Jaysus!

I hurry to my hotel room and fling open the door. An orange light blinks on the room phone. I dash to it and punch the number to retrieve the message.

I hold my breath, waiting.

It's Collin. His voice is dull and distant. "Vittorio's man has a gun to my head. Call this number ASAP or they'll shoot me."

His words fall on my ears like an avalanche of boulders.

Oh God. Lorenzo Vittorio has Collin.

At least he's alive!

I power on my SOS phone, pull up our intranet, and tap the geolocation icon. Hand shaking, I type Collin's burner number. A red dot appears, moving along a highway away from London. This was risky to do, as geolocation can track both ways. But I must know where Lorenzo's men are taking him.

At least they haven't smashed his phone and chucked it. *Yet.*

Clutching the SOS phone and my burner in one hand, I frantically toss things into my carry-on and abandon my hotel room. Lorenzo Vittorio had messaged my room phone—he knows where I am.

I need my weapons.

Finn had drilled the location of my SOS locker into me before leaving Rome. Hope I remember how to open it. Thank God the building is only a short distance away. I rush to the stairwell, hike up my gown, and pound down the flights of stairs with my duffle slung over my shoulder. Can't risk the elevator and running into Lorenzo and his goons.

Collin's Porsche is parked outside in the hotel's car park. As I exit the hotel and bolt toward the car, I tap Cousin Declan's number on my burner and leave him a message.

"Dec, I need your help. Get me all you can on Antonio Vittorio's twin brother, Lorenzo. Here's my burner number."

The next order of business is to text Mother on the SOS phone that I spoke with Dominika, along with the number of the hotel room my Russian sister had entered. I position the mobile on the dash. The car fires right up, and I point it toward the location Finn had instructed for me to access my SOS locker.

I'm back in full-blown assassin mode—but this is now personal. The brother of my mark has the love of my life. God help Lorenzo Vittorio if he hurts Collin Stedman. I will gut him like a fish, grind him into shark food, and dump him into the Mediterranean.

Heart thudding, I pick up my burner and tap the number Collin messaged on my room phone. If Lorenzo knows what's good for him, by God, Collin better answer.

Chapter 41
Collin

When Collin came to, it felt like sledgehammers pulverized his skull.

His hearing kicked in. Men talking. He tried to move. His legs were bound at the ankles and his arms stretched behind a chair, bound at the wrists.

It'll get worse when he opens his eyes. He pushed one lid open.

Shit!

Why bother opening the other? He knew he was in a fecked situation.

"He's awake," said a deep voice from across the room.

It appeared Collin was in a residence. A rather luxurious one, judging by the high ornate ceilings and crystal chandeliers.

An imposing goon with blond hair rose and stood in front of Collin. He held Collin's burner phone to his face.

"As you know, we shot your handler. Our boys are on their way to your woman to get Angel Fire. And of course, they'll kill her," said the wee bastard from across the room, with his feet up on his desk.

Collin recognized him as the dead brother's twin, Lorenzo.

Collin's burner vibrated in the man's hand.

"Talk to your woman. Tell her we'll kill you unless she gives us Angel Fire. We know she has it."

His tone sent chills up Collin's spine.

So, Lorenzo *had* been watching them at the fundraiser.

Blond guy tapped the speaker and held it out to Collin.

"Hello?" Collin croaked out.

"Hiya, Mickey O'Shea. You all right?" A woman's voice with a Cockney accent echoed through the room.

Didn't sound like Shayla, but who else would invoke the name of the delivery man from Cacciatore's in Rome?

If Collin wasn't so miserable, he would have laughed.

Good, she didn't use my real name…and these eejits won't get it out of me.

"Don't identify yourself. They plan to kill you!" Collin grunted out.

The blond guy backhanded him.

Collin's cheek numbed, and he licked the blood that seeped from his nostril.

Blond Asswipe pressed the muzzle of his pistol to Collin's temple. "Tell her."

Collin hesitated.

Asswipe pressed harder, shoving Collin's head to the side.

Collin winced. "They have a gun to my head. Lorenzo Vittorio wants the necklace."

"I want your name, woman!" hollered Lorenzo from his wing chair post.

Blond Boy nudged Collin's temple with the muzzle.

"Don't tell them!" Collin didn't want anyone knowing who Shayla was, especially when her mark had been this wee bastard's twin brother.

Lorenzo guffawed. "Identify yourself or we shoot him."

He nodded at Asswipe, who raised his pistol and racked the slide so Shayla could hear.

"Jealousy," said Shayla, keeping with her Cockney inflection. She enunciated as if addressing a toddler.

"The name is Jealousy, love. You hurt Mr. O'Shea and it'll be the last name to ever cross your lips."

Shayla's lively East London Cockney voice charmed Collin, and he waited with bated breath to see the response to her ballsy warning.

Lorenzo chortled. "Ooh, a threat. I doubt that very much, my dear girl, whoever you are."

"You want the necklace or not, love?" Shayla's tone remained light and casual.

"Easy as xyz."

Good, she used our secret phrase. Her way of saying she's in hit-woman mode.

Collin's pulse ticked up. He wasn't sure whether to take comfort in that aspect or what. But after seeing how she'd efficiently disposed of Lorenzo's brother, Antonio Vittorio, Collin felt certain she'd handle this situation.

"You don't give us Angel Fire? We shoot this Mickey person of yours."

A tense silence ensued.

"Go ahead. Shoot him," quipped Shayla. "And you'll never see Angel Fire."

Collin's heart thundered at the shock value of her words. He squeezed his lids closed, waiting for the fallout.

Lorenzo sniggered and made a careless motion at the blond man's pistol.

"Shoot him."

Asswipe eyed his boss, who motioned at the open window. He stepped over to it and fired.

Another long silence.

"That was a warning," said Lorenzo, stuffing a meatball sandwich into his mouth. "Next one goes in his brain."

"Deliver him alive or it's no deal, King Dick."

"Xyz," Collin choked out, conveying to Shayla he was prepared for anything.

"Shut up!" Asswipe backhanded him so hard he fell backwards in his chair.

Collin tasted more blood, and he wiggled his jaw to assess whether it was broken. Never mind the back of his already pulverized skull smacked the floor. He groaned.

Asswipe left him there and slapped a piece of duct tape over his mouth.

Collin closed his eyes, dreading whatever else they had planned. His heart stuttered at Shayla playing hardball with people who thought nothing of shooting Scorpio. But no way did Collin want Shayla to compromise herself—to hell with the Angel Fire.

These mother feckers don't know who they're up against.

"Must run, love. Be at the Blackford Hotel car park in an hour," she said, her tone light and calm. "And bring Mickey O'Shea. For your sake, he better be alive—or no necklace."

Shayla's calm demeanor impressed Collin, especially when he knew she was anything but. He'd love to imitate her casual manner, but it was a wee bit difficult with the blond baboon smacking the bejaysus out of him. Everything hurt.

"Come alone or we'll end you," shouted Lorenzo.

He eyed the baboon with the pistol.

"Send the men to the Blackford."

Collin had no choice but to trust Shayla.

Whatever she had planned, he prayed she would succeed.

Chapter 42
Shayla

I answer my SOS phone while sprinting to the building Finn had directed me to find. I scan my key card to let myself inside, and speed down a long hallway to my SOS locker. Thankfully, Finn had established it ahead of time, as he does for every Sisters of Sin operation.

"Hello, Mother." My voice wiggles as I sprint to the end of a long corridor.

"Jealousy. Dominika's working with dangerous individuals, so don't fly onto her radar. When I received your text, Finn dispatched his staff to surveil her. You verified she's staying there for the time being. That's all we needed."

"That's right. Blackford Hotel, tenth floor, suite at the end of the corridor."

I reach the end of the corridor and scan the locker numbers.

"What else are you doing in London? Finn saw a CCTV capture of you in an evening gown at the Galleria Hotel tonight. He loves tinkering with his facial recognition app. Secretly, he wanted to make sure you're okay, but don't tell him I told you."

"Tell Finn thanks for his concern, but all is grand."

I don't want anyone in the SOS to know about my involvement with Collin and the necklace heist. This isn't part of my assignment, and Collin is forbidden fruit.

"Finn has a soft spot for you, Jealousy."

My brows lift in surprise. Wouldn't have suspected that, the way Finn and I have argued in the past.

"Thought I might see Dominika at the hotel function." I'm impatient to end the call. "Mother, I have to go."

"But—"

"See you soon." I cut her off in mid-sentence and shove my SOS phone in my pocket.

Not much I can do. Collin's life hangs in the balance.

I find my locker and spin the combination according to the instructions Finn messaged me. The door opens, revealing another security measure, a retinal scan. I press the button and hold my eye to the flash of light. The door pops open to my deep locker. I pull out a long duffle containing a rifle, a couple of sharp blades, and two 9mm pistols.

Finn had even equipped me with a chest holster and a Kevlar vest. And, of course, my favorite ninja uniform of black spandex with head and face mask to hide everything but eyes and mouth.

"Thanks, Finn," I breathe, hefting the black duffle over my shoulder.

I place the Angel Fire inside my locker. I know it's a gamble not taking the necklace, but I'm confident I can free Collin without it. If not, then that means I suck as an assassin, and I'd be compelled to give my two weeks' notice—or however one quits this line of work.

If it's even possible.

I close and secure my locker, then duck into the women's toilet to change into my black spandex. I stuff my evening gown and black wig in the bag and run out to Collin's Porsche. I speed back to the outside car park at the Blackford Hotel and position the Porsche where I can see the entrance to the car park.

I stay in the vehicle and tug on my black ski mask

Lorenzo's goons don't know what I'm driving, therefore I have the advantage. Must work fast, they'll be here any second.

Sitting inside the car, I set to work, readying my weapons. I remove the two pistols, size up the magazines, and insert one in each Ruger. Then insert the extra magazine into my vest pocket.

T rounds should be enough for what I have planned. I put on my black ski mask and tug it down over my face. I wriggle into my Kevlar vest, strap on my chest holster, and

I lay one pistol in my lap and set the other on the passenger seat. Then I settle in and calm myself. I lie in wait, like a spider for a fly that happens into my web...except my web is more lethal than a black widow's.

This is the first time in my life I've planned cessations for someone I love. Unlike my assigned targets, this motivation is not the same. Love is the most powerful force on earth—now that I've found it with Collin—I'll do anything to protect it.

Even kill for it.

A dark SUV drives by with tinted windows. I can't tell who or how many are inside, but I can tell by the way the driver is slowing that they're looking for me.

The space on my left empties when a town car pulls out. I slink down in my seat. The SUV circles once more, then stops. It pulls into the space next to mine.

This couldn't be any more perfect. The fly lands on my web.

I grip my suppressed pistol with my right hand and rack the slide. I'm focused, and know my capabilities and limitations, as I have been trained. I hover my finger over the window button. When the passenger door opens, a big man emerges, pistol drawn.

I slide my window down and pump two bullets into his head.

He drops. Two more leap out of the SUV.

I snatch the other Ruger from the passenger seat, shove my door open, and spring to my feet. Gripping a pistol in each hand, I aim for center mass on each target and unload half the magazine without pausing between shots.

I shoot the one nearest at point blank range, and the man on the other side fires. The bullet whizzes past my face when I bend back. I sight, aim, and place two bullets in his chest as he advances.

With three men down and no more exiting the SUV, I grab my duffle, slam the driver's door closed, and scurry to the driver's side, pistols drawn.

I train them both on the driver, who scrunches down in his seat, eyes squeezed tight.

I scared the poor guy shitless.

Stepping over the man lying in a puddle of dark red, I climb into the passenger seat and toss my duffle into the back.

"Drive. Go!" I wave my pistol in the direction I want the SUV to go.

The driver exits the car park and drives into the night.

"Take me to Lorenzo Vittorio." I keep my pistol steady on him as he drives.

He doesn't speak. I've clearly rattled him after terminating his three passengers.

A phone rings on the dashboard. We both stare at it. Caller ID says it's Lorenzo.

"Answer it," I say. "Tell him you have the woman and the necklace and you're on the way back."

The driver recoils.

I raise the gun to his temple. "Tell him!"

The driver taps the phone and relays what I said.

"Good," says Lorenzo. "I'll be waiting."

"I'm sure you will," I mutter at the phone after the call ends.

In what seems to take forever, we wind our way out of the city proper, and follow the M25 highway. After twenty or so kilometers, we turn onto a quaint country lane and follow it between hedgerows to a lavish estate.

Someone with money lives here.

I worry about Collin, and my heart thunders—I can't let it get in the way of my mission.

Please be okay, Collin.

I wave my pistol toward an open garage to the side of the house. "Pull in there."

The driver does, and I rummage around for a roll of duct tape. An assassin's best friend, next to her weapons. I wind the wide sticky tape around the driver's ankles and force him to sit on the concrete floor. I tape him to a bench and slap a piece of tape over his mouth.

I won't take his life. He's only a driver who works for the wrong people.

Out here, away from the city, the dark is intense. I can hardly see my hand in front of my face. No streetlights. I'm used to the dark, same as back in Ireland; I prefer the cover of night.

I creep over a manicured lawn to the back of the home. A security person is on the stoop. He's armed, but if I can take him, I can get into the home.

I increase the magnification on my night vision goggles, and note the entry has a card reader.

A dense clump of bushes hides me as I sneak up close. I step out and aim my suppressed pistol. When I fire, the man drops. I scurry up and squat to raid his pockets. I lift the key card up to see which side to swipe. Then I grab his phone and small radio and jam them into my vest pocket.

The door clicks open when I swipe the card over the reader.

Once I'm inside, the house is quiet. I sneak through a sizeable kitchen, down a long hallway, then hear voices upstairs. I check the entire first floor to make sure all is clear.

Two security goons stand out in front of the house. Only a matter of time before they discover their back door compadre is down.

I debate whether to proceed upstairs or remove the front porch threat. I choose the latter. When I walk through the foyer, I take the radio out of my pocket and key it.

"Come inside and give me a hand," I croak in my best guy voice.

I watch through a window as the men exchange puzzled expressions. In the time it takes for them to enter the house, I stash my radio and stand on the ready with my second pistol.

My reflex kicks in when the door opens. I empty two rounds into each guard. The staircase leads away from the foyer, and I creep up the stairs. My one advantage is the element of surprise.

I reach the top of the stairs and inch my way down the hall. It appears the only people in the house are the ones in the large room at the end of the long hallway.

I don't hear Collin. I need to know where he is.

Blood pulsates through my veins. From what I can tell, there's only two voices—Lorenzo and another guy.

"They should be here by now," growls Lorenzo. "Where the devil are they?"

I hear movement, followed by a brief silence.

"Nicky doesn't answer. What the fuck?"

This is my cue. I raise my pistols, rack the slides, and tighten my grip.

Arms straight out in front of me, I slip into the room.

Where is Collin?

A scraping noise pulls my gaze to the floor. I spot Collin, tied to a chair resting sideways on the floor.

Threat number one sits on a chair to my left. Threat number two sits in a leather chair at a desk.

"Hello, love," I say to threat number one, aiming for center mass. I fire three rounds and his weapon clunks to the hardwood floor. He follows.

Threat number two is Lorenzo Vittorio, who fumbles his drawer open and lifts his weapon. I raise my pistol and put a bullet into his forehead before he can fire. He slumps and slides to the floor.

I run to the window to check for other potential threats. Seeing none, I rush to Collin, choking back surprise at his rough appearance.

"Thank God you're alive!" I manage, wanting to smother him with kisses. Instead, I yank the tape from his mouth, and he howls.

He's banged up pretty good, with bruises on his head and cheek, a cut over his brow and blood from his nose. His rented tux is in tatters, and his jacket hangs open, the white shirt bloodied. His bow tie is missing, but he's a beautiful sight.

"You can't get rid of me that easy," says Collin, his voice hoarse.

"Dress you up, can't take you anywhere," I admonish. "This is exactly why I should have stayed with you!"

"You're right. My bad, lass," he mutters, flicking his eyes up at me. "Remind me to listen to you from now on."

I reach into my daypack for the sharp blade. I slice through the cords binding his wrists and ankles. He lets out a long stream of air, stretches his arms, and rubs his wrists.

"There's a vehicle we can use. Follow me and stay close." I tug Collin's sleeve, and he does as I say.

Still on full alert, I shove one pistol into my chest holster and grip the other with both hands as I tap down the stairs, with Collin behind me.

"Holy hell, there's carnage in here." Collin gapes at the two guards lying in dark red pools on the wood floor.

I shrug. "Couldn't be helped."

I reach inside my vest for another magazine. Shoving the fresh ten rounds into my pistol, I step over the two and head out onto the portico. I swing my pistol in a one-eighty. Satisfied all is clear, we scurry to the car.

"So sorry. Afraid we must borrow your car," I say in my Cockney to the terrified driver, where I'd left him bound with a taped mouth on the floor tied to a bench.

The driver's door opens easily, and I grab the key fob, tossing it at Collin. "You drive."

I clamber into the passenger side of the black SUV as Collin removes his jacket and tosses it in the back seat. Once we're safely on the road back to London, anxiety smacks me like a pissed-off banshee.

A full-blown attack hits—I can't breathe. When I inhale, the air doesn't enter my lungs.

I panic.

"Collin!" I gasp, my hand clutching my throat. "I can't—get air!"

He glances at me in alarm. "What's wrong?"

"Stop—stop..." I rasp. Everything spins, I'm desperate for air.

Collin slams the brakes and pulls over.

He turns to me. "You're hyperventilating. Let's get this shit off you."

He claws at my gun holster and tugs the Kevlar vest off. He forms a closed cup with his hands and puts them over my nose and mouth.

"Slow your breathing. Deep breaths. Slow, slow," he says in a soothing voice. "Look at me, Shayla. Inhale, one, two, three, four, five. Now exhale, and count to five."

I glue my gaze to his, losing myself in his lovely blue eyes as I do what he says. I put my full faith and confidence in him, same as I did with Declan.

He breathes with me. Gradually, my lungs allow air to enter.

"That's it. Good girl."

Collin drops his hands from my face, reaches across me, and pushes open the passenger door.

"Take in some fresh air while I worship you—it's the least I can do for you saving my life."

I do what he says because it's Collin Stedman.

And I love him so much I would give my life for his.

Chapter 43
Collin

Collin opened his eyes, enjoying Shayla's warmth as she spooned into him. He slid his palm along her upper arm as she slept on her side, then down to the indent of her waist and rise to her hip. He brushed her hair off her shoulder to kiss it.

He was in awe of this woman—and proud of her. She'd come into her own these past several months, here in Rome, with her new organization. He was curious as hell who she worked for—but all things considered— thought it best to let it lie.

For now.

Seeing her in action last night and the danger she put herself into, helping him out of a situation he'd insisted he could handle—he respected her courage and professionalism.

However, nothing comes without a price.

She's an assassin who has panic attacks. Collin surmised he probably would, too, if he worked in her profession. His was bad enough.

A while back, she'd mentioned she was on the spectrum. He'd noticed it at first, but when he'd caught up with her in Rome, Shayla had not only come out of her shell, but her social skills had also picked up. Whomever her employer was, they had invested considerable time and training for her to be an effective asset to their organization.

He wanted to know who she worked for.

After helping her through the panic attack, she'd shared she always got them after her hits. And that she'd depended on Cousin Declan back home in Ireland to help her through them.

Collin told her he would be the one helping her from now on.

Now that Scorpio was dead, Collin had other problems. Not only had he lost his contact with the dealer who had hired him to steal the

Angel Fire, there was the matter of the Rokeby Venus painting. He hadn't been paid anything for it yet, per the terms he'd negotiated with Scorpio.

As far as Collin was concerned, the Rokeby deal was on hold. First, he'd see if they'd hire another handler. Since Collin had half of the forty percent already in his account, he was certain they would hire another handler soon, if not already.

The dealer would want Angel Fire and would contact him immediately.

Before leaving Rome, Shayla had given him the necklace she'd kept in a safe place, though she wouldn't say where—and he didn't press. He learned not to question her about certain things.

He'd grabbed the authenticity paperwork under the necklace when he'd boosted it from the Vittorio compound. It had worked so far, getting through airport security. He'd worn a fake badge and name plate with 'National Museum' on them, when he explained he was transporting Angel Fire for display in a museum gallery.

He just didn't say which country.

Despite both Vittorio brothers being gone, Collin expected continued interest in Angel Fire from other members of their family. The wife was vocal in the news, saying she would hunt down the thieves and make them pay. She seemed more concerned about the necklace than the death of her husband and his twin.

Shayla stirred, and Collin kissed her neck. She rolled onto her back, fixing her dreamy gaze on him.

"Good morning, Stedman. Oh..." Concern took over and she put a finger to her lips, then to the bruise on his cheekbone.

"Oh, my Lord, you're a sight."

Collin chuckled. "They worked me over pretty good."

"Mother feckers deserved everything they got," she said defiantly. She softened. "It's good to be home, here with you. Only..." She trailed off and threaded her fingers with his.

"This isn't really home though, is it?"

"Not in your Rome apartment. Feels like I'm in a royal palace. Speaking of home, I scheduled a flight home to Dublin for this evening."

She gave him a coy smile. "You'll never guess where my next assignment is."

"Not London, I hope." He bugged his eyes at her.

Shayla laughed. She did that a lot these days.

"Oslo, Reykjavik, and possibly Ireland."

"Why there?"

"That's all I can tell you. I shouldn't even be telling you that."

He thought for a minute. "Yesterday you said your name was Jealousy when Lorenzo asked you on the phone. Why did you say that?"

She stared at him. "It's a code name—assigned by my employer."

"A rather odd name. What's the significance?"

Shayla shrugged. "Nothing, really. Just a name."

He knew there was much more to it. Despite his being eternally grateful to Shayla for saving his life, he couldn't help wondering when she'd share more with him. But he wouldn't press—not after last night's life-or-death scenario.

"After my dance card filled yesterday and flying the rest of the night, I was too knackered to make love to you."

He kissed her on the lips, her fingertips light on his back as she dragged them up and down his smooth skin.

He winced when she hit a bruised spot on his shoulder blade.

She lifted herself over him to kiss it.

"I love that you're safe and sound here with me."

He kissed her forehead. "Me too, thanks to you."

She let out a heavy sigh. "I have to get dressed and go to my briefing."

"Ah, yes, the employer," said Collin. "Can you meet me for lunch before I fly out?"

"I won't have time, I'm afraid. I have things going on all day. But don't go until I finish my shower."

Shayla gave him a kiss on the cheek and climbed out of bed.

He enjoyed the sway of her beautiful arse as she headed into the bathroom. He was tempted to follow, but he had to check his messages.

After he'd dressed and made himself an espresso on Shayla's fancy machine, her phone vibrated. He spotted her burner on her nightstand. Curiosity piqued. Only Shayla and Collin had used these burners.

Who could this be?

Probably her employer, he reasoned. He stared at the phone, wanting to answer it. But he didn't want to snoop. Well, yes, he did, but didn't want to be a dick about it.

Listening to make sure Shayla was still showering, he waited for the phone to stop vibrating. Next to the phone was a business card. He picked it up. All it said was 'Conexus', with a gold and black logo below it, containing a filigreed 'C'.

When the phone stopped vibrating, the message icon lit without a caller ID. Collin tapped it and put the phone to his ear.

A male's voice spoke in a lively Irish tone.

"My sweet Shayla, are you all right? I'm worried about you. I have what you wanted. Can't wait to see your lovely face at the Pizzeria Roma near the Pantheon. Two p.m., right? Love you."

The message ended.

If steam could blow through both of Collin's ears, then it would at hearing this message. Who the hell was that? Did Shayla have an Irish biscuit on the side?

She doesn't have time to meet me for lunch before I go, but she's meeting this mother fecker?

He tapped incoming texts that weren't from him. Shayla asked for help. The response saying he'd help her with whatever she needed.

Sounds more lovey-dovey than business. Is she just toying with me?

Our little Shayla has become a worldly woman in more ways than one.

Collin didn't have time for this. He had business to take care of. He collected his things and scribbled a note before leaving Shayla's apartment.

Had to go. See you later. C.

He sure as shite wouldn't be chivalrous and sign it, 'Love, Collin.'

Not after what he just fecking heard.

Chapter 44
Shayla

I make myself comfortable in the SOS headquarters in Mother's office. Mother had it painted since I was here last. Pastel colors, which I find odd, but being underground, I can understand why Mother likes to lighten things up.

Mother and Finn enter together. I wonder if they connect at the hip. And if they're together in their off time. If they even have off time.

"Brief me on London," orders Mother.

"Not much to say other than what I told you."

"What did Dominika look like?"

"Like her photos, maybe a little thinner. No disguises that I observed."

"What was her demeanor like?"

"Demeanor?" I'm not sure what Mother is getting at.

"Yes. How did she seem? Friendly, hostile—did she say what she was doing?"

"It was only a brief encounter in the elevator. Kind of hard to get a personality assessment during a ride to the tenth floor."

I note Mother's no-nonsense face and I clean up my smartass act.

"I played a ditz with an East London accent. Hard to say whether she bought it."

Mother frowns. "If she didn't, you wouldn't have left that elevator."

"Why is that?"

"I think she's hellbent to go after the Sisters. And me. I believe each of us is a target now."

Mother pauses. "She knows who you are."

"Do you know that for a fact?" I ask.

"I sense it. I'm betting she's watching every move we make, and I'm sure she's watching video cams in Rome—she's observing all of us coming and going."

"Are you saying I'm now a target by a rogue Sister I've not officially met?"

"Yes." Mother and Finn trade glances. "Some dedicate their lives to perfecting violence. Dominika is one of those."

I look Finn square in the eye. "I suppose stink-eye won't work with this Russian chick."

He gives me a slow smile.

"We're in a situation where we must stay one step ahead. It's unfortunate, but that's what we're all facing now. You must keep training hard. We've taught you hand-to-hand fighting, but I'm assigning one of my people to help you brush up on your skills."

Finn hands me a file.

"Conexus has approved the five terminations of the cybercrime individuals you'd briefed us on. Normally, they don't consider recommendations from down the chain. But because of the excessive global impact these five engage in, they approved the operation."

My blood warms and I nod. "Good."

Finn briefs us on his further research.

"Besides his myriad of illegal online activities, the mark in Oslo operates a revenge porn website under an assumed name with the goal of destroying people's lives. He brags that he's a 'professional life ruiner' by hacking into email accounts and stealing private photos without consent. Then he posts the sexual, explicit photos on his website, along with their names, addresses, and social media accounts."

Mother lifts a brow. "And no one has stopped this disgusting degenerate?"

"No one can get his website taken down. He has a talented attorney, despite the suicides and destroyed lives he's caused."

Finn lifts his chin to address me. "What strategy do you suggest?"

I've given this considerable thought.

"I want to do the Oslo and Reykjavik hits. The Icelandic hit is a female who trafficks children online. Not a problem for me. I've dealt with her type back in Ireland."

Finn shakes his head, his face grim.

"Before I came on with the SOS, I helped bust a female-run trafficking ring in the States—they had families. It was awful."

I don't share how I still suffer guilt after ending the female trafficker in front of the Holden boy, after she stole him in Dublin. Finn doesn't need that info.

"I'll do the Oslo operation first, then Iceland. Our corporate jet flies faster than commercial, so I can be in Reykjavik within two hours of the Oslo hit. There's nowhere to run in Iceland anyway, even if she bolts. However, I need a Sister to do the Beijing hit. Who do you suggest?"

"Wrath is available," says Mother. "She just reported in, and lives for these kinds of operations. I'll introduce you. You'll have to synchronize with her time in China, taking into consideration the international date line difference."

"Not a problem," I say. "Thanks, Mother."

She scrolls her tablet and glances up at me.

"Who will do the Irish Newcastle and English Falmouth hits?"

"Cousin Declan and the Uncles will take care of those operations." I look up at Mother. "If that's okay."

"Yes. As you know, your family and the SOS have worked together before. We all go by the same code."

"Good," I say, breathing relief. "Declan will fill me in when I meet him for lunch today."

"Excellent," says Mother. "I've always liked him, and your uncles brag about his expertise."

I have a request that's been weighing on me, but I have to make it.

"Mother, I'd like a wee vacation after I execute my operation in Norway and Iceland. Uncle Casen is sick, and I want to go home to spend time with him. And—I really need a break."

"Who doesn't?" mumbles Finn.

Mother nods. "Actually, that is a good idea. I doubt whether Dominika will come for you in Ireland. Finn and I won't tell anyone that's where you are. As long as you don't share with the other Sisters or anyone else, things should be okay."

Finn speaks up. "Keep your Ruger under your pillow, just in case."

"I have to say this." Mother lifts from her desk.

"I can't emphasize enough the importance of never missing a target. No matter what weapons you use or how you eliminate your targets, stay one step ahead. Should you find Dominika has a missile lock on you, you'll be ready for her."

"I'll practice my stink-eye."

I wink at Finn, and head for the door.

Mother stops me.

"One last thing. Remember, there are no holds barred for assassins." Sadness crosses Mother's face. "I want you to know I've tried to encourage a family bond within the SOS. All it takes is one person to corrupt an organization and create distrust."

"I know. But, Mother," I say with a half-smile. "All it takes is one person to make it right again."

Mother lifts her chin. "One day we may wake up to find that our days of fighting for the greater good are limited—and it will be up to each of us to control the truth, and the concept of right and wrong."

"So, what are you saying? That we're fighting for an ideal that doesn't exist?" I ask.

"We'll never stop all the wrongs, the evil—it's too prevalent." Mother looks away, frowning. "History has a way of repeating itself."

"What do you mean?" My heart thuds at what she doesn't tell me.

"You may one day find that from now on, you may have to choose a side," she says quietly.

Before I can respond, Mother quickly switches gears. "You better get going. Complete your assignments and have a safe trip home."

Still processing what she said before that, I slowly nod. I understand the ways of the world, after traveling and working in this strange and deadly business. But what astounds me is how easily people turn on one another when vanity, greed, pride, jealousy, lust, and passion motivate them to do the unthinkable.

Not to mention power and money.

It's what Mother doesn't say that disturbs me.

Finn points his finger. "Inform us when the jobs are done, and we'll make the deposits into your account. Stay with your family as long as you need."

I think I've finally won him over. "Thanks. Appreciate that."

I walk out the door with an additional concern—that my life is now in serious danger from a bat-shit crazy assassin. I must watch my back and keep myself from becoming a victim of this Russian sister of ours who has gone rogue.

I'll take Finn's advice and sleep with my Ruger under my pillow.

Chapter 45
Collin

Collin sat back in his comfortable seat in a corner of St. Angelo's Espresso, in the busy and congested Via della Conciliazione district. He'd enjoyed strolling around Vatican City and St. Peter's Basilica.

So, Shayla had another guy on the string? And an Irishman at that? He should have confronted her about it but didn't want her to know he'd snooped, checking out her phone calls. He'd also been quick to anger because of the pressing matter of what to do with the Angel Fire.

He'd thought it best to leave Shayla's apartment, get his thoughts together, and find out his next order of business. He'd talk to her about it later.

Collin pulled his laptop from his carry case and powered it up. After last night's clusterfuck where his meeting with Scorpio had taken an ugly turn, he knew his inbox would have something in it today. And he knew it would be from the source who'd deposited the twenty percent of the Angel Fire value into his Moneytree app account.

What Collin wanted to know was, how did Lorenzo Vittorio find out Scorpio was the handler for the dealer who wanted the necklace? He obviously knew Collin had burgled it from his brother. Now that Shayla had killed both brothers—Collin shook his head on that one—had the brothers ratted out Collin as the Angel Fire thief?

Collin logged onto his message site using his VPN and typed in his key to unlock the message center. Sure enough, a message appeared. He tapped and waited for the decryption.

You have Angel Fire, and we must complete the transfer. You've been paid half of the negotiated percentage. If you want the rest, leave the necklace in a locker of our choosing at Da Vinci Airport.

Collin's fingers flew on the keys.

Unacceptable. First, you'll deposit the remainder of my fee, which has increased to fifty percent, after all my trouble. Personal transfer only, or no deal. Be at the Lufthansa VIP lounge at 4 pm, sharp. No agreement, no necklace.

He had this guy by the balls. He sat back and waited, knowing he was in the catbird seat. Not only did he have the necklace, but the new handler would have to undergo airport security, and therefore be unarmed.

He still had the authenticity papers, fake badge, and paperwork to get the Angel Fire through airport security. This time he'd say he was transporting the necklace to the National Museum of Ireland.

Which is where he wished it were going, instead of to someone who probably wanted it for his daughter's high school graduation or his trophy wife's twenty-third birthday.

A message appeared.

Forty-five percent.

Now Collin was agitated. Who was this joker, garage-saling him down on a nine-hundred-million-dollar necklace?

"That's it. I'm done," he muttered, typing furiously.

No deal. My fee is now fifty-five percent. Be there at four or I keep the necklace.

Collin hit the exit key and slammed his laptop closed. He shoved it into his leather case and checked his watch. He had to fetch his rental car, return it at the airport, and check in. Then take a nap in the VIP lounge before his mystery guest arrived.

He couldn't wait to see who it was.

Lifting the strap of his laptop case to his shoulder, he stepped along the wet sidewalk. When he glanced left, then right, his eye caught a blue motor bike following a string of cars. He squinted to see a long wine-colored stream of hair down the back of the rider.

Shayla's Vespa.

Collin pivoted toward the direction she was going. He'd followed her for half a block, then she pulled her scooter over to the curb and swung her leg over to get off. She'd dressed casually in jeans, not like someone going to an office.

Well, duh—she's an assassin, you idiot.

She lifted the front end of the bike onto the sidewalk and rolled it to an archway leading to an underground car park. She pulled out her wallet and showed ID to the attendant. He let her through, and she disappeared down the ramp. When he caught up to the limestone building, it was covered with scaffolding and apparently undergoing a remodel. He peered at a gold plaque attached to the stone: CONEXUS.

A round gold and black logo with an elaborate 'C' in the center.

Collin stood there wondering why this was familiar. It hit him like the cobblestones on this ancient street—Conexus was on the business card on Shayla's nightstand.

Collin did a double take, slack-jawed. This must be the front company for Shayla's organization. Surely, they wouldn't advertise an assassin agency only a couple of blocks from the Vatican...would they?

Hell, in today's world, anything was possible.

Collin thought about going inside the large double doors. He peered inside to see a security and an x-ray machine, as in most of the buildings here; he had Angel Fire with him, and he didn't need additional hassles going through security. It was bad enough that he had to go through the gauntlet at Da Vinci Airport with the necklace.

This must be the central headquarters of Shayla's employer, Conexus.

Collin hurried to his car, where he searched the Internet for Conexus on his phone. All he found was generic information found on many organization websites. A general mission statement, and a vague description of what Conexus did with global enterprises in the financial world.

There is money here. Many, many monies.

So, that's how Shayla's employer supplied her with whatever she needed to get the job done.

Collin started the car and pulled onto the Via della Conciliazione roadway when Shayla zipped by on her Vespa. She weaved in and out of traffic, heading east across the Tiber River. Collin lost sight of her but knew where she was going.

What a coincidence, Collin was headed there, too. He turned into a car park a short distance from The Pantheon and the nearby pizzeria Shayla was to meet her boyfriend, or whoever the feck he was.

Collin seethed, recalling their texts and the dickwad's breathy voice message.

He couldn't wait to see this guy.

After parking the Porsche—he wanted to own one of these—he hastened to the pizzeria, which only offered alfresco dining, as did most places around here.

Collin chose a small table at the espresso place next to it. He tugged a baseball cap down over his face and put on his sunglasses.

Shayla moved to a table at the pizzeria and sat with her back to Collin. Good, she didn't see him.

The guy across from her was of medium height, with curly brown hair to his shoulders. He beamed when he saw her and stood to embrace her.

Collin's skin prickled, and he had to control himself from leaping up to stop the guy from holding her for so long.

Dickwad gave Shayla a lingering kiss on the cheek. Not a quick peck either. Definitely lingering—one of those oh-baby-I-want-to-fuck-you kisses.

Collin lifted his cap and brushed his hair back, irritated. He felt like a dick spying on his—his what? *Lover? Partner? My girlfriend the assassin?*

The guy said something, and Shayla threw back her head and laughed. Her hand rested on Dickwad's hand, and they were leaning toward each other.

Collin knew body language, and this was no casual friendship. He couldn't take it anymore. He'd seen enough...he had a flight to catch.

He tossed back the last of his espresso, threw bills on the table, and strode back to the car. What disturbed him the most—how could Shayla be that way with someone else after all she and Collin had been through together?

He started the Porsche's engine, put it in gear and sped off toward the Leonardo Da Vinci Airport. Good riddance to Rome. And good riddance, Shayla Byrne. Or maybe her name really was Jealousy.

That's what he was feeling right now.

Jealousy.

Chapter 46
Shayla

I 've carefully orchestrated the execution of the five hits. Timing is crucial. I've enlisted the Conexus corporate jet for my Oslo-Reykjavik operations. At least the jet hadn't suffered damage in the bombing. It sits unharmed in a private hangar at a rural airport, one that celebrities and dignitaries of state use.

Plus, I can load as many weapons and personal items as I want to. No airport security.

I tried unsuccessfully to sleep during the three-hour flight from Rome to Oslo. I checked into the Hotel Continental near the Nobel Peace Center and took a quick stroll down to visit the center. I continued out on the long concrete docks, admiring the beautiful condos on the coast.

I must relax before tomorrow's synchronized five-mark operation. I must be rested and on my game. Finn had a car and driver waiting for me at the airport, and I'd scoped out the location in an upscale neighborhood near The Viking Ship Museum. He'd also sent one of his staff ahead of time to study the target's patterns, routines, and movements.

And relayed all of it to me.

I'm set to go. What I'm not set on is why Collin left Rome without saying goodbye. Just wrote me a lame note. I'm mystified why I can't get him to answer his phone or my texts. I've been trying to reach him since this afternoon, after my meeting with my cousin.

Declan had flown to Rome to brief me about everything he'd discovered. He and the other cousins have been working on these cybercrime syndicates for a long time. He was grateful to me for presenting the situation to Conexus and the Sisters of Sin.

And in return, I was grateful to him for trusting me to take care of it through the SOS organization.

Declan had lined me out with my two marks. Clean shots from a sniper viewpoint. Even showed me where to perch, clean getaways, the works. He felt responsible for the SOS undertaking such an extensive operation, and he wanted to help.

I mentioned to him Mother and Finn suggested he come work with the SOS, but Declan shook his head, saying he could better serve world justice by setting up cybersafe security systems and nailing the ones who hacked into them. I can't say as I blame him.

I want to know what Collin plans to do with the necklace; whether anyone has contacted him yet. I have a stake in knowing since I'd worn the blessed thing, and he'd nearly gotten himself killed over it.

I call him again using the same burner phone we used in London.

No answer. What if something has happened to him? How will I know?

All I want is to do this job and go home to Arklow.

Chapter 47
Shayla

Once onboard the corporate jet enroute to Reykjavik, I groaned at how my Oslo operation had nosedived into an unnerving experience.

I recalled how Mother had always emphasized, never, under any circumstance get emotional while on a job.

I fucked up on that one.

Besides the other four mother effing trafficking monsters, Declan and the Uncles had been tracking the Oslo mark for a long time. It was their idea for me to present their findings to the SOS, since they were scattered around the world; our Ireland operation only accepted one-at-a-time contracts. The Uncles were aging, and Declan didn't want to do the icky stuff that I used to do.

Using his computer from the comfort of his home, the Oslo mark had not only run his revenge porn website, he'd arranged human trafficking, stole money from countless charities and bank accounts, and destroyed lives in any way he wished through his identity theft and imposter tactics. One of his poser gimmicks was to masquerade as a utility company to bilk millions from the elderly who barely afforded a roof over their heads.

He did all this on a global scale.

I had pre-arranged and coordinated the five hits with Declan and my Sister of Sin, Wrath. Wrath was to do the Beijing hit, and the Uncles would do the operations in Newcastle in Northern Ireland, and Falmouth in England.

We all wanted these losers off the planet so they couldn't destroy lives ever again. So, I'd decided to scrap the sniper operation. Instead, I chose a proximity cessation with my pistols.

Up close and personal. I wanted this sadistic, hedonistic monster to see what was coming.

I had approached the mark's residence with visions crowding my brain—him trafficking children for the sex trade; his routine of inflicting pain on those same children; him raking in forty grand a month off his revenge porn website, reveling in how he'd ruined countless lives.

The jarring image of the Holden boy we'd saved in Ireland had crept into my brain. I'd been living with non-stop guilt for killing the little boy's traffickers in front of him that terrible night in Holyhead. I'll never shake this guilt, despite believing I'm a gladiator for the young and the innocent.

And so, I lost my shit.

I had enjoyed the mark's surprised expression when I entered his study, raised my pistol, and fired suppressed rounds at his arms, thighs, and groin, then waited for his agonized screams.

Not because I enjoyed his shrieks of pain—but eliminating this slime quickly was too good for him. I took my time to make sure he felt pain as he watched himself bleed out. Only then did I take aim and steady my hand, to pump two rounds into his chest, then confirm the kill.

Overwhelming emotion had crashed over me with such amplified intensity, I'd done the only thing I could think of—shot up his keyboard—felt good to see the keys explode into a million pieces.

The QWERTY had blown apart in slow motion—sending letters in a punctuated explosion sailing through the air. It had annoyed me to annihilate a perfectly good keyboard, but I was intent on destruction. It took several rounds to destroy the six monitors but obliterating the hard drives delivered the most satisfaction.

Afterwards, I calmly exited, climbed into my waiting car, and boarded our corporate jet at the Oslo airport.

An hour and a half later in Reykjavik, I ended the next target as she had soaked in the hot springs at Blue Lagoon, watching the northern lights. The Blue Lagoon was conveniently on the way to the Reykjavik airport, so I had boarded the jet and slept the entire flight to Dublin.

When I had landed, Wrath and Declan called to report they'd accomplished their missions. Mother and Finn were pleased. I'd taken the train down to Arklow Town, where Declan picked me up and drove me home.

After the planning and execution of my first multi-target operation, I heaved a sigh of relief and succumbed to exhaustion. Powering off my SOS phone, I tossed it onto my vintage nightstand and collapsed into my old bed in the Uncles' Arklow cottage.

I dreamed about Collin and the Celtic Sea Bookshop.

• • • •

I wake the next afternoon, fully dressed. After hugging the Uncles and stumbling upstairs in the wee hours of the morning, I don't remember falling into bed.

I wince at Uncle Casen coughing downstairs. I plan to spend the day with him. Uncle Brodie says his prognosis isn't good. Declan told me he'd contacted our cousin, Colleen, Uncle Brodie's only daughter. She was on her way from America.

I roll onto my back and stare at the familiar cracks in the ceiling, welcoming them like old friends—one shaped like a rabbit, and the other like a sheep. I hadn't realized how much I missed my home. After living and working in challenging environments for so long, I'd forgotten the easy cadence of Arklow, nestled on the coast of the Irish Sea.

Right where I left it.

Collin has been front and center in my mind since leaving Rome. I wonder if he's back at our old haunt—the Celtic Sea Bookshop.

He doesn't answer his phone.

I'm worried something else may have happened to him. I want to know he is all right.

Collin wouldn't ghost me, would he?

Springing from my bed, I open my dresser drawer and dig around for something to wear. I've outgrown the drab, outdated clothes from my old life.

Only now do I realize how much I have changed...from Shayla the girl to Jealousy the woman; and I embody both.

I turn to the oversized suitcase I'd toted from Rome and choose a bright-colored blouse and jacket. I pull on skinny jeans and a pair of white Dolce and Gabbana sneakers, dotted with navy blue stars.

After spending time with the Uncles, I give them pecks on the cheek and take my electric bike from the mudroom off the kitchen, right where I'd left it. I pedal down to the Celtic Sea Bookshop.

A 'Closed' sign hangs on the door.

Where the heck is Collin?

I have no clue where to start searching for him, but if I must call in reinforcements to help, I reckon I will. I'll start with Declan. He can find anyone.

Even people who don't exist.

Chapter 48
Collin

C ollin startled awake from his dream about film star Helen Mirren.

"Hello? Excuse me, I'm here for Angel Fire."

A woman's cultured British tone had him thinking he was back in London, talking with that same film icon.

He snapped his eyes open and shook himself fully awake, remembering where he was and why he was here. Collin immediately reached behind him to make sure his daypack was intact with the necklace inside.

He sat up straight and eyed the older woman standing before him.

She had perfectly coiffed silver hair, cut to frame her handsome face. Remarkably beautiful, reminding him of his grandmother—only impeccably dressed.

Collin's jaw dropped. "Did you say Angel Fire? As in—*the* Angel Fire?"

This wasn't quite who he'd expected. She gestured to the seat across from him.

"May I?"

"By all means, have a seat."

Shocked didn't cover Collin's reaction right now, although he'd come to understand anything goes in his business.

"Are you the one who messaged me?" he asked in a faint voice, studying her.

She nodded. "Sorry about your inopportune incident at the Galleria Hotel in London. I can see by your bruises and cuts things didn't go well for you. When we lost our handler, I thought it was time to step in."

"How do you know about all that? Are you the dealer who hired me?"

"Let's say I represent the dealer who paid you the twenty percent deposit to steal the necklace."

"I was expecting—"

She interrupted. "A man. The reason why the world is such a bloody mess. When something needs doing, a woman must do it."

She pulled off her gray gloves, one finger at a time. "Just as *your* woman does."

Collin sat back. She had his undivided attention.

"My woman?"

"Shayla Byrne. Our Jealousy." She stared at him, waiting for a reaction.

He didn't disappoint. "How do you know Shayla?" he sputtered.

His eyes darted to a business card the woman set on the table. She tapped it with her finger.

He switched his surprise to realization as he eyed the familiar logo—Conexus. He fit the puzzle pieces together.

"You're with Conexus." He picked up the card, studied it, and tossed it on the table. His eyes narrowed.

"What's an assassin organization doing in the middle of my necklace transaction?"

"One of our board members did a favor for a good friend of his, who wanted the Angel Fire back. It was stolen from the jewelry collection he'd inherited from his grandmother in Singapore. He was readying the collection a few years ago for an American Museum, who agreed to pay handsomely for it."

"Which one?" asked Collin.

"The Smithsonian."

"Go on," said Collin, his interest piqued.

"When he'd taken it to Christy's in Hong Kong to have it appraised, Antonio Vittorio hired someone to steal it. An impossibility, everyone thought. Miraculously, Antonio pulled it off, and unbeknownst to our Singapore associate, it remained in Antonio's residence for the last couple of years."

"Until he tracked it down." She stopped to scrutinize Collin.

"When our friend found out where Angel Fire was, he called out a favor we owed him. We hired the handler."

"Scorpio."

"Yes. He was reputable in the business."

"I had worked with him before. Only why did Shayla and I have the same target?"

She shrugged. "We handled that contract as well."

Collin now understood the bizarre connection.

"I see. Now what?"

"Scorpio said you were one of the best. He bragged how you could easily steal Angel Fire. He liked you." She gave him a thoughtful look.

"I find it a strange coincidence that you and Shayla are involved. In the past I've tried to discourage romantic involvement with my staff. Even ordered a hit on one."

This turned Collin's blood to ice.

"However." Mother leaned back in her seat. "These are extenuating circumstances. The fact that you and Jealousy had the same target was indeed a coincidence. If there are such things."

Collin's brow furrowed. "How did you find out we were involved?"

She snorted. "Darling, we make it our business to know everything."

"Who's 'we'?"

"The Sisters of Sin. I'm sure you know by now that Shayla is one of our operatives."

She smiled and patted Collin's forearm. "I know your family. Donegal—isn't that right?"

Collin's pulse quickened, and the pucker factor kicked in. "Are you threatening me?"

She laughed. "Goodness, no. Ireland is a small town. I spent time there back in the day. I also knew Shayla's mother. In fact, I worked with her some years ago."

"Why do you call Shayla 'Jealousy'?"

"She didn't tell you? Good girl." The woman paused. "Jealousy is her SOS code name. All the Sisters have them—Pride, Vanity, Greed, Lust, Passion..."

"The seven deadly sins. How quaint. And what's *your* code name?"

"Call me Mother."

She leaned forward and nodded at a nearby private room. "I've reserved that room, so let's step in and take care of business. And...if you tell anyone what I've just told you, then I'll have to kill you."

She shrugged one shoulder and flashed him a bright smile with her perfect teeth.

Collin's stomach ping-ponged. "Hold on a minute. First off, I know you aren't armed, but do you have other weapons that made it past security?"

His eyes strayed to her large Gucci bag.

She gave him a dour look and hefted her bag over the table.

"See for yourself."

Collin glanced at her, then pawed through the contents and felt the linings. He didn't find anything that could harm him. But that didn't mean squat with an assassin in the house.

"All right. Let's do this. I have a flight to catch," he said, glancing at his wristwatch. He'll either walk out extremely wealthy or extremely dead.

Collin's stomach swallowed itself as they entered the room. After Collin gave Mother the Angel Fire necklace, she made a phone call.

"Send the rest of the money to this Moneytree email address." Mother specified the email and thanked someone named Finn. She snapped her head up.

"You didn't hear me say that." She drilled Collin with an icy stare.

His heart skipped a beat as he stared back.

A cash register sounded on Collin's phone, verifying completion of the transaction. A hundred-million anvils lifted from his shoulders, and he wanted to scream happiness and relief. Instead, he remained professional.

Collin squared his shoulders. "Before we go, there's the matter of the Rokeby Venus painting in the London Gallery."

Mother hesitated. "That order was canceled, I'm afraid. However, I have another offer for you, if you're so inclined."

Collin slipped his phone into his pocket.

"And that would be?"

"Now that I know of your professional expertise, and your connection to Jealousy, I'd like to refer you to some other Conexus associates who are interested in recovering stolen items."

She slid the Conexus card across the table and tapped the phone number on it.

"Word on the street is several art galleries and museums are interested in paying handsomely for your services to get their valuable pieces back from past heists. For all I know, maybe some are things you've stolen yourself."

"Ha, funny, but I doubt it." Collin picked up the card and studied it. "You're saying there's lucrative work in stealing back what other thieves steal in the first place?"

He chucked the card onto the table. "Galleries and museums can't afford me."

Mother patted her Gucci bag containing Angel Fire. "Depends how badly they want their precious items back. The Rome galleries alone will keep you busy. Call that number on the card. I don't do things like this for just anyone. But since Shayla loves you—and for the life of me, I don't know why—I'm doing this for her."

She leaned over the table and leveled her gaze.

"I've known the Byrne family in Avoca for eons. So I have a special affinity for Shayla. If you so much as hurt one hair on her head or break her heart in any fashion—count on me ordering a hit for you."

She flicked another piercing stare at him, and the thought crossed his mind that since she had the Angel Fire, she could easily kill him and stop payment on her transaction.

He hoped that wasn't her intention; his arse was hanging out on a wire right now.

Collin figured she indeed meant it. He also figured it was best not to fuck with this woman.

"Shayla grew up without her parents, as you know. She doesn't know the truth about what happened to them. When I tell her, the truth will devastate her. She will need you to lean on. And that's an order. *Capisce?*"

"Yes, understood. Loud and clear. Thank you for not killing me," he joked. Collin flicked his eyes up at her. "Do you have a real name?"

"Yes, but I don't want anyone confusing me with Her Majesty, The Queen."

Mother stood and held out her hand. "Nice doing business with you. Now go home to your woman. She's waiting."

"I doubt it. I saw her being chummy with some other guy today."

He abhorred this feeling of jealousy but wanted to know who the guy was and what he meant to Shayla.

Mother scoffed, and a petulant expression crossed her face.

"Oh, for pity's sake! That was her cousin, Declan. He helped us execute a recent operation. Dear sweet Collin, pull your head out of your bum and go home to Ireland." Mother pivoted and clicked out of the lounge.

He stared after her, stunned at what had just transpired.

So, that was the infamous Cousin Declan that Shayla had always gone on about. Collin didn't know whether to feel relieved or stupid for misjudging her.

No matter. He'd get his bloody arse to Ireland, as Mother, or Queen Elizabeth—or whatever her fecking name was—advised him to do.

The reality of his being five hundred million dollars richer super-charged him. All kinds of new possibilities presented themselves. He was astounded that Shayla's fecking employer had turned out to be the new bloody handler.

His mind whirled.

Was this a karmic joke or had Shayla somehow orchestrated all this?

No, she couldn't have.

Collin didn't need to boost the Rokeby painting now. In fact, he was glad that order had been canceled. He liked the idea of flipping art heists on their head—steal valuable pieces from the rich—and return them to the galleries and museums for the world to enjoy and appreciate.

That action would reverse his go-straight-to-hell card into a get-into-heaven-free-card. He thought back to why he began stealing in the first place—to help his parents pay for his younger sister Bridget's medical bills. He continued stealing to donate his heist fees to the facilities that helped kids battle insidious cancers.

This new chunk of change would help him turn over a new leaf. Rob from the rich and return the art back to the galleries—for nominal fees, of course.

The first thing he'd do when he got to Arklow was to write a tidy check for another hefty donation to St. Bridget's Children's Hospital in Dublin—so named because of the millions Collin had donated through the years. The medical staff had done everything in their power they could way back then, to save his beloved little sister.

Collin had a new mission statement. Restore balance. Make things right. Steal from the rich and give to the masses. A noble cause if ever there was one. He couldn't wait to tell Shayla.

He glanced at his watch. His plane was boarding. He snatched the Conexus card from the table, shoved it in his pocket, and rushed from the lounge.

Feeling light as a feather and happy for his fifty-five percent, he practically skipped to his boarding gate, arriving just in time.

Collin was the last one to board the flight to Dublin.

Chapter 49
Shayla

D eclan comes through for me. He'd hacked into flight manifests at Da Vinci Airport and located Collin boarding a plane for Dublin. At least I know he's back in Ireland. But why hasn't he called? After my last assignment, I told him I'd be here.

I borrow Declan's car to drive up to Avoca. I'm able to visit there now without the anxiety attacks, but I still want to know what happened to my parents. Mother wouldn't talk about it when I asked. Uncle Casen is too sick, and I don't want to upset Uncle Brodie.

I pull into the Avoca Woolen Mill and saunter inside, remembering being here with Collin when he'd had business to do for his bookshop.

Before I left Arklow, I'd driven to the bookshop. Still a 'Closed' sign on the door.

After the woolen mill, I go to Fitzgerald's Pub and sit at the bar. I still don't drink much, but for old times' sake, I order a raspberry beer. When I finish, I drive to Castlemacadam Cemetery and weave my way around the ornate tombstones to Mum and Dad's graves. I sit on the stone bench where Mother had recruited me into the Sisters of Sin.

I have my SOS phone with me. I call Mother.

She answers right away. "Why are you calling? You're supposed to be taking a break."

"It's time you told me the truth about Mum and Dad's deaths. I'm at their graves, in the cemetery in Avoca. There was a reason you were here when I first met you. Tell me why."

A long sigh came through the phone.

I wait patiently.

"All right. But before I do, you need to understand that history repeats itself. There's nothing you can do to fix the past."

"I'm listening."

225

"As you know, your mum was my first Jealousy operative. She was one of the best the Sisters of Sin had. Quick, smart, charming—she maintained the Irish stay-at-home parent persona that worked well to fool everyone."

I fix my gaze on Mum's tombstone as Mother speaks.

She continues. "One assignment went terribly wrong with another operative, a Sister, who was extremely jealous of your mother and had gone rogue. The hit was assigned to both operatives by mistake. When your mum beat her to the mark and made the hit in Paris—which paid very well—the rogue Sister accused her of stealing her hit and vowed vengeance."

"She was bent on revenge. One night after your mum and dad drove home from a céilí in Arklow, their brakes failed. Subsequent investigation ordered by your uncles revealed someone had tampered with the brakes. No leads, so no charges were filed. Your uncles flew to Rome to meet with me, asking for help in finding who murdered your mum and dad."

Mother continues as raindrops fall on me. It always rains when I'm in this cemetery.

"The rogue agent bragged to the wrong people, and word got back to the SOS. I informed Brodie and Casen. They said they'd take care of it, and I knew what that meant. And indeed, they did." Mother quiets, and we're both silent for a spell.

Mother takes another breath. "You were in the back seat. By some miracle, you tumbled out before the car missed the curve and crashed down the embankment into the river. It is my belief your mum pushed you out before the car went over."

A sob escapes, and I close my eyes, recalling my three-year-old mind from the experience. Only jarred images and crying.

Lots of crying.

"Talk to your uncles, Jealousy. Tell them you know what happened and why. Casen and Brodie will be relieved that you know the truth."

"I will. Thank you—Mother." I squeak out, fully aware this is the first time I've called her Mother to her face.

My ears sting with this truth that I'd somehow sensed, after working for the SOS—that something wasn't right with the cause of my parents' deaths.

I struggle to hold it together until this call ends.

"Are you still there?"

"Yes." I sniffle away from the phone, so Mother won't hear.

"I knew it'd be hard for you to accept what happened. But remember how I said the assassin world is a no holds barred, ruthless business? Yes, it pays supremely, and gets adrenaline pumping for those who find thrills from it—but our danger quotient is relentless."

"Yes, I know." I stare at Mum and Dad's graves as my heart shatters. Unstoppable tears stream down.

"Now that we have another rogue agent, I am officially warning all the Sisters of Sin: Dominika is targeting all of you. Just know that you are now in her sights. Doesn't matter that she doesn't know you. You're guilty by association. Stay alert."

"I will. But why would she come after the other Sisters?" I'm not worried about Dominika seeking me out in Ireland. If she does, I'll be ready. She'll have a fight on her hands.

My entire family will see to it.

"Knowing Dominika, my guess is she intends to run a new organization and wants everyone out of her way. Oh, and another thing...I met Collin Stedman," says Mother in her off-handed way.

My head snaps up. "What? How? Why?" This causes all kinds of flutters in my stomach. Mother is full of surprises today.

She chuckles. "We had business to conduct. By the way, Collin saw you with Declan before he left Rome, and thought you were lovebirds. You better get things sorted with him. You broke his sweet little Irish heart."

"How do you know all that? Where did you see him? Is he all right?"

"You always have questions, my curious one. Yes, he's fine. Collin will explain. He's looking for you." Mother ends the call before I can get a word out.

I sit in the rain, the same as last time. Without an umbrella. I contemplate what Mother said about Mum and can't believe it.

A rogue agent ended Mum's life.

That's what Mother meant about history repeating itself. Dominika wants to eliminate me—eliminate all the Sisters. She doesn't even fecking know me.

Panic hits. I succumb to a full-blown anxiety attack.

I lose my shit.

Rising from the stone bench, I utter undecipherable sounds—screaming and raging like a lunatic. I aim my face at the sky and emit a long, lonely wail that leaves me short of breath. The pain is too great—the loss too real. I'll never know Mum. I'll never know Dad—what he liked, didn't like, how he talked, how he walked—what his voice sounded like.

There were no videos, no recordings.

What was Mum's voice like? I don't remember. What was her favorite color? Her favorite song? Did she love me?

The rain pours into my contorted mouth and pummels my eyes.

"God, why didn't you save them? Why did you let them die that way? Why...?" I fall to my knees on Mum's grave and wail like a child—as women used to do at Irish wakes, keening. Mourning. Grieving.

I want to know who the woman was that ended their lives.

I want to kill her all over again.

My wails I send up to God and the angels, so they'll hear me, and know what they've done. I shout at the heavens. "I hate you for allowing this to happen! I hate that Mum killed for a living, and now I do the same!"

I crumple onto the grass, a pile of saturated pathetic loneliness, not giving a flying feck how wet I am, not caring about anything. Hating the mother effing woman who stole my parents from me—hating Dominika for becoming just like her.

Curling into a fetal position, I cry so hard I have the jags, burying my face in the wet grass.

Strong hands slide under me, lifting me from the rain-soaked ground. I turn my head to see the love of my life.

"Collin! Thank God, you're all right!" I choke out.

Appreciative for his comforting presence, I wrap my arms around his neck, trying to control my jags, but they're controlling me.

Collin's hair drips as if he'd emerged from a swim. His raincoat is slick on my skin. He holds me tight—tighter than he ever has.

"I'm here, lass. I'm here. And we're home." His voice soothes my aching soul, and he carries me from the cemetery to his car—a new metallic gold Porsche. He stuffs me inside, then climbs in.

"I'll ruin your rental," I sniff.

"It's mine. I wrote a check for it."

My head snaps up and I stare at him, thankful he's here. With me. In the rain.

In Ireland.

"Let's get you dry and warm. You're shivering." He wraps a bright colored wool blanket around my shoulders and rubs my arms. I don't ask how he knew I was here—I don't care. He's here, and that's all that matters.

I hadn't realized how hard I was shaking. Didn't know how long I'd been crying in the rain.

"Your...assassin supervisor, or whatever she's called, said you'd need me," he says amid the pounding raindrops plunking the windshield.

"I do." My voice sounds small. I'm humiliated and embarrassed that Collin is seeing me so vulnerable.

There's no crying in the world of assassins.

I avoid his gaze and swipe at my cheeks. "I'm so glad you're here. Why did you leave without saying goodbye?" I stare ahead at the water streaming down the stone wall of the cemetery.

"Saw you with your cousin and thought he was your lover. I was jealous." He glances at me. "Seems jealousy gets the best of us."

He reaches across me and takes a cloth from the glove box and offers it to me.

"Tell me about it." Dabbing at my tears, I manage a smile. "I have a shite ton of questions. Let's start with Mother. How did you find her? Or did she find you?" My jags shake my chest, but I will them to lessen.

Collin starts the car and cranks the heat on high. As the windows defog, he explains everything—how his new handler turned out to be Mother—of all people! He'd transferred the Angel Fire after she agreed to pay him more, but more astonishing, she'd suggested that Collin work in reverse—steal from the thieves and return the artifacts to the galleries and museums.

Collin tells me that when Conexus agreed to help an associate in Singapore, they'd delegated the handler role to Mother, after Scorpio was shot. She and Finn had found intel that Collin was the professional thief working for the Singapore dealer.

I sit in disbelief, listening to Collin explain—astounded that the one I love and the person I work for chanced into each other in a separate capacity.

It seems God has answered my prayers by sending Collin to be with me.

And with a little help from Elizabeth Danvers—the woman I call Mother.

Chapter 50
Shayla

O nce my sobs subside and my jags along with them, Collin shifts the Porsche into gear and drives to the Meeting of the Waters in the Vale of Avoca, a short distance from town. He knows it's my most favorite place in the world; the one place that calms me and rejuvenates my soul.

The rain has stopped. Everything smells fresh and clean.

When we climb out of the car, I circle around to scrutinize it.

"I love your Porsche. It's prettier than the one in London."

I step to the front and grasp Collin's hands. "I want to make love on top of this car, too."

Collin laughs. "That is most definitely going on my to do list. But not now. I'm afraid it's a wee bit wet."

He leads me from the car into the same quaint cottage where I'd lost my virginity to him the first time we made love.

He closes the door and sets to work, starting a fire in the hearth, while I take a shower. I hold the warm washcloth to my swollen eyes, thankful Collin had shown up when he did.

I'll forever love him for it.

Afterwards, Collin loans me his t-shirt. He moves around bare-chested, all hot and sexy in his tight jeans. I eye him like a succulent piece of shrimp as he pours me a hot tea and spoons honey in it. We sit on the oval braided rag rug in front of the fire, sipping our tea.

Collin lifts a pint of Jameson and pours a generous amount into my teacup, then into his.

"This'll relax you."

"I relaxed the second I saw you."

I give him a coy smile. "You want to get me drunk so you can have your way with me."

"You're onto me. In fact, I do plan to have my way with you."

He stretches an arm around my shoulder, and we sit in comfortable silence, sipping tea and listening to the crackle of flame.

Collin stares into the fire. "All things being equal, it appears you have another mum who knew you when you were a wee one."

"What do you mean?"

"Your SOS boss. Now I understand why you call her Mother. She's the one who said if I ever hurt you, she'd come for me. She also said you were waiting for me, and I should go to you."

"She watches out for us and our best interests. Feels like I'm closer to her than the other Sisters, probably because I'm the youngest."

I think for a minute. "What about the Rokeby painting? Is that a no-go?"

Collin nods. "Yes, and it's fine by me. I like the idea of stealing *for* galleries, not *from* them. Have I told you I have an art history degree from a Texas university?"

"No, but it doesn't surprise me after you going on about the art and sculptures in Rome, and how they must be preserved for future generations. No wonder you work in the art business...so to speak," I add, tongue-in-cheek.

"So, that's how you learned to talk like a Texan. You had full-on immersion."

"Yessirree, y'all can hang your hat on that, ma'am." Firelight twinkles in his eyes.

"I love it when you do that," I say, watching him.

Collin's brow furrows. "Listen, Shayla, I apologize for being a dick—thinking your cousin Declan was bollocks, another guy in your life. My nose fell out of joint when I saw you with him."

"I probably would have reacted the same, had things been reversed," I empathize. "How were you to know who he was? I do wish you would have asked me about it when you saw us together. I would have cleared things up and Declan would have given you a grand hug."

"Think he'll like me?"

"He already does. I've told him about you." I squeeze his thigh. "From now on, let's be honest with each other...with all things," I say softly.

Collin bumps my shoulder with his.

"Duly noted. With all things. When you saved my life, I resolved to love you forever. I resolved to love you before that, but saving my life sealed the deal."

"Good, I can hold that over you, unless you return the favor."

A powerful feeling wells up. I can't contain it, and my voice tremors.

"Collin, I almost lost you. Some bodyguard I was. None of that should have happened. I should have stayed with you when you went up to meet Scorpio from the fundraiser."

"I'm glad you didn't."

I turn to him and rest my palms on his shoulders.

"Don't know what I would have done if I'd lost you. I'd not experienced much of the world until I looked upon you...and loved you."

My voice breaks.

He draws me close, and I twist into him, pressing my ear to his chest. His heartbeat soothes me, comforts me.

"Don't feel bad, lass. It's all history now," he murmurs, caressing me and stroking my hair. "I had to keep you safe."

"Also, thanks for that 'xyz' bit. Clever of you to use it as our secret communication."

I lift my head to wink at him.

"A bit of trivia not many outsiders know." He draws back to gaze at me.

"Frankly, I don't know whether to be glad you warmed up to my employer or nervous that you two actually know each other, let alone conducted business."

"Hell, your boss scares the shit out of me."

Collin lets go of me and rises to put more wood on the fire.

"She scares the shit out of most of us," I respond, my appreciative eye traveling him.

Collin turns to face me. "She said in the past she didn't want her employees to have love relationships. She gave me a 'pass' because of our unique circumstance, and the fact she knew your mum. She won't order a hit on me. I actually thanked her."

I chortle at this news.

"Mother actually said that? Well, that's grand. I was nervous about her finding out about us. That's a load off, isn't it?" I give him a bright look, loving the way he moves, loving how the firelight accents the contours of his back.

I watch his shoulder blades ripple when he lifts firewood and rests the pieces on the flames.

"Collin, do you realize how beautiful you are?" I say softly.

He straightens and his look turns feral.

"You have it backwards, lass—you're the beautiful one."

"Remember when you said we'd go on holiday, anywhere I wanted? I still want to go to Anacapri."

He smiles. "I have a friend who has a villa on the island of Capri. How about we take a few days, ride the funicular, and go sailing? I'd love to see you naked on a sailboat."

"I want to see you naked right now."

I can't take it any longer—I want my hands on him. Pushing to my feet, I take his arm and lead him to the queen-sized bed. His eyes take me in, his glorious bare chest gleaming in the firelight. I trace the outlines of his pecs with my forefingers, then move close to kiss them.

I love his goosebumps that spring up like Irish clover.

He lifts his t-shirt off me, and we stand facing each other—thief and assassin—opposites, yet kindred souls. And friends...even co-workers, on occasion.

But mostly lovers. Definitely lovers.

As we pull back the covers and crawl under, all cozy and warm, with the fire crackling across the room, it occurs to me I've never been this happy. Coming home makes my world normal again.

Collin offers me a heavy dose of stability along with my sense of normalcy, even though it's temporary until our professions summon us back into the game.

I love Collin, because from the beginning, he offered acceptance. And offered it a second time when he found out what I did for a living.

And then offered me love.

Collin rests my back on the bed and kisses me in a long sensual meeting of the tongues—like the Meeting of the Waters in the Vale of Avoca—waters that flow from two separate streams, alike yet uniquely different, as they join to form one river.

Neither stream judges the other. Neither care how the other got here. Or what happens along the way. Only that their merged waters run wild and free—a united, unstoppable force, stronger than before.

And, like the Meeting of the Waters, my love for Collin flows like the untamed river.

All the way to the Irish Sea.

I hope you loved Shayla and Collin's story! Please take a moment to post a review on Amazon, Goodreads, and/or Bookbub. Taking the time to post a review makes a huge difference for my author career and success as a writer. I would very much appreciate it. Thank you! ~ LoLo

Loving the Sisters of Sin series? Continue reading for a preview of LUST!

Lust

By Michelle Ventura

Rome

Zoe McKnight tapped her foot as her handler signed off on the last document needed to officially complete her brutal training for Sisters of Sin, shortened by half due to her intense training at Quantico, prior to her stint with the FBI.

He hesitated, the pen hovering over the document. "I am aware of your history...your childhood. There will be times when you have to use whatever means you have at your disposal to overtake your mark. This includes your body." He looked up at her, pen at the ready.

Zoe tilted her head to the side, eyes squinting slightly. She pulled the band from her blonde hair shaking her head to let the curly waves spill over her shoulders and down her back. She smiled seductively. "You mean I have to have sex with men to distract them long enough to kill them?" Her blue green eyes narrowing narrowed as she moved closer to him.

His gaze took a trip over her body and then back to her face. He nodded. "Exactly. Can you do that, given your past?"

"Yes, sir, I can do that *because* of my past," she answered without hesitation.

Compartmentalizing was something she'd learned to do at a very early age although it wasn't until her psych training in college that she understood what so she'd easily done as a child.

She had this.

While it went against everything she believed in, she had a job to do, and she would use any means necessary to succeed. She vowed to right the wrongs of man, and to honor and serve the strict code of the Sisterhood.

After several hours of questioning and a final weapons meeting, Zoe received the stamp of approval from the Conexus board.

Her earlier meeting with Mother had resulted in her first assignments, and Zoe was eager to get started. She left the almost fully renovated headquarters building, feeling a mix of excitement and apprehension. Mother had warned her about Dominika not being someone she should trust or even engage at any level.

Zoe shivered as she stepped outside, taking a moment to adjust to the wind. She pulled her long blonde curls away from her face, slid the ever-present hair tie from her wrist, and wrapped it around her hair. Her eyes narrowed as a dark shadow stepped into a doorway across the street. She shook her head and turned the corner toward the apartment she'd occupied for the last few months. She had just enough time to pack and catch an Uber Black to the airport for her short flight to Milan. She packed her sparse belongings into her suitcase, and added her laptop to her backpack.

Once Zoe had settled into her first-class seat, she pulled out the laptop to review the details of the chateau owned by one very mean son of a bitch who liked to prey on young models. She'd worked out her plan to surveil him, studying his habits and haunts and committing them to memory.

Milan, Italy.

Zoe watched through the tiny sliver between the closed drape panels as Niko Bianchi yanked the young woman from the passenger seat of his Ferrari. Zoe couldn't see the weapon he held against her side, but she assumed it was his favored Glock. Three weeks of surveillance, and four missing women, had finally brought her face-to-face with the monster who'd been stalking the runway models in Milan for more than a year. Zoe reveled in the adrenaline coursing through her veins. She took a deep cleansing breath and exhaled to slow her heart rate as she waited for him to step inside the chateau he rented in the name of a shell company he thought no one would discover. He hadn't counted on her dedication and commitment to her duties as a Sister of Sin.

Niko opened the door and pushed the woman inside.

Zoe, dressed in black leather from head to toe, her face hidden by her dark sunglasses and low hanging hat, waited until he used the same key he'd unlocked the massive wooden barrier with to re-lock it before stepping from the shadows.

"What the..." He hit the floor before he could finish his sentence, Zoe's bullet hitting him in the center of his forehead. His hostage, eyes wide with shock and fear, stepped back.

JEALOUSY

Zoe holstered her gun and held up her hands.

The girl and rushed to Zoe, almost knocking her over when she wrapped her arms around her. "Grazie," she whispered, clinging to Zoe.

"Prego." Zoe gently set the young woman aside, reached down and with her gloved hand and picked up the key, unlocked the door, pocketed the key, and ran into the forest.

A sudden flash of her past popped into her mind: A younger version of herself, fleeing from the scene of another death, so many years ago on a cold winter's night in Lake Tahoe. Zoe shook off the memory. She desperately wanted to turn back and comfort the terrified woman but that wasn't an option. Concealing her identity was foremost in her mind. She couldn't risk botching her first assignment.

Adrenaline pulsed in her veins—the rush of killing a man both nauseated and empowered her. He was evil. She'd saved the young model from certain death, and that knowledge reinforced her belief that becoming a Sister of Sin was the right decision.

Zoe broke through the last copse of trees and slowed as she approached the rented Maserati. Once convinced she hadn't been followed and that no-one was in the car, she climbed inside, started the ignition, and jammed the sexy beast into gear, speeding away toward freedom.

She exhaled with relief when she was safely on the motorway.

Ten miles to the airport and then she'd be on her way back to Tahoe and a much-needed couple of days with Marcus. She couldn't wait to see him.

She reached into the console and pulled out her cell phone. "Siri, check messages and voicemail."

Siri's voice read a voicemail from a Devon Kincaid, claiming to be a friend of Marcus Sherwood, and to please call him as soon as possible, then Siri replayed three text messages and a voicemail from Marissa Becker, her best friend. "Zoe, please call me as soon as you get this message." And the last message from Jeff Lynsey, informing Zoe there had been a change in flight plans, and she should go straight to hanger 458 in the private airfield at the Milan Airport.

Something in her friend's voice sent a shiver up fear up her spine, but so did the fact that none of the messages were from Marcus. They'd talked as often as she was able while in training and texted frequently when they couldn't talk. Not hearing from him for a couple of days seemed odd.

"Hey Siri, call Marissa."

"Calling Marissa," Siri responded.

"Zoe?"

"Marissa, what's wrong?" Zoe took the exit for the airport, watching for signs leading to the private hangers.

"They killed him, Zoe." Marissa's voice shook with sadness.

A shiver much more violent than the first skittered up Zoe's back. She bit down on her lip. "Slow down, Marissa."

"I am so sorry, Zoe." Marissa choked on a sob.

Goosebumps raised the hairs on Zoe's arms and neck. "Who is him, Marissa?"

"Marcus," Marissa said quietly. "They found his car in a ravine yesterday. They're calling it an accident, but Jason is convinced it was intentional."

Special Agent Jason Reese was Zoe's boss during her employment with the FBI in the Crimes Against Women and Children division. Zoe sucked in a shaky breath of air, struggling against the tears. Her hands shook, and she tightened her grip on the steering wheel.

"I'm pulling into the airport. I'll text you when wheels are up."

Zoe disconnected. She focused on the road, ignoring the pain in her hands as her nails dug into her flesh. She took a curve too fast, weaving into the other lane as she drove around the perimeter of the airport toward the private hanger which housed the jet provided by Jeff Lynsey. She was supposed to go straight to Venice, but Jeff had reassigned that mark to another Sister, in light of this news.

A sob escaped her pursed lips as Zoe careened to a screeching stop in the hanger. She threw the car into park and dropped her forehead to the steering wheel, allowing the tears to take over. She sensed someone at the window and forced herself to let go of the wheel. Zoe swiped at her eyes and sniffled as she climbed from the car. Shock caused a pervasive chill to take over her entire body, and she shuddered. The man she assumed her pilot didn't ask questions as he escorted her to the plane and helped her settle in.

"I was notified of Mr. Sherwood's passing, Ms. McKnight. I'm very sorry for your loss," he said once she was seated. He handed her a box of tissues. "Wheels up in fifteen minutes. Mr. Lynsey suggested we take you to your home in Tahoe. Our expected arrival is 4 PM Pacific Standard Time. Can I get you anything?"

Zoe shook her head, unable to speak as her lips trembled from the emotions assailing her. Conexus knew about Marcus before she did? How was that possible? She leaned back into the comfort of the plush leather seat and stared out the window, choosing not to call Marissa but instead, reaching for her phone to text her with their ETA to Tahoe. Marissa responded with a plea for her to come straight to San Diego, explaining details for the planned celebration of life.

After assuring Marissa she would call when they landed, Zoe shut off her phone, not wanting to deal with this new reality. A small part of her wondered if this was her punishment for taking a life earlier, but she reminded herself that Marcus had died yesterday.

The unstable air, a result of the Alps rising high into the sky to the north of Milan caused turbulence that matched Zoe's mood. Once at altitude, Zoe leaned her seat back into a full reclining position.

Sleep wouldn't come. Every time she closed her eyes, an image of Marcus appeared in her mind.

She forced herself to remember, to feel the emotions she'd learned from a young age to suppress, and she cried until so emotionally drained and exhausted, sleep whisked her away into sweet oblivion.

Look for LUST by Michelle Ventura on Books2Read.com

Join our Sisters of Sin Reader group on Facebook! Let me know what you think of this series. I'd love to hear from you! Email me at lolo@lolopaige.com

Check out LoLo's website at www.lolopaige.com to get a free book for signing up or scan this code to sign up for LoLo's newsletter to learn more about her books!

Want to connect and learn more about LoLo's books? Visit Author LoLo Paige online on Facebook, Instagram, Twitter, Goodreads, & Bookbub

Acknowledgments

So grateful to my real-life Sisters of Sin who invited me to write stories for this fun romantic suspense thriller series. We've had each other's backs all the way, which has made all the difference to keep going when things got tough. Grateful to T Wells Brown, Sofia Aves, Michelle Ventura, S.C. Principale, and D.A. Nelson for creating this series and writing fantastic stories for it. It's truly been an honor working with these wonderful, talented authors.

A grateful shout-out to my wonderful editor, Maria Thayer, and my beta and proofreaders: Ray Braun, Judy Winslow, and S. R. Cyres. And many thanks to the Cops and Writers Facebook community for helping me to keep accurate, and to my readers who have stuck with me through my Blazing Hearts Wildfire series. Thanks to my Irish friends from the Emerald Isle, Elaine Nolan and Marie O'Halloran, for all things Ireland.

My biggest thank you goes to my husband and love of my life, who shared his creative and brilliant insights to help me create Shayla and Collin, for Jealousy.

About The Author

LoLo Paige is an award-winning author and former wildland firefighter, whose debut novel, *Alaska Spark,* received several awards, including an Indie B.R.A.G. Medallion, Eric Hoffer award, a Next Generation Indie Book award for romance, and a Kindle Book Review Award.

Alaska Spark and *Alaska Inferno* have ranked No.1 on the Amazon Bestseller Lists for action adventure and romantic suspense in the U.S., Canada, and Australia. The true story about LoLo's fire crew escaping a runaway wildfire won an Alaska Press Club award and inspired her debut novel, *Alaska Spark.*

LoLo has other books under the romance umbrella. *Hello Spain, Goodbye Heart,* and *Irish Thunder,* are two romantic comedies being published by The Wild Rose Press. Lolo lives in Alaska with her husband and golden retrievers.

ALSO BY LOLO PAIGE

Want more romantic suspense reads? Try my other books!

Winner of the Indie B.R.A.G. Medallion Award, and finalist in the Eric Hoffer, and Next Generation Indie Book Awards

Tara Waters loves being a wildland firefighter and the adrenaline rush of fighting wildfires is her calling. She must be on her game to join an elite hotshot crew in Montana. But when Tara is sent to fight fires in Alaska, her dream falls out of reach.

Blazes are ravaging Alaska's wilderness. Firefighter Liz and fire investigator Jon must find an arsonist while their own inferno smolders. As Liz and Jon race time to find the arsonist, they battle the lethal forces hellbent on keeping them apart. Fire is unpredictable, and so is love—but will Liz and Jon's second chance at love get extinguished before it's even lit? Romance, fire, and arson...another deadly mix!

Cinematically plotted in a spectacular, dangerous setting...smoldering passion where fire isn't the only heat! —New York Times bestselling author Cherry Adair.

COMING SOON...ALASKA BLAZE!

The epic firefighting adventures continue when Cohen Tremblay and the Aurora Crew battle flames near the mighty Alaska Range, in the shadow of Denali Mountain. They must protect the lives and property of Iditarod mushers. When Cohen meets the fearless and feisty sled dog owner, Riley Atwood, sparks and barks fly!

Don't miss out!

Visit the website below and you can sign up to receive emails whenever LoLo Paige publishes a new book. There's no charge and no obligation.

https://books2read.com/r/B-A-MQPK-WKEYB

BOOKS 2 READ

Connecting independent readers to independent writers.

Did you love *Jealousy*? Then you should read *Alaska Spark*[1] by LoLo Paige!

[2]

Can a chance encounter on a wildfire lead to true love under the midnight sun?

Tara Waters loves being a wildland firefighter and the adrenaline rush of fighting wildfires is her calling. She must be on her game to join an elite hotshot crew in Montana. Troubled from a tragedy on a wildfire, Tara is reassigned to fight fire in Alaska, and her dream of being on a hotshot crew falls out of reach.

Sexy Alaskan smokejumper, Ryan O'Connor takes Tara under his wing and counsels her when she fails to save someone on a wildfire. She owes him one, but not her heart just because of his irresistible charm

---

1. https://books2read.com/u/3kPxan

2. https://books2read.com/u/3kPxan

and good looks. Ryan has his own story with plenty of demons in his past. And Tara may be the spark his life needs.

But when a sinister rival sabotages Tara on the fire line, she discovers a threat far more dangerous than fire—a threat that can destroy everything she's worked for and her second chance for a love that could be extinguished before it ignites.

Romance, sabotage, and fire...one explosive mix!

Read more at https://www.lolopaige.com.